"Unashamedly various without being feeble, a series of exercises in voice, perspective, and style, deal in violence, exile, and much else besides. . . . Deftly switching perspectives is his most impressive technique . . . yet Perlman's work isn't all juggling tricks: at times, he manages to pack whole lives into a few paragraphs."
—*The New York Times Book Review*

"Hopelessly conscious of embarrassing personal truths—the sort we realize, then yearn to forget—Perlman's characters are erudite specialists of anomie. Hyperliterate and brutally funny, alternatively self-assured and self-loathing, they are mostly noble and deserving of our sympathy, even if we're implicated in our schadenfreude. The effect might be depressing if Perlman didn't show such care in imbuing his characters with devious charm. . . . Scant evidence exists to suggest that casual flirtation with Perlman's fiction will not end in total obsession."
—*The Believer*

"Perlman has a winner with this collection of nine eloquent short stories that examine the various natures of the human condition via a cast of remarkable characters."
—*The Sacramento Bee*

"Perlman mines pure narrative gold. . . . Insistently readable . . . provocative and powerful fiction from one of the best new writers on the international scene."
—*Kirkus Reviews* (starred review)

"Readers intrigued by Perlman's well-received *Seven Types of Ambiguity* will be delighted that he has upped the ante with nine stories whose characters range from lawyers to immigrants. . . . This story collection showcases the talent of young, Australian-born Perlman. . . . Expansively written with admirable control and generous detail, this is an excellent collection and is highly recommended for fiction collections."
—*Library Journal*

"Perlman has a rare gift for keeping the pages turning while never giving up on his vision of an encompassing and incisive social satire. . . . The Aussie equivalent of the Franzens, Roths, and yes, Austens of the world." —*Elle*

"Compulsively readable." —*The New Yorker*

"A brilliant book." —*The Miami Herald*

"This serious, searing character study . . . rotates through seven astonishingly intimate character studies revolving around one act by a charismatic but depressed former schoolteacher. Novelist Perlman, a Melbourne lawyer, must be hugely commended for the excruciating depth to which he follows the conflicts from Simon's mistake, and his writing is often piercing. A love story, domestic drama, and courtroom thriller . . . richly rewarding." —*People*

"Nuanced, dynamic storytelling, layered with essential digressions on everything from psychiatry to the stock market." —*The Washington Post*

"A dazzling thriller . . . *Rashomon* style." —*Newsweek*

"Perlman . . . has created a novel with just the right amount of meaning, intelligence, and beauty." —*The Boston Globe*

"[A] brilliant, absorbing novel . . . breathtaking but so intimately involving and densely plotted that it becomes that anomaly of a literate and urgent page-turner." —*New York Post*

"A big, ambitious novel." —*GQ*

ALSO BY ELLIOT PERLMAN

Three Dollars

Seven Types of Ambiguity

RIVERHEAD BOOKS *New York*

GOOD MORNING, AGAIN IN THE TIME OF
THE DINOSAUR YOUR NIECE'S SPEECH
NIGHT **THE REASONS I WON'T BE COMING**
MANSLAUGHTER THE *HONG KONG FIR*
DOCTRINE I WAS ONLY IN A CHILDISH WAY
CONNECTED TO THE ESTABLISHED ORDER
SPITALNIC'S LAST YEAR A TALE IN TWO CITIES

STORIES

elliot perlman

THE BERKLEY PUBLISHING GROUP
Published by the Penguin Group
Penguin Group (USA) Inc.
375 Hudson Street, New York, New York 10014, USA
Penguin Group (Canada), 90 Eglinton Avenue East, Suite 700, Toronto, Ontario M4P 2Y3, Canada
(a division of Pearson Penguin Canada Inc.)
Penguin Books Ltd., 80 Strand, London WC2R 0RL, England
Penguin Group Ireland, 25 St. Stephen's Green, Dublin 2, Ireland (a division of Penguin Books Ltd.)
Penguin Group (Australia), 250 Camberwell Road, Camberwell, Victoria 3124, Australia
(a division of Pearson Australia Group Pty. Ltd.)
Penguin Books India Pvt. Ltd., 11 Community Centre, Panchsheel Park, New Delhi—110 017, India
Penguin Group (NZ), cnr Airborne and Rosedale Roads, Albany, Auckland 1310, New Zealand
(a division of Pearson New Zealand Ltd.)
Penguin Books (South Africa) (Pty.) Ltd., 24 Sturdee Avenue, Rosebank, Johannesburg 2196, South Africa

Penguin Books Ltd., Registered Offices: 80 Strand, London WC2R 0RL, England

This is a work of fiction. Names, characters, places, and incidents either are the product of the author's imagination or are used fictitiously, and any resemblance to actual persons, living or dead, business establishments, events, or locales is entirely coincidental. While the author has made every effort to provide accurate telephone numbers and Internet addresses at the time of publication, neither the publisher nor the author assumes any responsibility for errors, or for changes that occur after publication. Further, publisher does not have any control over and does not assume any responsibility for author or third-party websites or their content.

The author gratefully acknowledges permission to quote from:
T. S. Eliot, "The Love Song of J. Alfred Prufrock," from *Collected Poems, 1909–1962*, Faber and Faber Ltd.;
Osip Mandelstam, "I Was Only in a Childish Way Connected to the Established Order," from *Selected Poems*,
translated by James Greene, Penguin Books (UK); "I've Many Years to Live," from *The Moscow Notebooks*,
translated by Richard and Elizabeth McKane, Bloodaxe Books (UK); and "Poem on Stalin," reproduced by
permission of The Harvill Press. Vitaly Shentalinsky, *The KGB's Literary Archive*, first published by The
Harvill Press in 1995. Copyright © Editions Robert Laffont, SA, Paris. English translation Copyright © John
Crowfoot 1995.

First Riverhead hardcover edition: December 2005
First Riverhead trade paperback edition: December 2006
Riverhead trade paperback ISBN: 1-59448-223-3

The Library of Congress has catalogued the Riverhead hardcover edition as follows:

Perlman, Elliot.
        The reasons I won't be coming / Elliot Perlman.
          p.   cm.
        ISBN 1-57322-321-2
        1. Australia—Social life and customs—Fiction.   I. Title.
    PR9619.3.P3619R43   2005   2005048023
    813'.54—dc22

PRINTED IN THE UNITED STATES OF AMERICA

10 9 8 7 6 5 4 3 2

CONTENTS

GOOD MORNING, AGAIN IN THE TIME OF THE DINOSAUR YOUR NIECE'S SPEECH NIGHT THE REASONS I WON'T BE COMING MANSLAUGHTER THE *HONG KONG FIR* DOCTRINE I WAS ONLY IN A CHILDISH WAY CONNECTED TO THE ESTABLISHED ORDER SPITALNIC'S LAST YEAR A TALE IN TWO CITIES

Her sinuses are blocked and she doesn't know. She would be embarrassed if she did. I shouldn't know, either. At four o'clock in the morning, with a new friend asleep beside me, I remember standing in the rain that night feeling angrily disconnected as you cried with incomprehensible frustration at my failure to agree that group therapy was just as likely to be of benefit to someone—someone unnamed—as private sessions. We had just eaten Thai food. It had been a good day in spite of the rain towards the end.

At four o'clock in the morning I haven't slept at all but when she wakes up I will have to continue the date as though I had slept—part lover, part waiter, part *Tonight Show* host. After sheltering from the rain for a little while, sharp and brittle, apart, I could tell that you were going to cry but you were not sad, not yet, you were frustrated and I was equally frustrated. It's just that I don't cry at those times. What time is it now? Way past four. She sprawls diagonally in bed, leaning towards me, assuming an inequitable familiarity. As tempting as it may be to mistake this for an accelerated form of love, I quickly attribute it to her youth, her previous experience or lack of it, her urgent need for more experience. She is the young friend of a friend, my new friend, and I will learn soon that neither she nor I really need any rude awakenings at the moment. The neighbors have started making a racket again. They never care what time it is. They sell antique furniture not far from here and he gets up early every weekend to make it. His wife takes their young son into the garden, where they can perfect his tantrums without the artificial restriction of walls. My new friend won't be able to sleep through all of this. You never could.

Why was it so important to either of us? You were trying to tell me something and I was trying to tell you something else. We didn't trust each other and that was reason enough to make each of us right. You thought I was too rigid. I thought you were too open—prone to putting your faith in something just because you wanted to, even when you had been shown it contained some logical flaws. But you are intelligent and the contradictions hurt you as much as the fact that it was me pointing them out. Your eyes became red. I should have hugged you then in that rain but I was never one for public displays of affection, was I, except in comparison to you, that is. I discovered this when we met. It had been such a long time since I had met someone who didn't care what my star sign was.

"Good morning," my new friend says with one eye open.

"How did you sleep?" I ask.

"Great," she says, putting her hand gently to my forehead. She's breathing through her mouth now.

"Did they wake you?" I ask her, indicating towards next door. There is a throbbing in my head.

"Something did, I suppose. What *is* that noise?"

"It's just a local amalgam of irritating sounds. There's a hammer, a sander, of course, and a circular saw. He's building some really delightful Victorian pieces. They'll be ready by noon. And that shrill hysteria which occasionally approximates language— that's his wife and their new gargantuan son. It was bad enough before he was born but now it's impossible. One day she was merely a scrawny suburban shrew enjoying the simple pleasures of humiliating her anemic husband in the garden, and then, all of a sudden, without giving anyone a chance to lodge an objection with the council, she was pregnant. The fetus gestated for about an hour and a half and then there were three—a cacophony of three, first thing on a Sunday morning—with matching washstand, recently varnished, ideal for indoor plants that are hard of hearing. Would you like a cup of tea?"

I am avoiding her.

"They must be crazy to be up at this time making a noise like this," she said.

"*They're* just selfish. The really crazy ones are on the other side. He sells insurance and she sells cosmetics. If she can't restore your skin's natural smoothness in six days, he has a policy that will refund fifty percent of the retail price. Of course, this is only available to approved customers, and I think they know that I don't approve at all."

She nestles just below my shoulder. She thinks my attempt to amuse her is a compliment when actually it is the by-product of other things.

"I think *you're* the craziest one in the street," she says, snuggling beside me. But she doesn't know you. Anyway, you're not in this street anymore.

It's not true to say I didn't sleep at all. I must have, no matter what contrary arguments are put by the throbbing in my head. My eyes would have moved rapidly, perhaps in time with my new friend's breathing, because I dreamed that stupid dream again, the one that particularly embarrasses me. It must be based on something that happened or else on a composite of many things, because its form doesn't vary. You would chide me if I told you about it, even if you were not somewhere else now. How can I put it? I have come home from somewhere. It is cold outside but you are waiting for me in this bed. It's dark. I have this dream too often, I know that. Joseph Brodsky put it best, as though the dream was his:

. . . For darkness restores what light cannot repair.
There we are married, blest, we make once more
the two-backed beast and children are the fair
excuse of what we're naked for.

There, I said it, albeit in someone else's words. Are you flattered? Is it pathetic or just out of the question for us now? Many times I have dreamed of having children with you, not just sleeping with you, although, of course, I think about that too.

My new friend has drifted off to sleep again, this time in my arms. I can't really move without disturbing her. That's how it's seemed since we got into bed all those hours ago. There is some kind of code or etiquette for sleeping with someone for the first time but it is constantly changing and I never knew it in the first place. Do you keep any clothes on, even if only for a little while? Can the temperature of the room be taken into account? If you disrobe too quickly, does it look presumptuous or crassly eager? You have to feign at least a little surprise at being in this position with someone when you've never known them this way before. On the other hand, you have to behave as if you're under the influence of the other person's body with an insatiable hunger to know their soft and hidden parts, as though this person was the apotheosis of everyone you had ever lusted after.

Our clothes are scattered on the floor. We could not have done it more randomly. Once the pretense that we might not sleep together had evaporated, everything else followed with the grace of a runaway train. If she brought her own condoms, I was too much of a gentleman to let her offer them. But when I reached for my own, it suddenly occurred to me that the ease and system of it might appear a little slick and too practiced. I didn't want to insult her gratuitously. So I kissed her as though she meant everything to me that I had wanted you to always mean to me, only without the need to protect myself, and she kissed me back, in gratitude, as though I was going to rid her of all the pain she had ever known and would tell me about when this was over. Although she was lovely and welcoming, her hair spilling out all over the pillow, I wished she wasn't here. Consumed by her moist gratitude and what must have been exaggerated passion—it was as though she had come straight from a dentist's waiting room having just read "Twenty Ways to Please Your Man"—I felt under the same obligation not to climax as I will feel to drive her home at the end. She has decided to give older men a try, and, as old as she makes me feel, on behalf of all the older men who won't sleep with her but who will merely follow her step as she passes by, I must show her the utmost courtesy. That is the attribute used to "market" us. It's how older men get a look in.

The curtains are completely drawn, just as you liked them to be, so that we could trap the night way past midday, getting up only to have a pee, make a cup of tea or put on the Django Reinhardt you'd bought for me. You told me one Sunday, when we were running late for one of those daunting lunches at your mother's, to act embarrassed when we arrived late in a way that would give your family the impression our lateness was a consequence of our carnal appetites. You said it would stop them asking why we were so late and, at the same time, give your mother some small pleasure at the promise of more grandchildren. Your mother liked me, especially next to your sister's husbands. But how does one suggest obliquely to someone's mother that fucking is the fair excuse of what her roast has burned for? Anyway, it would have been a lie. We had been fighting, do you remember?—not about your smoking—and when I had finally chosen a shirt, you were still on your knees by the dresser, looking for the antidepressants.

I am trying to remember your cruel irrationality and that coldness you smuggled out of boarding school, hidden like everything else under your tunic, hidden so well I thought you were me. I have thought of you at home, watching television by yourself with a plate of something colorful on your lap, unable to work the video recorder, and it has made me angry. It didn't have to be like this. I have wondered what would really happen if I visited you. You're so much better at this than me, I had thought. I hadn't known why at first, so, stupidly, I had envied you in this regard. At four o'clock on other mornings, I have thought of you asleep in your house, the house I knew so well. I liked it more than you did and talked you out of selling it.

I am cold but if I reach for a T-shirt, my new friend will wake up. She's breathing through her mouth again. When she wakes up she will tell me about her past boyfriends, the early ones, the exotic ones, the ones who hurt her most. She will be lonely when she wakes up. I am sad for her. She deserves to have someone. I am stroking her hair very gently. I am sad for us too. I wonder if I am lonelier now than I was at the end. Are you lonely? Perhaps you don't have time. There's a crack in the curtains and the light is getting in. Of course, one day I will come around and see you.

You said that no one else ever made you so angry, but you were flattering me and I didn't believe you. I don't feel it diminishes anything to admit that other people have made me cry, but I'll concede that admissions are hard. They are hard until you have to admit that the thing stares you in the face, until it's all around you like the weather. It's you now, just you.

Whatever is going on in my chest has woken her. My new friend looks up at me and sees you in my face. She doesn't ask any questions. She doesn't ask why you have made my eyes glisten in the light that comes through the gap in the curtains.

"Good morning," she says. She asks just this when I don't have enough love for the three of us.

"Good morning, again."

GOOD MORNING, AGAIN **IN THE TIME OF THE DINOSAUR** YOUR NIECE'S SPEECH NIGHT THE REASONS I WON'T BE COMING MANSLAUGHTER THE *HONG KONG FIR* DOCTRINE I WAS ONLY IN A CHILDISH WAY CONNECTED TO THE ESTABLISHED ORDER SPITALNIC'S LAST YEAR A TALE IN TWO CITIES

Nicholas doesn't remember anything. He was still a baby, really. There's no point even asking him. I have to remember it all myself. Nicholas had just stopped wetting his bed. We lived in the flats near the chocolate factory. Standing in the street at night, you could smell the chocolate cooking. Dad and I would go for a walk while Mum was getting Nicholas ready for bed. Sometimes the wind would take the chocolate into the flats and I could smell it from our room. When I went to bed Dad would read me a story and turn the light out. I'd close my eyes and, with dinosaurs in my head, I would sniff in the chocolate till I was asleep. (I always breathe through my nose so that nothing gets into my mouth without my knowing about it. Bill Economou from upstairs once swallowed a fly in his sleep. He said his window was open. He was dreaming about chocolate.)

The books Dad and I read were always about dinosaurs. I couldn't get enough of them. At that time I wanted to be a dinosaur scientist when I grew up. Dad said he thought it wasn't a bad idea and that I was well on my way already. He said it beat making shoes in a shoe factory, which is what he did. I think he had a fair amount of respect for dinosaurs too.

The first dinosaurs lived on earth more than two hundred million years ago and so you can't even imagine how things were for them. I tried to imagine them in Australia, because there were dinosaurs here before Captain Cook and the Aborigines or anything you can see around now. They weren't stupid, either, like a lot of people think. Bill Economou said they had to be stupid because they became extinct, but he couldn't come up with another group of backboned animals that lived on earth for more than a hundred and sixty million years. The facts stared him in the face.

Dad calls me Luke but my full name is Lucas. Once I told Bill Economou that I was named after a dinosaur, the lukosaurus. I think that shut him up for a while. The lukosaurus lived in southern China and was two meters long, not counting his horns. A couple of weeks later Bill Economou came downstairs to our flat all of a sudden, knocked on the door and announced to Mum, Nicholas and me that he was named after a dinosaur, too, the billosaurus. I told him there was no such dinosaur but he said there was. Mum shirked it the way mums do. She said she hadn't heard of the billosaurus but that there might be a dinosaur called that. I went to Nicholas's and my room to get the books. There was no such dinosaur. I would've known about it if there were.

Bill Economou said it was a Greek dinosaur and that I wouldn't know about it. That's when Mum laughed. Nicholas doesn't remember this of course. Then she said that maybe it was a Greek name for a dinosaur and would he like some cordial.

Bill Economou never says no if you offer him something. Mum should've known that. It was probably his sister who told him to say that about a billosaurus. It didn't sound like something he'd think of on his own.

Bill Economou has two sisters, two brothers and his mum and dad. One sister, Mary, is the oldest and the other is almost too young to talk. His brothers, Con and Nick, are older than him too. Nick used to play cricket with us for a while but then he stopped. I usually keep away from Con. I think Bill Economou does too. Mr. Economou likes to get you in a headlock. It's not so bad sometimes. The Economous live directly above us and we hear them. Mum says we don't need to watch TV on one of their good nights. They don't sound like TV. I don't know why she says that.

Mary Economou fights with Mr. Economou. Sometimes Bill Economou invites me up if it's a good one. She's seventeen and still cries. She yells at him in English and he yells back in Greek. I hear a lot of Greek words from Mr. and Mrs. Economou, nearly every day. Never heard *billosaurus*, though. Bill Economou says Mary's boyfriend always makes Mr. Economou shout in Greek even when he's not there. He can often predict when it will start. The best ones were when Mary wanted to leave school and when the police came asking for Mary to talk about her boyfriend. Bill Economou rang me up as soon as he saw the police car pull up in front of our block. He did the right thing.

Bill Economou was in the same class as me at school. He had always copied me in lots of things but tried not to let me know. I always knew sooner or later. Earlier in the year we did a couple of projects together, but Mrs. Nesbitt knew that I'd done most of the work. Bill Economou was even a bad colorer. Lines meant nothing to him. I was actually pleased when Mrs. Nesbitt said Bill Economou and I had to do one project each. I don't think he should've asked her why. Later he agreed with me about this.

Of course I chose dinosaurs. I had big plans. I knew my project would take days and days, some days just for thinking. There were more than three hundred and forty types of dinosaurs. I knew I couldn't include them all. I didn't actually like them all. As well as the lukosaurus, I liked the tyrannosaurus, the brachiosaurus and the stegosaurus best. My favorite period was the Cretaceous period. This was the heyday for dinosaurs. There must have been hundreds of different kinds of dinosaurs just roaming around chomping on things during the Cretaceous period. Mum said this was my Cretaceous period. I asked Dad when his was. He said it was before he was married. He must've eaten a lot then. Dad's a big man and when he's hungry there's no stopping him. Mum said that before they were married there was no stopping him.

I had figured out that some kids would just do lots of drawings of something and call that their project. Others would copy out slabs from a book and call that their project. These projects would be all right, they might even get two or three red ticks or even a silver star. But I wanted gold for my dinosaurs. One gold star was my personal best. I wanted to beat it. It had got to where red ticks meant nothing to me. Mrs. Nesbitt was giving them to sucks for behavior and to milky girls for a chart of "The Fruits We Eat." Dad said that dinosaurs would be hard because there were no pictures of them in magazines to cut out. Mum tried to get me to swap to dairy products but I just couldn't. You don't get the gold for pictures of milk. It had to be dinosaurs. Dad said he admired me, which was good I thought. He said, "Luke, I admire you."

I had decided to write out my own theory of why dinosaurs became extinct and to do a drawing of a lukosaurus. Then Dad gave me a great idea. He suggested making cardboard cutouts of different types of dinosaurs. He said I could fit the dinosaur cutouts into slits in the top of an upside-down box. Then I could move each dinosaur in a different slit to show how slowly they must've moved and which ones came first after the beginning of the earth. This was a great idea. It could get me the gold. It probably would. Mrs. Nesbitt would never have seen anything like this in her life. Dad said he would bring some shoeboxes and cardboard offcuts for me from work. I asked him not to say anything about it in front of Bill Economou.

Dad gave me the idea on one of our chocolate walks. I was pleased he hadn't tried to talk me out of dinosaurs and into dairy products. He didn't like milk much. I've never seen him drink it. He said he'd drink it if it was on tap. Then he laughed and lifted me up high in the air. I was way above his head in those hands at the end of his thick arms, sort of near the moon. He held me up there for a good while in the chocolate wind and we didn't speak. His arms didn't waver so I was perfectly still in the air. Only the sky moved, just enough to give tiny shakes to the stars. That was the last chocolate walk we had. I don't remember a chocolate wind much after that, either.

Nicholas doesn't remember the chocolate winds. But I remember them. I remember that one too. We came back to our block and before we got to the front hall we heard shouting and a door slamming. Mary Economou ran down the stairs. She shouted "I hate you" in a new voice that sounded like someone scraping a tin roof. She didn't mean me, though. She didn't mean Dad, either. She hated someone upstairs. I knew Bill Economou would tell me everything the next day so we let her run out into the street and I went to bed really happy and sleepy.

I don't think anyone really knows for sure exactly why the dinosaurs disappeared. I know I don't. The books shirk it a bit really. It seems that about sixty-five million years ago they just disappeared. I was thinking of maybe being the first dinosaur scientist to know for sure what happened.

It's hard to know where to start trying to figure out something like that. You would probably have to work out a whole new code or way of thinking, maybe something combining maths and the dictionary. Between maths and the dictionary you've pretty much got it all covered. I was thinking about the dictionary a fair bit. I think there's a trick to it that no one ever tells you. When you look up a word, like *dinosaur,* you get "Reptile (freq. huge) of Mesozoic era." Where does that get you? More words. So you look *them* up and you get *more* words. Well, sooner or later you have to be lucky enough to *already* know at least one of the words you've looked up or you'll never understand anything. No one ever says anything about this.

One theory says the dinosaurs disappeared because of a great catastrophe which affected the whole world. Perhaps they all choked from dust in their throats as the earth passed through a swarm of comets or from bits of rock and sand from an exploding star. Some people think the earth might have been hit by a giant meteorite. Sometimes I think that might've happened. It's hard to explain these things. A great catastrophe.

I had nearly finished the writing part of my project. Even though it was his idea, Dad kept forgetting to bring home the shoeboxes he'd promised me. I asked him every day and every day he forgot. I had to change my plans. Dad wasn't cooperating. It was at about this time that Mrs. Nesbitt and I started having discipline problems. I had told her that she was really going to like my dinosaur project and that she might even think of gold stars when she saw it. (She keeps them in a tin in her desk drawer.) But I had also told her that it was going to be a bit late. She asked me why. I didn't want to tell her. I told her that I couldn't say because it would spoil the surprise. I didn't want to tell her about Dad's box idea. She said that she was already surprised that my project was late. I asked her if she would hang on. She gave me three days. (Bill Economou had asked for three more days, too, and he'd already handed his in. It was on "Fish of the Sea.")

I knew I would just have to change my plan. I tried to explain it all to Dad but I could tell he wasn't listening. He was all silent. He'd been that way for a while. Mum was silent too. She only said what she *had* to say, about things like washing or peas. On the third day I came to school with my project, but it was different now. I had two sheets of paper with writing about dinosaurs from the books and a big model of a megalosaurus, a two-legged meat-eater. Since the writing was just *stuff*, all my hopes for the gold pretty much rested on the model megalosaurus. I had taken two wire coat hangers and threaded them through seventeen beer cans Dad had. (They were empty, so I didn't even ask for them.) The can at the head was flattened for a snout and the whole thing could bend so I could show how dinosaurs had walked. (I kept the movement part of the first plan.)

Bill Economou loved it. Mrs. Nesbitt was angry. I was surprised. She was angry in front of the whole class. She asked if I had needed the extra three days to get enough beer cans. The class laughed when she said that. She looked at them and said that she was very disappointed with my project. Then she went down the aisles between the desks asking to see other projects. She'd already seen all of them three days before. She was just doing this to make me feel bad. It worked and I felt bad, really sick. I thought maybe I'd caught an epidemic, a throat one.

At lunchtime I went home without asking. I just wanted to get away from school for a while. Mum had given me a pear in my lunch. I'd told her not to but she didn't listen and put it in my bag anyway. When I got to the front door, I felt inside my bag for the door key. I felt the pear all squashed up. The megalosaurus must have done it. I really just wanted to be home with a peanut butter sandwich, some milk and maybe some TV. I opened the door and Dad was there. This was my third surprise in half a day if you count the pear. He was watching TV on the couch.

Dad stayed home in the days now and looked after Nicholas. It's what his work had told him to do. He told me that they'd asked him if he could stay home with Nicholas for a while and not make shoes. That's all he said and then he went back to a TV show about hospitals. I wanted to know who was making the shoes now but didn't ask. I had my sandwich and milk. Then I started to scrape the pear off the inside of my bag. Dad forgot to ask why I was home at lunchtime.

After that, everything seemed different. Mum and Dad would be all quiet when I was in the room with them, but then they'd shout when I'd gone. I couldn't hear the Economous. Dad made plenty of cans but I didn't need them. Things were different at school too. It was like Mrs. Nesbitt was always thinking about my megalosaurus. I just couldn't get back in her good books and I got sick of trying. Bill Economou got a silver star for "Fish of the Sea." He kept showing it to me.

I suppose that's why I did it. It all happened so fast like it wasn't really me and I got caught. Mrs. Nesbitt caught me at her desk, in her gold-star tin. She shouted. It hung in the air and made my sweat jump. Everyone looked. She held my fingers out and showed the class. There were gold stars on my fingers. My face got very hot. She started writing a note to Mum. It was about me. I didn't let her finish it. I left. I ran all the way home again. It still wasn't me, though, not really. My bag was still on the pegs.

The front door wasn't locked and I pushed it open. Dad was in the lounge room. His shirt was off and he was puffed like I was, out of breath. He said he'd just been for a run. Mary Economou was there too. Her face was red and her hair was messy. I was confused. I stood there looking at them. Then I cried, first in yelps. I felt really strange. She'd never seen me cry before.

Dad took my face and pressed it into his chest. He put his fingers in my hair. He told me nothing was wrong and that he and Mary Economou had just been for a run. He kept telling me not to be upset. He asked me to tell him that nothing was wrong. He told me there was nothing wrong with going for a run. Then he squeezed me so hard it hurt. He smelled of sweat. Then he cried and told me nothing was wrong. His chest moved up and down. It slapped me. I couldn't see anything past his chest. He told me he was sorry.

Two days later I came home from school and Mum was there, not Dad. He had gone. He wasn't coming back for a while. They'd swapped again. Mum would be home with Nicholas, and Dad had gone to look for another shoe factory where he could make shoes again. I asked her where he was. She said he was looking for work in a level playing field. I asked her where that was and if I could go there. She said I would never find it. Bill Economou had borrowed an atlas from the library for "Fish of the Sea" and we went to the map of Australia to look for Level Playing Field. We couldn't find it. Bill Economou said she must have meant the Southern Tablelands. When I asked her, she said yes, that was it. I tried to imagine Dad living on a huge flat table, making shoes and writing me letters. She said we would get letters.

If the earth was hit by a giant meteorite it would've made so much dust that the sunlight wouldn't have been able to get through and the dinosaur food chain would've been wrecked. Without any sunlight they would've frozen too. Even the biggest of them would've needed protection from the cold. Everyone does. It's just a theory. No one knows for sure about the meteorite. If you don't know something for sure, you might as well just dream it.

Bill Economou dreams all the time. He dreamed Dad was outside one night, outside our flats in the wind doing nothing; leaning against the wall of the empty chocolate factory, staring at our flats. At first, he tried to tell me he actually *saw* it. Mum said there aren't many letterboxes at the Southern Playing Fields.

Nicholas dreams but he doesn't remember. When we shared the same room I could hear some of his dreams. I told him I heard them all. I've got our room to myself now. He's been sleeping in Mum's bed since he started wetting his bed again. He says he doesn't wet the bed. He says it's Mum. I wanted to check this out because he lies much more than me now. I went in and checked one night when they were both asleep. I wasn't sure about him, but Mum's side of the bed was wet. Her pillow. Nothing surprises me much anymore, not really. It's because I'm growing up, I suppose. That's *my* theory.

GOOD MORNING, AGAIN IN THE TIME OF THE DINOSAUR **YOUR NIECE'S SPEECH NIGHT** THE REASONS I WON'T BE COMING MANSLAUGHTER THE *HONG KONG FIR* DOCTRINE I WAS ONLY IN A CHILDISH WAY CONNECTED TO THE ESTABLISHED ORDER SPITALNIC'S LAST YEAR A TALE IN TWO CITIES

Why is it later than you think so much more often than not? Many questions arise here in the dark, interrupted only by the polite applause, questions like "Where are you?" Do the high terrazzo walls of the cubicle take you back, put you in your place? They must. Is that it?

I am assuming you find it comforting or at least thought-provoking in some way to be sitting in one or other of the cubicles tucked away deep in the bowels of this great stone monstrosity that housed you all those years ago and in which you were taught, inter alia, Latin, French, algebra, some English history and deportment. But your deportment seems to have failed you momentarily just as something else about you, something I had never suspected, has failed me. I would apologize for seeming angry, but you are not around for any rudimentary apology that, in any case, I would not mean, which is why I am angry in the first place; in *your* first place, your alma mater.

I am sitting in a school hall, your old school's hall, with your sister, your brother-in-law and one of their daughters as they wait for another of their daughters, the eldest, to accept some award, or perhaps she is to sing. I am not your husband. He gets out of these things now, and so—at the last minute, I find—do you.

I do not know why I am here, although I would be able to recount with great accuracy *how* I got here—not that this is something you need to be told. It was arranged some time ago. Even had you not disappeared inexplicably, leaving me literally in the dark, it is hard to imagine feeling more uncomfortable. Your sister, poodle hairstyle—is it just for the evening?—pearl earrings with a matching brooch and matching breasts, each perfectly shaped and straining to make a point in cashmere reminiscent of more genteel times; does she always chew gum? It does you no harm being her sister—you are not your sister's keeper and you look good next to her—just as it does you no good to be ashamed of her. She should have married an astronaut and it looks as though she has. Her husband, as if freshly returned from an audition for the part of Dad in a U.S. situation comedy, replete with painted-on hair and perfect teeth and intoxicated by his own congeniality, bobs around us in the foyer of the school hall like an apple in a barrel of water. You were here then, I know that, touching my arm briefly and by accident. He tells me what he does for a living but I am having trouble remembering his name. I do not want to sit next to him in the hall during the assembly for fear that, in his bliss at being a father at his daughter's speech night, he might reach for my hand. But I am spared this fate and find myself seated between your immaculate sister and you—that is, before you got up to leave.

I would have had no expectation of anything but kitsch coming down at us from the stage tonight had I turned my mind to it, but the truth was, I did not and could not have turned my mind to it and still have agreed to accompany you here. It seemed important to you that we attend—or, rather, that you attend not alone—which has meant, of late, going with me. It has never before meant leaving without me, but perhaps I am precipitate to draw this conclusion. Perhaps you are in the wings, waiting for some response from the chorus before reappearing. Or is it the chorus from whom you are hiding?

When I first saw you, by the lift well, it was for an instant and I was not even sure that you were working with us. So what was it that I noticed in that instant? I had already been divorced for quite a while, and my female registering reflexes were permanently cocked, ready for quick action in the sense at least of acknowledgment, the lightning start of an Olympian being one of the few consolations of the truly lonely long-distance runner. Do you, wherever you are, want to know what it was that I noticed in that first instant? Yes, you do have a kind of beauty that is more than merely physical, I have told you that; but it wasn't that. The smile, I have seen it so many times since. The smile that plays around your lips and cannot be counted on kindled a curiosity in me that I had not felt for some time. The smile, and something with a life of its own residing in your eyes, suggested that you knew something most of us did not know, something which made you unsafe. Of course, there are many things we didn't and still don't know. These days I don't even know if I'm meant to be in Sales or in Marketing. But unfortunately I do know something that you don't. I might tell you if you come back from your ill-timed nocturnal creep down memory lane.

"It's a small world after all . . ." sing the girls from Mrs. Dowager's Year Seven music class. Is that really her name? Couldn't be.

It sounded like *Dowager* when the Principal introduced her. But she's hardly a dowager, is she, smiling side-on to us like that, seated at the piano in a tight skirt and white blouse looking barely old enough to be either married or fully qualified to smile side-on at us from a piano. What charm she brings to a melody so banal it can only have been composed to drive people mad. Surely it was not her choice. If you are not back by the end of this, I may have to seek her out. Perhaps if there were teachers here like her in your day, this seat beside me might be warmly occupied instead of conspicuously empty.

A small world after all? Perhaps, but after all *what*? After all the sanctimonious middle-class fund-raising and collegial and national flag-waving in all the speech nights ever orchestrated? Was it Dorothy Parker you were paraphrasing when, in describing your school milieu, you said that if all the girls that ever went to this school were laid end to end you would not be a bit surprised? But they surprised you once, didn't they? It began with an invitation not received, then another and another. For a bright and capable girl, pretty and later beautiful and famously coordinated, there was no excuse for not being selected by your peers for sporting teams and pubescent pyramids formed for the purpose of commemorating one or other school camp in photos ready-made for the back of a drawer. You found yourself, without warning, out of season.

You were the last to know your father had lost his money and these young women, ribbons in their hair and hearts so full of spring, already knew enough to know that your newfound afflic-tion warranted, at the very least, profound abandonment. So why do you do this to yourself? Why do you visit this place pretending that it holds something for you, something pure and joyous? And why have you dragged me here only to abandon me?

But that is not it, is it? That's not all of it. I don't think you have ever realized that what is left out forms part of the story. You don't need these people, and even then only part of you thought that you did, the part that was left out. How is it that I came to know so much of what went on all those days ago inside these sorrowful gates? I have listened, put things together and hung on to them and you didn't notice this because you were too busy either pretending these stories were meant to be funny or else that they were in lieu of what you had meant to say while undressing for bed or leafing through a street directory in the front passenger seat. Just when you thought I suspected the value in pursuing something, you would pull us both up short: "There is probably more than one way of getting there," you might say, "but why are they always digging up the road I need?"

I am not so dull as to draw conclusions about you from the fact that at fifteen or so, in extremis, you turned state's evidence, sending scores of young women to their detention for smoking. And it *is* funny that you convinced an influential echelon and perhaps even a few teachers that your archrival was infected with a highly contagious disease so rare that no one could be sure of its name. Eventually reaching a new equilibrium, you survived and then prospered academically. I know all of this, if it matters to you. But now you have felt the need to touch the iron gates again and breathe deep the disinfectant that stained your youth. We never completely lose our childhood appetites; we just add to them and, in doing so, they become a little less conspicuous. After a half life of apparent conscientiousness, are you finally indulging a taste for truancy? Don't do this to me, not now, when I have something to tell you.

Your presence at the lift well was no coincidence. We soon learned that you worked on our floor, and since our floor was one of five the company leased in their entirety, you had to be working for the company. This was somehow reassuring, perhaps because you were so unlike the rest of us. For a start, you seemed unafraid. I had been unafraid for some time, too, but with you it was different. You were efficiently unafraid. There was no mindlessness or sycophancy in your efficiency either. It was as though you were working for yourself. Head Office was not even in your firmament. This is the kind of state most of us had hoped for, years ago when we started our working lives.

When you begin, you always think that having done everything right as a child, adolescent, secondary and then tertiary student, you're going to be the one that success will snuggle up to while you are busy, that it will grab hold of your leg and never want to be without you. We know of course that very few among us will achieve this but, at least initially, we also seem to just *know* that we will be among the few. We will be the ones. Someone directly above us might be intractable; we hadn't planned for this, but we can handle it. In fact, as we walk down the carpeted passageway, the perfect generator of static electricity, to present our work to this person, we begin to imagine our colleagues in the tea room expressing amazement, admiration, envy, that only we seem to be able to handle him or her. "It's just a matter of reading them," we say nonchalantly, knowing this skill is innate and cannot be taught. And if, in addition, we possess those skills that can be taught, well, there will be no stopping us.

But there is always *stopping* us. Whether it is the tempera-
ment of the direct superior which we thought we had handled
but had not; the office politics of which we were unaware; sexual
politics, be it harassment or inopportune indifference; time-
honored racism, religious animosity, paranoia, a hungover economy, our personal appearance or the perception that we were not
really like them after all, the walls we streamed past first thing
on those first mornings turn into barriers, broken only where
necessary to allow the passage of air. So, after a while, we just
hang on and do not bother ourselves too much about success.

My figures had been down and I had just about given up on
rising any further within the company. In fact, it is not too dra-
matic to say I was working on surviving, just hanging on. My
marriage had ended not with a bang but with a Wiltshire, the
now famous last argument concerning specifically a putative
need for steak knives, and touching more generally on con-
sumerism and various forms of hunger. By the time you appeared
I was no longer living my life properly and was in grave danger
of having it taken off me. When I first saw you something awoke
within me, an inexplicable nervous pain which got me to work
early. We soon learned that you were married but that did not
bother me. I did not anticipate any kind of outside relationship
with you. In my prime you would have been out of my league,
and I had been relegated a number of times by then. It really
would have been sufficient just to watch you around the office, to
be your friend within it and to maybe start to rehabilitate myself.
I was droll around you but not unhelpful. Your suggestions at
the section breakfast meetings did not evoke my usual contempt.
Across the conference table I would detect, I thought, a swift

glance of inquiry from you, perhaps of apology. Had I approved of what you said? Had I detected that it was a performance? You *can* fool many of the people all the time.

But what do you call this performance tonight, this disappearing act, and what is it in aid of? Young Mrs. Dowager has long since vacated the stage, leaving behind a feast of expectation and unanswered questions; what is it about *Mr.* Dowager, whoever he is, that this musical patron saint of Year Seven will do no more than sit side-on at the piano for anyone but him? So certain am I that I will not forget the image of her in that white blouse that I feel I must have seen it before. Perhaps you have one like it? It is a small world after all.

The Principal is back onstage. Once he was a teacher, now an MC always with an eye to the sponsor. Soon he could have his own show. Or is this his own show? There *is* a great turnout tonight. In this he is completely correct. Looking like he is out of the same mold as your sister's husband, the astronaut, the Principal invites us to sing along with whatever is coming up next. Perhaps it is your niece? Your brother-in-law stirs. The Principal is working the auditorium. He will sing along. One can only hope he relinquishes the microphone before this happens. "Just doing his job," you would say, far more accepting than I of people making fools of themselves for money. But he has to work particularly hard tonight. There is disquiet among the faithful. Ten days ago a young girl was dragged to the bushes, still within the grounds, and raped. There is nothing reassuring about the police caravan set up by the side of the front gate. Notwithstanding that it has been on the news, in the papers, and that all the parents know about it, the police caravan serves to remind everyone how helpless we all are. The Principal has the mike in both hands. He is panicking. *All together, now!*

Somewhere at this moment, while the young girl, who has not returned to school, plays jacks on the end of her bed with a family friend she calls "Auntie," the man who did this, who took away her nights for years to come, is doing something else. It is too easy for us to picture him as we would like to paint him. Perhaps he is reading the newspaper, and if he is not, one day he will, as we do, and something will appall him. *Now* we say he is demented, sick. The trick is to call it that before the screams, the nightmares and the shivering. But we never do because we are too busy buying real estate from him, playing golf with him, wishing him a happy anniversary or coming to him for a personal loan. What is going on inside the caravan while I am sitting here? Police are on the lookout for a man who looks like everyone.

They are just doing their job. I know. I can hear the way you would say it, such a convenient expression. It is redolent of long suffering, but this, I have learnt, is not your forte, not when you are just doing *your* job. I am angry. You have been gone too long for comfort. Should I say something to your sister? I was not always angry, and even now, sitting here like an idiot, embarrassed, bored, I know I will not always be angry. I have something to tell you.

It was not so long after you came that it seemed, just for a moment, that I had reached a turning point. You had reached it for me, just by being there the way you were. You were an affirmation of life, and the weight of the last few years felt as if it had lifted. Everything seemed somehow possible again. And this was before we became—what have we become?—involved. You wore a silk scarf around your neck. It had colors that had never been seen before in this building. Your voice, confident but friendly: it was a pleasure to hear it no matter who you were talking to or what you were saying. It suggested, in the way you spoke to a secretary or someone from Accounts, that perhaps I would be all right. The prospect of lunch with you infused in me a kind of golden exuberance. Your interest, even your professional interest in me, reminded me of what I had wanted, hoped for, when I had started with the company. It was almost as though I respected them more for your association with them or rather their association with you.

Why did I start with them? Why do any of us choose one company over another as an employer? The money? At the beginning they all offer more or less the same, and no one knows how it will go after that. I guess it is often not so much your prospects at a particular firm, because these are essentially unknowable, but whether people will think you have done well to get the job there, that determines your choice. That was largely it in my case. It was really the prestige. They gave good letterhead.

But you know what can happen. You work their hours and sometimes it pays off, sometimes it doesn't. Usually you can't tell how it is going so you give it just a bit longer. You set yourself a deadline to be somewhere or something by a certain time but you don't tell anyone, so you can shift the parameters and no one knows whether you have failed. If they throw more money at you, you upgrade your car and get a bigger mortgage. That's how they keep you. You are not the same person anymore. Immaculately dressed over a skin irritation and chronically time deprived, you have jettisoned all those interests you talked about at your first interview all those years ago. You have deadlines to meet or budgets to fulfill and you're not going anywhere, unless or until you find yourself microeconomically reformed and slumped catatonic in the ergonomically designed chair of some employment consultant talking about the possibility of taking up painting again. Until then you are getting in earlier and leaving later, never finding the time to stop and smell the Prozac.

Who are the people who thrive on this? How do they do it? I think you knew from the first day at the lift well and only us chumps could have failed to notice it. And the biggest chump of all fell in love with you, slowly and awkwardly, to the gentle breeze of the desk calendar fanning the days. I do not hold you responsible for this insofar as responsibility is equated with intent. You were not flirting with me, or rather, that was not your intent. I know this now. There is little else I know to be as true as this except, of course, that which I was going to tell you tonight before you took off. Now here is something right up your alley. A magician is onstage. Bright-colored silk kerchiefs appear and disappear through his sleeves. Rabbits become acquainted with the insides of hats. Everyone seems to be enjoying it, your brother-in-law most of all. I am not. In infancy I was dropped by a nurse and ever since I have not been mystified by magic tricks. I smile in case someone is looking at me. But no one does. They are all enraptured, unaware of the greatest trick of the evening: the one in which the lady vanishes.

———

You courted me, slowly but undeniably, and I never questioned your interest. Since we were not yet lovers it was even easier to believe that you saw something in me that I had seen in you. This was enough. I did not need to see you after hours—does this seem naïve?—and the longer it went on, the healthier it appeared to me. It seemed honorable to be so fond of you without ever being with you at night, without ever touching you. I impressed myself greatly. You rarely mentioned your husband, and when you did, it was not with bitterness but a sad resignation. Even when you kissed me in the basement car park—and it was *you* who kissed *me*—I did not allow myself to make too much of it.

Then you called me at home one Sunday evening and asked me to come over. I'd wanted to have an early night. I had an appointment with the specialist the next morning. Your husband had left you. He packed up his estimate of half the contents of the house and went. I had, of course, never been to your home before. You wanted to go out to the movies or somewhere—anywhere. "Let's not talk about it now," you said. "Maybe one day I'll need to tell you everything, but right now I need not to." But you told me a great deal and we nearly missed the film, one of those vehicles that enables Anthony Hopkins to regret everything.

"Is there time for one more Joni Mitchell song?" you asked rhetorically.

There wasn't. Has there ever been time for one more Joni Mitchell song? But who am I to talk. When my wife and I first separated, I found myself often waking up in a shitty 1970 Whitlam-something Mazda hatchback—she took the sedan—barely moving on the South Eastern arterial, only to be reminded via the cassette player that *freedom's just another word for nothing left to lose.* All that remained of my marriage was a compilation country-and-western tape that had gestated for about eight years between the driver's and front passenger's seats, only to rise phoenixlike from the ashtray.

I was surprised to find myself in your home, flattered you had called. I think I had met him once, just briefly, at an office Christmas party, the one they invited spouses and partners to. I thought I had observed him thoroughly, given the limited opportunity, but I would not have guessed at his hunger for bric-a-brac. The place seemed more than half empty. We drank Swedish vodka and you filled me in, told me of an affair you'd had more than a year earlier, before you joined the company, and how it had hurt him, how he couldn't trust you after that. But I felt sure, even then, that his mistrust was older than that. When you went to get changed I sat, glass in hand, waiting for him to come back nonchalantly through the front door, as though he had forgotten something. What would I say to him?

Don't we love her unfaithfulness, just once or twice anyway?
Then her forgetfulness cleans her hands of all those deeds that we
have tallied so faithfully. It enables her to keep going. I know
her well enough and you know her even better. I can understand
how it is that you come to take these things, all these little
things. I know her well enough. You had better not come back.

He did not come back and I don't know that I even thought these things. Not at that time. These are just some thoughts, short of advice, on the occasion of your niece's speech night.

You had taken an interest in me well before this, before I could be of any obvious use to you. Before I had befriended you, I was completely computer illiterate, whereas now I can impersonate the employee who warrants all the expensive hardware the firm seems incapable of resisting. And isn't impersonation the key? Whoever the hell we are—and we never know—there is now the creeping suggestion that it no longer matters. If we can imitate the current faddish gestalt of success then money will surely follow. And even computers still matter less than money, although now it is only in computers that we prize memory. For us memory has become a burden. For you in particular it has been this way for quite some time, since before you sat here, in this auditorium among those young women with ribbons in their hair, suddenly out of season, so depreciated. Memory has been a burden for you since you first bristled at the stern admonition by your father that you must be happy in some *other* way. The money had gone.

Your sister was winded by this, left flat and lifeless. All the possibilities of civilization from gastronomy, travel, appreciation of certain previously ordained pieces of sculpture, haute couture and even sexual fulfillment that she felt would have been within her reach had your father done something differently, something about which she has never really bothered to find out—all these possibilities had vanished. There is a warmth in blame which blanketed her until you, the younger sister, took her under your wing. You had survived by reinventing yourself.

In your early university days you became the floral-skirted queen of alfalfa and buckwheat, an acoustic-guitar-strumming braided bohemian. You tried to teach your sister the guitar, probably without much greater success than your foray into that black hole that is my affinity with computers. There were many cross-legged circle-sitting music sessions in which your new friends tried to view things alternately from a Marxist or feminist perspective without any of them ever really mastering bar chords.

It must have been at one of these midnight-to-dawn sessions that someone introduced you to the songs of Joni Mitchell, presumably with malice aforethought, songs for which there is always time for one more, the one we just have time to hear when your husband has recently left you.

Then it happened, far more suddenly than the first, another metamorphosis. It happened so suddenly it might have created headlines in the student newspaper: *Sisters released from a year and a half on a D minor chord.* Your sister quickly recovered her *Vogue Living* sensibilities, the ones that led her to marry this astronaut here on my right. And you? I don't know where you are.

Only you know. You are not merely unknown to me but unknowable. It embarrasses me now to recall the way I permitted myself to admire you for your fluent command of a pseudotechnical managerial jargon for which I have contempt. So easily done in the first thaw, we became intoxicated with the you-and-me-against-the-world of it all, forgetting that it never stays that way. It became ultimately a tag-team match wherein sometimes you sided with the world. I watched you color your office and the whole of the floor with your presence, shrugging off without noticing all that had for years tripped me up or slapped me in the face. I wanted to believe in a likeness between us despite everything I saw, and this is how there came about the corruption of reason which, in this instance, permitted me to admire you for your capacity to impress Lloyd Walker, whom you persisted in calling Mr. Walker until I ribbed you for it without mercy.

Lloyd Walker is my vintage. We started at more or less the same time. A ruddy bespectacled man who speaks in forced high-pitched gusts of wind as if he had several pieces of fruit permanently lodged in his neck and speaking was only a method that had been recommended for dislodging them. With his exaggerated side-to-side gait and the inexplicable dowdiness of another time and place, Walker quickly became the object of often very funny but unfailingly cruel jokes. While his wife stayed robustly home, knitting casseroles from women's magazines and pruning the children, he was taking offense inoffensively year after year and punctually, steadfastly, not rocking any boats. There is a temptation to locate such a physically unfortunate-looking character somewhere around one's sympathy, pity and even affection, believing him, after everything that you have seen or imagined him to have felt, to be incapable of cruelty himself and perhaps even to be endowed with some vestige of a kind of *In Which We Serve*, Noël Cowardly honor.

Did any of this occur to you in that breakfast meeting as you put your now famous suggestions to this lymphatic papier-mâché head of the department and the assembly of double-breasted morons below him? What did you think they were thinking as they looked at you over black coffee, cardboard croissant and the *Financial Review*, these gentlemen of commerce, each with his own car space and synapses that are still waiting to be formally introduced to one another? Walker's secretary was already reading the minutes of the last meeting and I still hadn't found my seat, having sauntered to your side of the table to lean casually, conspiratorially, and whisper, "Hey, you know why they call this the bored room."

Feeling, unusually for these surroundings, not alone, I stumbled to my chair and fell into it. It was early morning, after all. No one noticed. The meeting had come to that hushed, fearful state described as order.

Walker thanks us for our attendance as though perhaps some

of us had considered sleeping in. Even I know the importance of this weekly orb-of-day charade. The minutes are read. Some circular from Head Office is distributed and discussed. This usually involves most of them, or at least the intellectually weakest of them, clambering over each other to most fulsomely praise with no-name-brand sincerity whatever inanity has come down from on high this week. Only Atherton is creative enough to restrain himself every now and then. Perhaps he is still asleep. There is often a sullenness to his affect at these meetings which has made me think we could have been friends.

Targets, projections, monthly, weekly, for the company and for the section, are read. Well done but we can do better. We can always do better. All talk of what Walker euphemistically calls the horizontal merger is, he says, premature. We must not believe what the press is writing about it, and if we are approached by any of them, we are neither to confirm nor deny. Refer all inquiries to Head Office. But what could we possibly tell the press? They know everything before we do. The little we are told is in the weekly epistle Head Office sends us, and every other department, to make us all feel we matter.

I was eating cantaloupe and honeydew melon. It slipped from my fork on to my lap. I shook involuntarily and it hit the floor. Had anyone noticed? I was gazing out of the window when you began to speak. I came back from the tiles and the flag on top of some distant building, in through the window, and past my reflection to see you lip-synch to your own voice. "Go ahead," Walker encouraged you. The words came out with polite certainty, a mix of reverence and the imperative. It was an idea and a statement of the bloody obvious dressed up as a question. Create a new market, by which you didn't mean exporting to countries where previously we were unknown and all of the population had until recently sat in loincloths up to their necks in their own shit but where *now* five percent live better than we ever did by co-opting the other ninety-five percent into slavery. This was a common idea. Everyone was doing it. We were already doing it. You meant something else, something local. Create a market somewhere between wholesale and retail. Since much of what we did was based on turnover, why not offer some form of discount to certain traders who either bought unusually large quantities or else bought far in advance? The principle was applicable to most of our lines. Walker liked it. You sang it like a song.

I wondered then whether it was something off the top of your head. As genuinely pleased as I was to see Walker take to it, I had difficulty reconciling it with the person I knew to be you. In the first place, it was trite. Did you really think this was a new idea, to offer products at a discount in order to increase the volume of sales? You had never mentioned it to me before. Were you worried that I would talk you out of it? Or steal it? I am not capable of stealing anymore, if I ever was, and am even less capable of dressing up something like this as new and original. It would embarrass me. And what a waste of time that would be, to feel embarrassed. I do not want to waste any more time. Where are you?

Con-sider yourself one of us, sing the Year Nine girls or those of them who graduated from Mrs. Dowager's Year Seven class and still harbor the suspicion that their future may lie on the stage. I feel the need to tell someone I don't know how much more of this I can take but your sister is hugging herself, both arms crossed against her chest, one hand gripping her shoulder, the other tugging on an earring. Your elder niece, our elusive but undoubtedly charming raison d'être, has not yet, to my knowledge, graced the stage. Perhaps you are with her, and she with you? Your sister's astronaut, sitting beside her, is tapping his knee in time to *We don't want to have no fuss. It's clear—we're— going to get along.*

I was in my office late one evening and, strangely, you were not around. You had not gone home but you had gone for the day, I remember being aware of that. The sun was going down, refusing to stay back late for love or money, and the skyline was delineated by the usual sterile fluorescent light of the city. I was not working but tinkering or perhaps tampering with my computer. I love the look of a spreadsheet against the dusk sky. By changing the data we can change the picture. If we do it often enough and fast enough we can make our own cartoons. The data is of course meaningless, so the skyline is the limit. I was checking my e-mail, just for the hell of it, because you had recently taught me how. Even the term *e-mail* sits uncomfortably with me. It always sounds like a brand of white goods. Previously my secretary was the only link between me and all those thousands of computer-literate people who desperately needed to contact me but who did not feel sufficiently confident with the telephone.

For all of my newfound computer skills, formatting, scrolling and saving, I can never remember my password or whether it is mine or yours. You will remember we used yours while you were teaching me. My first instinct is to use yours and I did that time, too, so that it was not my e-mail I was receiving but yours. Discretion may be the better part of valor, but serendipity should not be lightly dismissed, either. I was not searching for anything. My discovery was more in the form of an honest mistake and I would gladly have turned back from it had that been possible. It was one of these things you come across by chance, and though you are, at that moment, unable to grasp it fully or in context, still you are unable to turn away, fascinated by what it means, by what it is going to do to you. Something is triggered in your nervous system, something akin to that triggered when, as a child, you walk in on your parents in bed. No amount of shame or self-rebuke or the cursing of chance can overcome the sweet pulsating ache of your discovery. Walker had been writing to you.

It was so unutterably disturbing to see memos to you from "Lloyd" or from his secretary suggesting a familiarity with you I found astounding.

Nice work this morning. Regards, Lloyd.

What the hell was going on? What had you done so well that particular morning? If he was referring to your splitting of the atom at the breakfast meeting, he was clearly flattering you in the way that inadequate men with power and with the most transparent of motives often do. Surely you were not flirting with Walker? Were you simply permitting him to flirt with you, a proposition not quite as repulsive to contemplate but one still necessitating further explanation? You had not said anything about it. I know you would have been at least as revolted by this as I am. Why wouldn't you have said something? Were you planning to do something about it and, in the interim, thought you would spare

me? Of course I wouldn't have been jealous of a sensitively handled rebuff of his unwanted attentions. You could have told me.

But there was more. A memo containing your bright "creation
of a new market between wholesale and retail" idea was there on
the screen, word for word as you had expressed it at the meeting.
All right, what I would call sycophancy, you would call job security, or more likely, just "getting ahead." But this was a memo
from Walker to you. I couldn't understand this. Was he passing on
your idea to someone else and checking it with you, making sure
that he had captured the concept in all of its complexity? Was he
about to pass it off as his own? If so, why would he tell you? Why
would he check it with you first? I kept reading it, hearing the
words in different keys. By now it was night; most of the staff and
even the cleaners were gone. There was nothing to focus on but the
terminal and the high-rise clinic outside: cold, sharp immutable
representations of all that we have collectively striven for.

Were you giving it to him? Were you feeding him ideas and
if so, why? In order that he might grow? Why would you do
this? I still had it in the back of my mind that perhaps he was
stealing from you, although this would make no sense. If he was
stealing from you and I had discovered it, I would have to tell
you. Wouldn't I? So why wouldn't *you* tell me? I have nothing
he would want to steal. But this is nothing anyway, just some
bit of trite marketing you have dressed up. Why didn't you discuss it with me? Was it because it was just some puffery you
came out with that morning to alleviate your boredom, sitting
as we were in the bored room, and you have the ability—let's say
capacity, a more neutral term—to sell it to an idiot like Walker.
Then I read it again and noticed the date. He had written the
memo to you a week earlier.

There are friendships in which neither person gets to finish a sentence because both of them are so completely attuned to the other that they will finish each other's thoughts. We have never been like this. To know each other this well, there has to be a level of trust that we had not reached. When we met, I was more or less in the fetal position inside my suit; but by the time of my terminal discovery, I had made great progress, at least by my own standards. What was I to think of a memo from Walker to you containing some trivial commercial alchemy that, a week later, you parroted first thing one frosty morning as if it were your own? Why would you do this? Why the pretense?

My mouth was dry. I felt as one does when one is on the verge of becoming aware of something unbearable, something from which one never recovers. I didn't know what to do. It was about nine by then. I hadn't eaten anything. There was no sound but the ubiquitous hum of a large building, probably the lights, the occasional fax coming in and Atherton's muffled voice making what I assumed was an overseas call. I was breathing at a rate consistent with running but I was seated, still looking at the screen. I went to turn it off but it wouldn't go blank. I kept hitting the wrong button. I tried to reach you on the telephone but I couldn't. It was not because I didn't know what I would say. Not knowing what to say has never stopped me before. I could not call you. I was unable to. The first time I dialled I got the wrong number, a child's voice. "My mother can't talk to you." The second time, an older woman spoke on an answering machine. I became very alarmed. This was a nightmare. Checking my address book, I was reassured to see that I was not misremembering your telephone number. But when I went to redial it I found that I still couldn't. I kept misdialling. There was a numbness down my left side. I went shakily along the passage to the darkened tea room. I had to have a glass of water. I needed to talk to someone. I thought it was you. Your answering machine came on when I tried again and you will remember an almost percussive voice from an arid mouth asking, "Where are you?"

Mrs. Dowager is talking quietly to someone by the side of the stage. I can't make out whether it's a man or a woman. An elderly man is onstage now. He is speaking from a lectern. I wasn't paying attention when he was introduced and it isn't clear to me whether he is a retired politician or a war veteran. It has been too long. You have been gone too long. From the corner of my eye it appears your sister is asleep. I am tempted to wake her. There is a coarse ache at the back of my eyes. The formerly important older man seems to like being onstage. He has drifted to one of everyone's favorite topics, law and order, and he touches a raw nerve with the audience.

Should I say something to your sister? Someone should go to look for you. I have no idea how long you have been gone now but it is unacceptably long, unacceptable to both of us. What's your sister's name? I don't remember. I just remember how different the two of you are.

The man's voice does not have to grate, does not have to cause a pulsating pain in the back of my head, but it does. It carves a wedge in my consciousness. His voice itself is an offense. Then there are his words. *It has come to this, ladies and gentlemen and students. It has come to where we do not feel safe in our own community, in our streets, in our homes. I don't want to spoil the splendor of this wonderful family evening here at this proud educational institution, but let me just say this: We really do need more rigorous law enforcement. I know you would all agree.* I get up to look for you.

What was I hoping for? What do we ever hope for, and isn't it fortunate how innocent we are in hoping for it? Sunlight suddenly hits the earth, warming it till something grows, something we had not thought about, had not thought possible but now see and see it to be beautiful. The weather is unexpectedly balmy. We quicken our step and the smallest thing excites us. Your smile, have I mentioned it? It can awaken a tenderness in me that had lain dormant for a longer time than I can measure. We are in quiet agreement on all that matters. Everything is quiet and warm. We are not afraid to close our eyes, and while there is nothing at all contrived about this moment, we have been waiting for it all our lives. We close our eyes together. No one is offering advice: there is no need. We lie together on the cool dry grass, partially entwined and gently breathing in our own felicity. Do you remember? We lay on the cool dry grass and it was as if it were before the fall. Can you remember?

I had developed a taste for your electronic mail, particularly your correspondence with Walker. You may have noticed, I don't see how you could not have, but I was often agitated and irritable. An increasing proportion of my remarks were of a kind that would burn or corrode organic tissue. I was shaking more. Grabbing a coffee from the tea room, I would stop off at Atherton's room and make small talk for longer than I ever had before, leaning in his doorway with a new familiarity. He must have been a bit surprised. There are no pictures of his wife or kids on his desk. Atherton hates small talk. So do I.

What distinguishes Atherton from everybody else is not that he is so perceptive but that everybody else is so uncritical. Atherton is unbewitched by the cult of managerialism. I do not really know him and I have to imagine what his marriage is like or what he does on weekends. Is he in the garden, is he perhaps sanding down a hardwood cabinet of his own making, playing golf somewhere or reading Montaigne by the French windows in the chair his father left him? Perhaps, wearing corduroy pants and a checked shirt, he is shifting the furniture in the lounge room while his wife, one hand to her chin, tries to imagine some other configuration. The kettle boils and he makes a pot of coffee, finely ground, rich aroma, the kind he likes. On the other side of the window, his children are leaping over what was once a pile of leaves. It was a pile he had collected. He pours the coffee into two large blue mugs his wife had bought a couple of years earlier at a fair in the country. Perhaps there is still something of the little girl in her. He has always liked that about her. We really don't know much about Atherton. But he is going, too, isn't he? He will have to go.

I have no idea where you are, but you have no need to hide anymore.

Although we can never know all that there is about anyone, I know enough now. Migraine laps at the back of my eyes. Even though the corridors of the school are in almost complete darkness, there is a burning light behind my face. I call your name and hear your voice come back at me. It is a child's voice coming from the distance. This is not really dialogue but, stumbling as I am into the walls of your old school, it is the best we can do. Or is it? Can we do better? Walker says we can do better.

What would have happened had I not had your password? What would you have told me and when? I have been of so much use to you. A smart-arse, observant, alienated, subversive type like me, it was likely I would be of use. But you didn't quite know just how much you would call on me till your husband left you. This made things a bit sticky, even for you, and now you are hiding. But the game is up and sooner or later I will find you. It's a small world after all. It was extremely unprofessional of you to provide even an idiot like me with access to your private correspondence. Who knows what I might find out? I could discover what you earn, something we have never discussed precisely, never put a figure on, although this would not really be at all embarrassing for you. But I might learn who it is that pays you. This is far more damaging, especially since we are not, after all, employed by the same company. My company pays someone else for your services. Then that company pays you. You are, in the naked light of day, a consultant, and your work is just about complete. When you leave, so will Atherton and I and many more. It was all a performance.

From the auditorium I can hear the distant sound of a cannon or a kettledrum. A small student orchestra plays cabaret music. At least, that's what it sounds like. Berlin in the twenties: on it goes. Weimar revisited. But when the Reichstag finally burns this time it will be on pay TV. This night is forever, or at least that part of forever that you experience when everything else is on hold and there is no one above us to press Play. I have no idea where I'm going. There is no place I can think of that you are likely to be. So the darkness is appropriate. But it won't calm the nausea. It feels like gastric juices coursing through my eustachian tubes, seeping into my eyes. The cannon is in my head.

It is fuel to the fire behind my face, licking at my ears from the inside. I want to be rid of my tongue. My movement is staccato, out of time with the cannon. I grip the handle of one locker after another to keep upright. If I do this long enough, will I touch a locker that was yours? What have you done? Downsizing is the current panacea, and you had been hired to advise on its implementation. Why can't I hate you for it? I had something to tell you.

With the full weight of my body, I push open the door to what can only be the girls' toilets, slam my palm against the wall looking for the light switch. Nothing. The wall is cold. I can slam it all I like. It will not answer. The room is dark. I call your name. My voice is a gasp of air pushed over bark, a sickly afterthought from my neck. Do I really think you are in here? Now? Ever? I push open the door to each cubicle. There are five of them. They don't all swing back with equal force. I can't see them but I feel the difference in the movement of the air each time. The hinges squeal differently, individually. This is their moment. They won't share it. I am good at this, repeating it. I am getting to recognize them by their sound. I try your name a couple of times for no reason at all until I stumble and hit one side of a cubicle wall. On my knees now, I vomit. The floor is damp. The cannon pounds inside me but I vomit arhythmically. My tongue is in the way. My nostrils are clogged and I rest my head on the toilet bowl. Do you know this one? I hear nothing for the crashing inside me. I will cry here till I bleed.

My breathing arrests me once I am empty. This is the worst it has ever been. I raise myself up and flush the toilet. My knees are sore and damp. I am hot. The floor is damp everywhere. The cleaners must have mopped the floor here not long ago. I can hear the soles of my shoes rejecting the moisture. I go to wash my face in the trough. I had something to tell you. Don't you want to know what it is? The mop sits inside the bucket on the draining board beside a whole lot of plastic cups. Did you use these? I can hear the street, people. The tap is on. Water escapes hurriedly, dying for air. Furious. Never seen a trough before. I am wet, my face and hair, my chest, through my shirt. I shudder and lose balance. The mop is out of the bucket and both are on the floor with me. It crashes down. I lie there. It is dark. The left side has shut down again. I am numb there. How long will I lie here? I don't know. I was looking for you.

The door is kicked open. I hear the crack of a shoe against the wood. The light is on. I squint. It is a woman, a uniformed policewoman. I can't imagine what it is she sees looking down at me. I am ridiculous on the floor. She could be watching me die. They want to check, to do a scan. They want to check for a shape on my brain which would too easily explain everything. The policewoman wants to know what I am doing here. She draws her gun and requests backup on a two-way radio attached to her lapel. I am unable to speak and she is scared. Go on, shoot. I have no answers. She will have to wait for the scan like everybody else. Can barely say it anyway: a possible glioblastoma. The suspect has a name. No need for backup. I wanted to tell you. This is what they're looking for. Perhaps it will show up on my screen, when I'm more proficient with the terminal. Are you going to shoot or not?

It's clear—we're—going to get along.

They give you coffee in the police caravan whether you ask for it or not. It's their way of apologizing to the potential suspects for the recent spate of police shootings. It would be better if they shot you. I am shivering. They don't let me see myself. She starts asking me questions. I'm good at the early ones: name, address. What am I doing here? It is your niece's speech night? I don't know her name. What are her parents' names? I don't know, met them tonight for the first time. Can't remember. What year is the girl in? Eleven or twelve. I make it up. No, I have never been here before, of course not. Why "Of course"? You idiots! Are you really drawing a salary to suspect me? Ask me something sensible and I will do my best. They do. She has neglected to close the caravan door. The carnival is over. I hear people talking. That's what I want to know, too: Where is she now? Where are you?

I hear voices, women's voices and their laughter. Through the crack in the door I can see people passing; they come in waves, in bunches. They look in as they pass. They look at me. I see you with a group of girls. They are in school uniform and have ribbons in their hair. I hear them laughing. You look in at me through the gap in the door. We look at each other. Your face is blank. Say something. Tell them why I'm here. Tell *me*. But you don't say anything. You are wearing the school uniform. Only it is not you. It is your niece. She looks so like you, much more than like her mother. I call out your name to her but she walks on. It was her speech night and all went well. Her friends adore her. The world's at her feet, starting with me. I have never heard her speak. A policeman slams closed the caravan door. He frowns. They must be joking with all of this. I have the right to remain silent. He feels obliged to mention it.

Have I ever loved you? Yes, before there was reason, and still later, when there was none, even though, as it turned out, the best thing about us was the person I would have become had you been as I had cast you. I am broken now, feeling the wind on my skin till it pushes my bones to mock me, when there is no wind. I am burnt dry by the sun till the feeling is gone on one side, when there is no sun. They tell me these are the symptoms. Your betrayal is as clear to me now as our Swedish vodka, but I cannot allow you to be so far removed from the person I thought you were that I am unable to love you. You see, I realized something when you came along. It was not a realization that pays. It would be of no interest to Walker and it has no tax implications for anyone. But I realized that I needed to love you. It defined me, and if you did not exist I would have had to invent you, minus the betrayal. But perhaps that is all of you, the sine qua non of you.

So why is it later than you think so much more often than not? They will not give me a mirror but I see from my forearms, my wrists and hands that my skin is the color of wet ash. This place is not known as a war zone. It is the leafy suburb in which you and your sister were educated. Your father sent you here and then went about his business. This is your community. It has become a war zone for me and soon everyone will know.

I sit by the wall in a police caravan, a good night's work for someone. My feet, our feet, are sore and we have only travelled one day in our new school shoes. But we have travelled that same day over and over and over, only without ever noticing it. We fill our day, our one repeated day, with distractions, clothes, cars, orgasms, a job. A job for Atherton, for me. You will sleep and live the day again and again. But remember the cool dry grass. That's what I had to tell you.

GOOD MORNING, AGAIN IN THE TIME OF
THE DINOSAUR YOUR NIECE'S SPEECH
NIGHT **THE REASONS I WON'T BE COMING**
MANSLAUGHTER THE *HONG KONG FIR*
DOCTRINE I WAS ONLY IN A CHILDISH WAY
CONNECTED TO THE ESTABLISHED ORDER
SPITALNIC'S LAST YEAR A TALE IN TWO CITIES

People seldom have a genuinely clear understanding of probate. They are full of misconceptions about it. I've grown accustomed to this. It doesn't surprise me anymore. It shouldn't after twenty-four years with the Office of Probate in what is now called the Department of Justice. Maggie says people are afraid of it. She says that since they associate it with death in some way and don't really understand it in the first place, they're afraid of it. People are afraid of what they don't understand. Maggie often says this. She's angry with these people. I've told her that most people don't understand most things. She says that most people are afraid of most things. Maggie is a social worker by training but she works for the Department of Treasury now.

The topic arises when people ask me what I do. Maggie and I look at each other and then I start at the beginning, with the basics of probate. The Supreme Court grants a certificate to the effect that the will of a certain deceased person has been proved and registered in the court and that administration of the deceased's effects has been granted to the executor proving the will. Maggie says I've lost them by this stage. We never get to what I actually do.

We must have known the Gibsons for almost thirty years. Maggie thinks it's more. I actually prefer Fran to Brian, but whenever we're out with them there's always that preliminary stage where Maggie talks to Fran and Brian talks to me. It's there right after the hellos. It can take up to half an hour. Brian starts off with the state of his business, which he then links to the economy. He owns a news agency. He quotes figures and talks about trends, both in his business and in the economy generally. He goes through phases. A while ago he seemed very fond of the *trade-weighted index.* More recently it was the *current account deficit* and *microeconomic reform*, which he wants to introduce in his news agency. He puts his arm around my shoulders and talks earnestly about the *fundamentals* which are or aren't in place (I can never remember) and about our *major trading partners.*

This preliminary stage usually ends with Brian attracting the attention of Maggie and Fran, and then, with a mischievous grin, he asks what I do, again. He has a very loud laugh. Maggie thinks it's more than thirty years.

They have been our good friends for a long time. Maggie and Fran used to work together before Maggie went to the Treasury. They were really there for us when we lost Sarah. That's when you see what people are like. Brian wouldn't go home. He said he didn't think it was good for us to be on our own and we never were. He said he would keep the media away and he did. If it wasn't Brian and Fran or Maggie's parents, it was the police. We seemed to be constantly putting the kettle on. The police were really terrific. We don't blame them. Maggie says blame is useless. Some things are unsolvable. They worked long and hard on the case. Some have become close personal friends of ours. I don't think the public really appreciates the work they do. When they started the Neighborhood Watch in our area we were one of the first to join.

Not long ago, we received a printed invitation in the mail to the Gibsons' thirty-fifth wedding anniversary. The paper was tan and the lettering was gold. It said we had three weeks to RSVP. I've always wondered how they worked that out. Why three weeks and not four, or two? The Gibsons had booked the Regency Room at the San Remo Reception Centre. It was to be black tie. Maggie had left the invitation on the dresser in our room. She didn't mention it through dinner. She was talking to Griff, her father, about the ozone layer. He's not very concerned about it. She's been trying to make him more aware. Griff has lived with us in Sarah's old room since Maggie's mother passed away about two and a half years ago. He's not bad for seventy-eight. He's been trying to teach himself the guitar ever since we all heard a special on Radio National about a year back. Maggie's very good with him.

We listen to the radio together quite a lot, particularly Maggie and me. We listen in bed at night before we go to sleep.

One night in bed as we lay on our backs, having turned the radio off, Maggie asked, "Do you ever wake up with an inexplicable . . . panic inside you?"

"Panic?"

"Yes, a sort of general, nonspecific panic . . . in your stomach . . . that quickens your pulse?"

I thought about this for a moment. Although it was the middle of the night and her question was apropos of nothing in particular, I knew I had better give my answer some thought. Maggie can take people very seriously. She often does. Where

was she leading with this question? She was waiting for my answer. She was probably describing something she has felt. Perhaps it is a feeling she is ashamed of. She doesn't always want to
have to be strong. She has told me this.

"Yes. I have experienced something like that."

"I thought you had," she said, and rolled over on her side.

Although it was my annual leave, I had taken work home. You
realize as you get older that you're really only hurting yourself if
you put off your work, annual leave or not. We had formed a
committee at work to undertake a client services program. It
was I who had pushed for the committee to be widely represen-
tative. Although it wouldn't be meeting until a few weeks after
my return, I thought I would take the opportunity of this quiet
time to draft a few proposals, nothing definitive, perhaps starting with a working definition of *client*.

Maggie had a flexiday so she slept in while I worked on the
draft proposals. At ten o'clock I brought her a cup of tea. She
had been listening to the radio but had turned it off when I
came in with the tea.

"What were you listening to?"

"*Life Matters*."

"What's that? I don't think I know that one."

"It's the new name they gave to *Offspring*."

"Oh," I said, and put the tea down on her bedside table.

"What was it about this morning?"

"Breast-feeding," she said, bringing the teacup to her mouth.
"Is Dad up yet?" she asked.

"Yes, I've made him some toast and he's taken it outside. Are you still going to take him to the library today?"

"Yes. I'd better. He's got a couple of things that will be over-due soon."

"What else?"

"What else what?"

"What else are you going to do today?" I asked.

"Well, I've got shopping to do . . . and I'd wanted to write to Bruce."

"Haven't you started that letter yet?"

"No. No, I haven't. He wants some more money, you know."

"Yes, I know."

"How did *you* know?" she asked.

"He said it, didn't he? Doesn't he say something about money in his last letter?"

"*I* got the impression he wanted money from the phone call, when he called me at work."

"Do you want to give him more money? How much does he really need in Nepal?"

"You've decided, haven't you? You have an agenda," she said.

"No, I haven't decided. I haven't decided."

Maggie sat up with a pillow at her back and said after a while, "I haven't decided, either."

"It's terrific that he still writes. . . ."

"And calls."

"From Nepal of all places, after all this time."

"He wasn't calling from Nepal."

"Still. He's a good boy."

"He certainly knows how to take care of himself. Nothing

more we can teach him," Maggie said, pulling the sheet up to her neck.

"Will you be working all day?" she asked.

"Not *all* day."

"Would you do something for me today?"

"What?" I asked her.

"I'd like you to write to the Gibsons, to RSVP to their wedding anniversary invitation."

"I could just call them, except I'll never get off the phone if Brian answers."

"I'd like you to write to them telling them we won't be coming."

There was an awful banging sound coming from another room, like a hollow wooden box being slapped. It startled me.

"What the hell's that?"

"It's Dad. He's been having terrible trouble with notes because he won't press the strings down hard enough. He gets the muffled sound because he won't press them down hard enough. It's important that he feels he's achieving something, making some progress, or he'll get discouraged."

"Why do you say he *won't* press hard enough?"

"He could but he won't. He's too soft. Is there any more tea?"

I don't think Maggie has been enjoying her work recently. It's not so much the administrative component. She knew this would be a feature when she accepted the position. I think she even takes comfort in it now. I can understand that. I suspect when Fran accepted a position with the Australian Council of Social Services, Maggie was privately concerned that Fran's contribution to the community would be greater than hers. No matter what I said, I don't think anything has really dispelled that concern. There's a strong policy analysis component to Maggie's work. She's even privy to certain inside information. She knows in advance the proposed expenditure cuts, their size and where they'll fall. She sees the guidelines for the proposed Human Resources cutbacks. She even sees the lists of personnel, in all government departments, whose services will no longer be required. She has her finger on the pulse of public policy in a macro sense that I would have thought she'd find rather exciting. She used to find it exciting, but not lately it seems.

I must admit I've had my moments, too, moments when I've felt I'd lost that sense of challenge. When you're caught up in a new program, though, it's hard to remember ever having felt that way, but I have felt it from time to time. You can even get blasé about things. I remember that within only a year of being granted a Higher Duties Allowance I took it for granted.

Sitting there in the study one day last week, with the sunlight coming through our trees and falling softly onto the pages of the draft proposals, I had to work hard to be at one with Maggie's dissatisfaction. Griff was in the garden with his guitar. He likes to hold it to him.

Maggie came in from the car and unloaded the shopping bags onto the bench beside the sink. When Griff heard her he brought his guitar inside and looked in the plastic bags. I was listening to the rustling and talking. Maggie put the kettle on. Griff put the guitar on the kitchen table. Maggie ran the tap water, not hard but firmly over certain fruit and vegetables in our sink. I couldn't see it from the study but I knew this was what she was doing. I thought we might have a salad for lunch.

I was first in bed that night but not by much. Maggie was sitting at the dresser, taking off her face. It was a bit nippy so I brought out the flannel pajamas, my stripy ones. Maggie saw me in the mirror and gave a little smile.

"Those pajamas are so . . . you," she said.

I smiled a little. "What do you mean?"

"They are just . . . *you*," she said, and went back to her face. "But they're too stripy. I can't look at them."

I got into bed and she couldn't see much of them anymore. Then she got into bed. We listened to Phillip Adams on the radio. I thought Maggie seemed sad.

"What are you thinking?" I asked.

"Lots of things . . . and nothing."

"Should we talk about some of them?"

"Did you know that Sarah had once asked how we got married: about the decision to get married, the mechanics of it, the proposal and who was told first, et cetera?"

"I didn't know that. She was very romantic, wasn't she? I mean, right from the early days."

"There were only early days."

"Yes, of course. I know, Maggie." I reached for her hand.

"You told her the way it all happened?"

"Yes," she said, removing her hand to apply her moisturizer.

"You always knew what you wanted, didn't you?" I said, resting my hand on her shoulder.

"Why . . . why do you say that?"

"Because of the way it all happened. I was much too scared. I would never have said anything without your . . . encouragement."

"But you did," she said.

"I just said yes. Do you remember? It was about the time we were meant to be going camping, near Mount Disappointment."

"What do you mean you said yes?" Maggie asked.

"Well, I obviously didn't say no or we wouldn't be here, would we?"

"But I didn't ask you anything."

"Yes you did," I insisted. "I remember it clearly. It was night-time. We were in your parents' front room. They were in the kitchen. We were talking about what your parents would say about us going camping. We'd never been away alone. You said they wouldn't like it and that we might just as well tell them we were getting married because, as far as they were concerned, couples shouldn't go away alone together until after they're married."

Maggie sat up. "Yes, I remember. You said you didn't agree with that. You said it was old-fashioned but that you would re-spect it."

"And *you* said we shouldn't respect it . . . then you asked me if I was ready . . . and that's when I said yes," I reminded her.

I took Maggie's moisturized hand and put it between the covers and my stripy flannel pajama top. She sat still. We were quiet for a moment, remembering.

"There's a logical inconsistency there," Maggie said.

"Where?"

"Even the way you tell it now—"

"Which is the way it happened," I jumped in.

"Even the way you tell it now, it sounds as though I was ask-ing if you were ready to disrespect my parents' views for the sake of our camping trip, not if you wanted to get married."

"Look, I don't remember the exact words after all these years but I remember the effect it had on me, and I said yes. Don't you think it's getting late?" I said, turning off the bedside light and snuggling up next to Maggie, who stayed sitting upright.

"But I would know what I was asking!" she said.

"Yes, of course," I said, tucking my nose into her hip, "but you might not remember *now* what you meant *then*."

I was getting sleepy warming up next to her. The moisturizer smelt nice.

There are two forms of probate that may be granted, the common form and what may be called the solemn form. It's only when there is a dispute as to the validity of the will that probate in solemn form is employed.

I listen to the news. Maggie's away. There's a flood alert for rivers north of somewhere I don't think I've been. Bad news on the debt front is faced squarely by the Prime Minister. He says we can't keep living above our means. I guess that's true. He says the government will set an example in "belt-tightening." It's the harsh medicine we have to have to make up for the excesses of the last decade. I feel a bit sheepish. The all-ordinaries are down. Griff's in bed. He's not feeling the best. He doesn't understand why Maggie's not here. There's something about the recent Uruguay round of GATT talks. Where are my golf clubs?

She said she just needs some space. That's all she really needs at the moment. I can run things alone for a while. We're out of that multipurpose spray stuff. We use it on the kitchen table but it says it's appropriate for bathroom use as well. I might take my work into Sarah's room, just to keep an eye on Griff. There's nothing I can get for him. It's probably best that he keep dozing. The more he sleeps the better. I'll get him some lemons when I go out. I don't mind the supermarket. It's got everything you need. Poor thing.

I gather some pens and my papers and take them in to Griff. He's sleeping soundly. I've got the mail too. Never anything exciting. Nothing but envelopes with windows. There's one from work, too, from the department. I'm on leave; what do they want? They never write to me.

When there is a dispute, it's usually determined pursuant to Part IV of the Administration of Probate Act. The Act provides a lot of room for the exercise of judicial discretion, which is probably a good thing.

I should respond to the Gibsons' invitation. I wouldn't go on my own. I wouldn't like to. I'd have to hire a dinner suit and everything. I'll drop a present around sometime. It feels silly writing to them. What do you say? I don't write many letters. Never did. Perhaps I'll give them a call? Maybe Brian can get away for a game of golf. He works very long hours. They have to in that game. I don't like leaving Griff, though. He doesn't look good. We're out of lemons. How can a family be out of lemons? I'll give Brian a call. *Our major trading partners!* He's so funny. Who are our major trading partners?

GOOD MORNING, AGAIN IN THE TIME OF
THE DINOSAUR YOUR NIECE'S SPEECH
NIGHT THE REASONS I WON'T BE COMING
MANSLAUGHTER THE *HONG KONG FIR*
DOCTRINE I WAS ONLY IN A CHILDISH WAY
CONNECTED TO THE ESTABLISHED ORDER
SPITALNIC'S LAST YEAR A TALE IN TWO CITIES

Scared! Yes, I heard you, the line's bad but I heard you. You said you were scared. There's no need to be. Of course I understand it, but there's no need to be. You've got nothing to be afraid of. You're not really scared, are you?

The dumpy woman, fleshy, soft—*fat*, for those in a hurry—sits listening at one end of the long bench that makes up the second back row. Her hair is gray and shaggy. She wears a blue-and-white pin-striped shirt with the top button done up. Her neck spills out over the collar. The room is hot but she wears a blue blazer over the shirt. It has no lapels and had been bought at a sale. She never dreamed she would be wearing it under circumstances such as these. She cannot remember when she last dreamed at all. But now, in the middle of so many things, she is always imagining.

In front of her sits the informant and in front of him at the bar table sits counsel for the prosecution. His instructing solicitor sits on the opposite side of the bar table, facing him, ready to do whatever it is instructing solicitors from the Office of the Director of Public Prosecutions are meant to do. They are all nice men with fine manners. Even with all that they have on their plates, each of them has said good morning to her. She feels a bit alone but she is far more alone than that.

The Court officials look like no people she has seen before. There is neither malice nor humor in their faces. This is where they work. Theirs is an invisible art, the seamless achievement of efficiency without undue haste. They have a show to run. The less they are noticed, the greater their success. The Tipstaff wears a gray coat with military bearing. It looks like nineteenth-century European army-surplus and it hides the shape and definition of his body. The Associate sits directly beneath the Judge and, except for the wig, is dressed exactly like him, a Junior League clone. The plump woman listens as the Associate addresses the jury with the precise enunciation and impartiality of a newsreader.

"Members of the jury, Raymond Barry Islington is charged with murder. To this charge he has pleaded not guilty and for his trial has placed himself upon God and his country, which country you are. Your duty is to say whether he is guilty or not guilty. Hearken to the evidence."

There were twelve of them and they would not all hearken equally. There was a woman in the back who tried to be excused from jury duty. She told the Judge that it was a busy time for her at work and that her employer would be displeased if she were selected to sit on a jury. Her employer was her son and she did not want to talk about her difficulties with him in a room full of strangers. But the Judge informed her and everyone else in Court that to discriminate in any way against an employee because of their jury service was an offense against the Juries Act. He refused her application to be excused and she had gone back into the throng of the Court with the other members of the jury pool, dissatisfied with the protection afforded her by the Juries Act. When her name was chosen at random from an old wooden ballot box by the Associate, she hoped the accused's solicitor would have enough sense to challenge her selection. But he did not and she became one of the chosen twelve.

Another woman, much younger, sat in the front row of the jury box with her hair tied back in a ponytail. She was wearing a low-cut singlet with her bra straps exposed. Each of her eyes wandered around the room independently, from the floor to the ceiling, around and around. Her attention seemed to fix for a long time on the knee of the juror to her right. She was not understanding anything.

When the man who was to become the jury's foreman had his card chosen at random by the Associate, he stood proudly erect but then, momentarily stunned by the publicity of his own presence, he froze slightly hunched, like a rabbit at night when a torch is shone in its eyes. He listened stilly as his name and occupation were called. *Donald Hamish McPherson, engineer retired.* He walked as directed by the Tipstaff, slowly passing the accused, up the stairs and into the jury box. *Kenneth Arthur Halliday, storeman*, was much younger and with thicker limbs. He wore jeans and a yellow T-shirt as though, with this informality, he might reduce his unease at being there. He rolled his newspaper up like a baton when he was called and took it into the jury box without making eye contact with the accused.

The dumpy woman looked at the foreman. She thought he looked kindly and that a man like this probably appreciated the authority with which the Judge spoke. The Judge was polite to the jury. He spoke to them with a deference unexpected by many of them, explaining that they were the triers, the judges of fact. He would explain and rule on any questions of law, but ultimately they would have to decide whether the Prosecution had proved all the elements of the offense of murder beyond reasonable doubt. If the Prosecution had done this, the jury had no option at law but to find the accused man guilty. If not, they were equally bound by the law to find the accused not guilty.

The first witness was a doctor, the forensic pathologist who had conducted the autopsy. He wore gray pleated trousers, a white shirt and a green tie with small yellow cats on it. The jury began to learn about the deceased, a man of one hundred and seventy centimeters and eighty-two kilograms. The plumpish woman wondered how many of the jurors would know that this meant five foot seven and twelve stone twelve in the old scale. She knew what it meant. The pathologist described the various injuries and said that they were all consistent with injuries caused by a shotgun. In the skull he had found shotgun pellets. Death was due to head and neck injuries caused by these pellets. It would have been instantaneous. The deceased had a blood alcohol reading of 0.24 percent. There was no evidence of any defensive-type injuries on the hands of the deceased. The injury to the head due to the pellets went upward from below the jaw toward the right ear at an angle of forty-five degrees to the vertical.

Senior counsel for the defense cross-examined him. The pathologist agreed that no gunpowder residue was found on the skin of the deceased. The lack of any residue on the body could be

explained by the gun having been wrapped in the car seat cover
that was shown in the police photographs, the pathologist further
agreed. But this was not the only possibility, he continued. If the
barrel was right up against the neck, it was also possible that all
the residue had been expelled into the wound site or out through
the exit areas. He conceded that, nevertheless, it was possible that
the gun was still totally wrapped at the time it discharged. The
juror with the bra strap and the wandering eyes tore dead skin
from her index finger with her teeth.

*It's warm here too. No, not as warm as Melbourne. Because you told
me. And anyway, we get your weather on the TV news. Because you're
there, of course. Why else would I care about Melbourne's weather?*

A Senior Constable, taller than necessary for a firearm exam-
iner with the Forensic Science Laboratory, took the oath and held
the Bible high in his right hand as though wanting to slam-dunk
it into the mouth of God. He had attended the postmortem and
described the shot found in the skull to be consistent with that
from a Number Four shotgun cartridge, specifically a brand of
French cartridge used in twelve-gauge shotguns. It was difficult
for the Senior Constable to say precisely where the man with the
gun would have been standing, but he believed the muzzle was
in contact with the body of the deceased when the gun was fired.
His colleague, a forensic scientist whose area of expertise was
bloodstaining, was more subdued taking the oath. Based on an
examination of the bloodstaining on the partition wall, he con-
cluded that the deceased was standing at the time he was shot
and was no more than thirty to thirty-five centimeters from the
partition wall. The foreman of the jury had thought he had been

paying perfect attention but now wondered whether he had missed the significance of the partition wall. Perhaps it would become apparent. The Judge might mention it. Already he was behind. He felt a fraud.

In cross-examination, the bloodstain expert admitted he had not examined the car seat cover. Referring to one of the police photographs, he said it was not unusual for a victim to have blood on his mouth or nose as a result of being shot. It was not unusual at all. It's not unusual. The juror in the yellow T-shirt swivelled uncomfortably on his seat and, smiling, tried not to think of Tom Jones. *It's not unusual to be loved by anyone.*

No one had thought to ask the plump woman to leave the Court after the Prosecution opening when, on the Judge's instruction, the Tipstaff had announced that all witnesses were commanded to leave the Court. She had heard the order but had not thought it applied to her and no one had said anything to her about it. When she was called to give evidence, the Associate stood, turned and murmured something to the Judge. After a brief whispered exchange the Judge decided to let it go and the plump woman slowly ascended the stairs to the witness box and took the oath. She was the wife of the deceased.

She had met Yadwiga Quinlan in mid-1990. They became friends, close friends. The woman spoke slowly. Yadwiga had separated from her husband, Ricky Quinlan, in January 1993 and Ricky subsequently went to Tasmania. The witness and her husband, Geoff, the man everyone else now referred to as "the deceased," and their children continued to visit Yadwiga and her children. She and Geoff visited at least once a week, usually on Saturday when their daughter, Amy, and Yadwiga's daughter, Carly, went horse riding. Geoff would take them there and pick them up several hours later. Before he left for Tasmania, Ricky Quinlan had given Geoff permission to use their garage to work on his MG. Yadwiga had seen no reason to revoke this permission after Ricky had gone, and Geoff was frequently at Yadwiga's house, talking with her, playing with the kids and working interminably on the MG. Occasionally the witness and Geoff would join Yadwiga in a few drinks, "making up a party." Because he was there more often than she was, Geoff and Yadwiga drank together more frequently.

The dumpy woman was careful to emphasize that her husband rarely drank excessively. He was a moderate drinker. He had always been only a moderate drinker. He would perhaps drink two or three times a week at the Criterion Hotel but not to excess, and he rarely drank at home, unless they had guests. Her husband did not own a firearm. She volunteered this.

On Wednesday the second of March she had been at home. She had been sharing a car with her husband and had had the use of it for the day. Their son was home from school with a chest infection. The dumpy woman jumped backwards and forwards in time. The Prosecutor let her go. About six months after Ricky had left, Yadwiga formed an association with Ray Islington, the accused man. The witness and her husband, Geoff, subsequently met Ray on several occasions. She understood that Ray and Ricky used to work at the same place. On the previous Boxing Day, Ray had dropped Carly Quinlan and her brother off at their house to play. What did they play? Different games. The boys and girls played separately, she remembers. It probably doesn't matter, does it? She was sorry for wasting the Court's time.

Yadwiga would call her at home sometimes on the telephone. After Ricky left she had called more frequently, usually distressed.

Geoff was good at calming Yadwiga, settling her down. He was better at it than she was. When Yadwiga was on edge or particularly upset, she would ask Geoff to come over. They would have a couple of drinks and he would be home within an hour or two. Of course, she could have accompanied Geoff to Yadwiga's home, which was only around the corner, but someone had to stay with the children, and since Geoff could help Yadwiga more than she could, it made sense for him to go. The plump woman asked for a glass of water.

Geoff usually came home from work at around seven o'clock unless he was having a few drinks at the Criterion, in which case he might get home some time between eleven and twelve. He worked as a technician with an electronics company, in their R&D section. They had been working on some big project for a while that would often keep him back late. It had something to do with telephones. He had mentioned it often but it was really all a bit beyond her. It was something about a mobile terminal. He might well have mentioned it to Yadwiga; she wouldn't know. He probably had. They all saw each other quite frequently. She herself had been to Yadwiga's many times, just knocking and entering. Their friendship was on that kind of basis. The woman wanted to know if the Prosecutor understood this. If no one was in the lounge room, she would walk through to the kitchen.

The dumpy woman and the reluctant juror caught each other's eye. The juror instinctively wanted to help her. They had pitched in together at weekend working bees at the local primary school. They had gone for their driver's licenses together and both had failed twice; they had waited up as young girls for their parents to come home from anniversary dinners; they had kept busy at home when their contemporaries were out on dates with boys; they had tried out different recipes for orange cake and prune muffins. They had tried all the diets. They had each married the first man to ask them; they had given birth soon enough to avoid the embarrassment of annual holidays and nothing to talk about, and they had made many of their own clothes from material that had been greatly reduced from a price no one had ever paid. The reluctant juror could picture the large woman's home, always tidy, and so quiet whenever her husband worked back late on a mobile terminal or something or other, for better or for worse. In an instant they recognized each other even though they had never met.

The reluctant juror had never been cross-examined. Neither had the dumpy woman before this, which was another thing they had in common. But the juror had a husband and the dumpy woman was a widow now. On the day of her husband's death, her son, who would normally have gone to school, was at home ill. Geoff had said that he would call her during the day to see how their son was feeling. He did not make that call.

He had said in the morning that he would try to get home earlier than his usual seven p.m. She prepared the evening meal for him but he did not come home. With one car between them, they had discussed the possibility that her husband might have to come home early to take their son to a doctor. He would have known if their son's health had deteriorated during the day because she could have called him at work. She would have interrupted him if it was important.

He didn't like to drink at home. Some people are like that. Her husband was like that. He would have a few drinks at home only if they had company. If a person left the Criterion to go to their place, they would reach the Quinlan home first. The Quinlan home was on the way. It was convenient. You might say that. The woman left the witness box disappointed. She was starting to understand a few things about the workings of this room and the people in it. There were so many things they should have asked her. Her husband would not be defended here, either. They were going to kill him again.

Yes, of course you can. You know you can stay here anytime. You know there's room, plenty of room. Don't ask stupid questions. Yes, anytime. No. Not now. Of course, you can't come now. Not till it's over. No, not just your bit, all of it. Yes, the whole thing. It's important you stay together. Till it's over. Then you can come. I promise. Yes. No matter what happens to him. I promise. Of course I love you.

She resumed her seat in the body of the Court and sat, smoothing the flanks of her blazer, just as quietly as she had before she had given her evidence. She had never met Albert Bird, nor had she heard of him, and as he took the oath she wondered how this man came to be talking about her husband. He was the manager of the Criterion Hotel. He had seen the deceased on the night he was killed drinking pots of full-strength beer. "Five or six pots of heavy, maybe more. Drinking alone. He generally drank on his own. That night he came in sometime between seven and eight. He stayed for a couple of hours. Asked him if he'd just finished work. The man said he had. Would have left by nine thirty."

Otto Milosz was a technical colleague of the deceased. The dumpy woman had heard mention of him from time to time over the last three years. The day Geoff died was also a memorable day for Mr. Milosz. They had just solved the problem they had been working on for almost two years. Geoff had left saying he was in a bit of a hurry. He had to pick up his son. Mr. Milosz had told him that this was all right and the deceased left at about seven thirty p.m.

In cross-examination Mr. Milosz explained that the project they had been working on for so long was very important to the firm. It was going to have export ramifications. There had been a problem with it that, according to preliminary tests, had only been solved that day. But they still had some further confirmatory tests to undertake.

"Geoff came in with his briefcase and just said he was leaving. I was about to set up the tests but he said he was in a hurry and had to go. I had expected Geoff to do the tests with me. It was about ten past seven."

The woman pictured the briefcase, maroon, wearing thin. How many times had he had the clasps repaired? "Cheaper to buy a new one," she had told him. "Perhaps," he had said. She had planned to replace it for him for Christmas, birthday, whatever.

Tomorrow? Are you sure? There's nothing to worry about. I have, actually. I've given evidence on a few occasions. Before your time, my girl. Before your time. Well, you never asked. Good to hear you laugh. It'll all be over soon. I'll call you tomorrow night. Try to remember everything that happens. No, so you can tell me. I'll call you tomorrow night. Be strong for her.

The next witness was Yadwiga Quinlan. An insurance assessor, she had married Ricky Quinlan in 1971 and had lived with him at their present address till their separation in January 1993. They had two children, Brian, thirteen at the time of the night in question, and Carly, then eleven. She had met the wife of the deceased when they were enrolled in the same adult education course. They became friends, and when their children met, they, too, became friends. The deceased and his wife often visited the Quinlans with their children. Sometimes Geoff would come on his own to tinker with the MG Ricky had allowed him to garage there. After the separation, Yadwiga saw no reason to revoke the permission.

Geoff usually came over on a Saturday afternoon and they would take it in turns to drive the girls to horse riding. Sometimes he and his wife would call past after they had been to the market on a Saturday. Alone or with his wife, it was normally on a Saturday that he came. Shortly after Ricky and she had separated, Ricky came back to Melbourne for a brief visit. It had been an upsetting visit for her and particularly for the children. She was under the impression that Ricky had contacted Geoff, the deceased. She had phoned and asked Geoff's wife if Geoff could come over so that they could discuss Ricky and whatever it was Ricky might have said to him. Geoff came and they chatted for about an hour or so, drinking coffee. It was about eight p.m., sometime in February or March.

On another occasion Geoff dropped by at about ten p.m. one night, just to say hello. She had been on her way to bed. They had a cup of coffee and a cigarette and then she said that she would have to go to bed. He had said that was fine and left. She had smelled beer on him but he was not drunk. Yadwiga said that she remembered the night because it had been a Scout night and her son was late to bed. She could also recall Geoff dropping by a few months later and being a little upset. He had been drinking. Yadwiga paused for several moments. She looked down. The foreman took the opportunity to clear his throat. He thought it all a terrible business.

Geoff had said that although he appeared to be a good husband and father, he felt he was living a lie. They talked for possibly two hours, at least two she thought. It was sometime before October. They drank some Southern Comfort and coffee. He just talked.

On another occasion—it was a Sunday afternoon—Geoff came over after she had telephoned him to tell him that she had flooded the car, the engine. It wouldn't start. Geoff knew about cars. There was another time a few weeks before Geoff died. It was a Saturday and she and Geoff had taken the girls riding. Afterwards Geoff stayed for a while at the house. They had a few glasses of wine and she had put on some reggae music. They had danced, "not close," she said. It was only later that Geoff got too close. She told him to back off and he became upset. The children were running in and out of the house. The telephone kept ringing so they went outside to talk. Geoff said that he wanted to hold her close. She told him that this made her uncomfortable. He laughed, a kind of laugh, when she told him this. "Don't be stupid," she had said. They had both had five or six glasses of wine by this time but they were not drunk. They stayed outside for a while and he told her that he felt a lot more for her than he should. When he asked her whether she felt the same way about him, she said that she did not. Yadwiga had told Ray about Geoff getting "too close" the day after it had happened.

By the middle of the year before his death, Geoff was coming over to the house two or three times a week. Ray, the accused, met Geoff for the first time at Easter that year. Geoff was in the garage one evening—it was not Good Friday—when Ray visited. Her relationship with Ray was warming but he had not yet started staying over. After Ray arrived, Geoff stayed no more than five minutes before leaving. They did not see each other again until Boxing Day that year at a gathering Yadwiga had arranged. Sometime in January or February of the year Geoff died, she and the accused went around to Geoff's home to collect her children. This was about two or three weeks before he died. The juror with the bra strap was asleep.

That's it? There was nothing else? About anything? Nothing, say, about the gun? Yes, of course, when it's over. And I love you. Call you tomorrow night.

On the night of Geoff's death, Yadwiga was at home with the children and expecting Ray for dinner. He called at about eight thirty from his mobile telephone to say he was on his way and would pick up some takeaway chicken for the two of them and the children. She assumed he was calling from the car. He arrived at nine bringing the chicken, baked potatoes, coleslaw and a bottle of red wine. The four of them ate the meal and talked. It took about half an hour. She doesn't remember what they talked about. The children went to bed a little after ten. They opened the wine after that. Ricky had phoned earlier that evening sometime between eight and nine and she and he had fought. The children, particularly her son, Brian, had been upset by the call. Yadwiga had gone to comfort him after he went to bed. The plump woman knew Brian, his voice, his laugh, how much he missed his father. He was her son's friend. She sat alone in the second back row holding hands with herself. The courtroom was inadequately ventilated. She didn't notice.

Yadwiga had returned to the lounge room. Ray had opened the wine and poured about half a glass for each of them. After sitting on the floor for a while, she joined Ray on the couch. They had hugged, perhaps they had kissed. She is sorry but she finds it hard to remember such small things now. "Please continue, Mrs. Quinlan," entreated the Prosecutor. "You are doing very well."

They had been together that way on the couch for some five to ten minutes when she heard the sound of the sliding door at the rear of the house. A few moments later Carly came in and said that there was someone on the back verandah. Yadwiga told her to go back to bed and that she would take a look. She told the jury that she had not been concerned. Ray was behind her by this time. He told her not to go. She went anyway, out through the sliding door from the lounge room to the driveway and in the direction of the garage, which was at the back of the property. A white car was parked outside the drive in the street. Geoff's car was white. She had assumed it was his car. "It's only Geoff," she said, assuming Ray was behind her. She looked through the garage window, thinking that perhaps Geoff had crept into the garage. Geoff was not there.

The witness had the full attention of each of the jurors and, indeed, of everyone in court. The plump woman's hands felt cool on her face as she heard how Yadwiga had whispered, "Geoff, where are you?" Why had she whispered? To avoid waking her son perhaps. Carly was not only still up but very upset by the time Yadwiga got back to the lounge room. She told her mother simply, "Geoff is in the back." The witness said she did not know where Ray was when Carly had told her this. She told the court how she ran to the back of the house and into the rear hallway and it was there, outside her son's bedroom, that she saw Geoff slumped on the floor.

Yadwiga had taken his hand to help him to his feet. Then she saw a pool of blood. Carly was screaming by now that someone should call an ambulance. Yadwiga told the jury that she did not see Ray during this time. From the time she came back into the house to the time she found Geoff on the floor, she had neither heard nor seen anything. She remembered wondering where Ray was sometime during everything that happened and even looking in his car but she was unable to say whether that was before or after the ambulance arrived. When she realized he was no longer there, she phoned him at his place but got his answering machine. Then she took her children with her into her bedroom. What did they all do in the bedroom? Nothing. They held each other and waited.

I know you don't like thinking about it. I understand why. I was the one who told you not to think about it afterwards. Remember? Come on, you remember that. Good. I am on your side, Carly, but just for a few days you have to remember as much as you can. That's all you have to do and then it will be over and you can forget about it again. Yes, I promise. Yes, you can go swimming. And horse riding. There's a place not far from where we live. Where I live. I don't know why. I meant not far from here, where I live. How's your mother taking it? It'll be over soon. Anything about the gun yet?

Although Ricky had owned various guns, Yadwiga said there were no guns on the property on the night Geoff died. She could identify the material shown in the police photograph as some kind of cloth car seat cover but it did not belong to her or to Ricky and she had never seen it before that evening.

Yadwiga remembered Geoff coming over about two weeks before his death. He was upset and had said, "Don't ever leave me, always be there for me." She remembered his words. Counsel for the defense asked her how she had responded to this. She said that she thought Geoff was being a bit "over the top" but she gave him a hug as a friend would and told him, "I'm there for all my friends." At various times throughout the year Geoff had seemed dissatisfied with his work and with his lot in life generally. He would often tell her about a problem he was having at work with some project involving satellites. He seemed to regard his work as a series of challenges to be met. Yadwiga found that admirable. On the last few occasions before his death that Yadwiga had seen him, he had said nothing about his work. On that night two weeks before his death they had been drinking but they were just merry, not drunk, and he told her again that he had feelings that he should not have. He didn't mention the project at work that night, the one about satellites. Yadwiga had been embarrassed. She thought this was understandable. The day after it happened she told Ray about it. It was understandable that she should find it embarrassing. The plump woman ran her finger between her collar and her neck.

Yadwiga said that she was not particularly upset by Geoff's declaration and neither was Ray. It was just that it would make things uncomfortable for them in the future, for all of them, that was all. Ray was staying over two or three nights a week by this time. There had been some discussion about him taking a caravan to Bruthen and living in it there. This option had come up because of his work. It would have had the benefit of cutting down his living expenses. He would not have been able to see Yadwiga as frequently if this had eventuated, but at the time, she said, they had had no plans to change the nature of the relationship.

Counsel for the defense suggested that although the curtains to the lounge room were drawn, there might have been gaps. She agreed. The light was on? She agreed. Someone outside could have seen her and Ray on the couch together. Yadwiga agreed. At the time that Carly had said to her that Geoff was in the house, Yadwiga now knows, Geoff was already dead. She could no longer remember whether Carly had initially said there was a prowler outside or just that someone was outside. Carly had been concerned that someone was moving around outside the house and she wanted her mother to do something about it. After looking in the garage at the back, Yadwiga had gone to the front of the house where the white car was parked. She had peered inside the car before going back to the house.

When she found Geoff on the floor, she did not think he was dead. She had heard nothing in the two or so minutes between leaving the house to search outside and returning to find the deceased in the hallway outside her son's room. At the time she left the lounge room to search for Carly's "prowler," she was not aware of Ray coming with her or being in her presence with any kind of wrapped parcel in his hand. She was not aware that he had brought in any parcels, other than the food, when he had arrived with the chicken and wine. Yadwiga explained which parts of her house were shown in each of the police photos: the kitchen, the lounge room, the porch and outside sliding door where wood was kept for the fire, tools, a broom and spade. The juror with the bra strap thought of the barbecued chicken and coleslaw she liked to have in summer. Red wine goes well with potato salad. Beer too. She had been at the beach one night when someone had died. Drowned, she thought. Coleslaw has mayonnaise. Best kept out of the heat.

When Yadwiga had bent down to lift Geoff from the floor,

she did not see any wounds on him but she did see the pool of blood on the floor in the hallway. Everything had happened so quickly. Counsel said quietly that he understood this and checked the order of the pages piled on the lectern of the bar table. When she saw Geoff in the hallway, he was slumped as though he was sitting down. This was not the way he was in photograph seventy-three.

The juror in the yellow T-shirt wondered about this. What could it mean? How could she not remember the car seat cover? It was right there in the photograph. They all had it in front of them. Unless she was going to try to suggest the police put it there: was that it? But why would they do that? Was it Ray's car seat cover? The cops don't really do things like that. Unless they already knew this bloke, Ray. But if he had a shady past, it would've come out already. Look at him in the dock. Stupid bastard. He's gone. Why *couldn't* he have killed someone, someone touching up Yadwiga and someone storing that rust heap of an MG in his garage, Yadwiga's—in Ricky's garage? He could have. Didn't the police plant a glove or something in the O.J. Simpson case? A glove. What kind of man wears gloves, except for driving? That's okay. Michael Jackson. Can't laugh here. That poor bastard is no Michael Jackson. Look at him. Why doesn't he say something. When is he going to say something? Where did the car seat cover come from, you faggot? She's bull-shitting us.

Carly was screaming. Yadwiga remembered that clearly. It was around then her son had woken up. He had slept through the struggle and the gunshot, if there was any struggle. She didn't see any. She got there too late to see any struggle. Her son had jumped over the body. He was in his pajamas. She sent him and Carly into her bedroom. The telephone was kept in the hall-way. The kids had taken to making prank calls. Ray had never been the jealous kind. He didn't own a gun. He had never men-tioned owning a gun. She said her children knew Geoff well. They had always called him by name. She could not understand, even now, why he didn't respond.

Ray didn't move to Bruthen, after all. She was still with him. They were still together. The dumpy woman moved her hand down along the gap between the two sides of her blazer, fingers feeling for the lapel. There wasn't one.

Just do your best. Be polite. Answer all their questions, and if you can't remember something, just say you can't remember. If you're not sure, just say you're not sure. The only thing you have to be sure of is that you saw him do it. Just like you told me. Well, ask her for something to help you sleep. But don't say it was my idea.

On the morning Carly was due to give evidence, the plump woman brought her son and her daughter, Amy, with her to court and sat them on either side of her. During the morning break Carly and Amy stole glances at each other through the traf-fic of adults in the court, but they did not speak. Carly tugged on her right earlobe and her tongue came out of the left side of her mouth. A tug to the left ear made her tongue slide to the right. Her friend smiled. In return, she pulled the skin around one eye away from the other eye. Carly was almost twelve when her friend's father came to visit one night and was killed.

Carly told the Court that she had been ill that day and had not eaten anything except jelly beans until the dinner Ray had brought. After dinner she had gone to her bedroom, where she had read and listened to the top forty for a while. She had been half asleep for about an hour when two headlights shone through the window from the street near the drive, waking her up. They were left on for a few seconds before being turned off. There were no sounds. She lay awake in her bed. Someone came out of the car and walked slowly towards the front of the house. Carly looked out of her bedroom window into the driveway. There was an adult near the rose garden. She thought it was a man.

He walked towards the rear sliding glass doors and then back towards the car and out of her view. She did not think he actually came through the sliding doors, only up to them. Perhaps she had not been sure it was a man. It's hard to say because of what she knows now. She could not recognize him and she went into the lounge room to tell her mother someone was outside. As she left the bedroom it seemed to her that the person outside was walking back towards the car. Her mother and Ray were sitting together on the couch. "Somebody is outside," she told them.

They got up to go to the lounge room sliding door and outside. She followed them as far as the door. Her mother went towards the garage at the back, Ray towards the drive at the side. Carly stood still. In the driveway light she saw Ray go to the driver's seat of his car and pull out an object wrapped in some kind of dark material. The object was obscured by the material. She could not make out what it was except to say that it was about a meter long. Ray then caught up with her mother, who was now walking back in the direction of the car parked in the street. She heard her mother say, "Oh, it's Geoff's car." Carly saw her mother go back towards the house before losing sight of her. Throughout this time she had not moved from the lounge room sliding door. She does not remember where Ray went.

Carly went back to her bedroom and stayed there for about five minutes before going into the hallway. As she turned right to enter her brother's room, she saw, in the dark, a figure in a business suit leaning against the wall of the hallway. Geoff wore business suits and she assumed it was him. She said hello. There was no reply. She went back to the lounge room to tell her mother that Geoff was there. Her mother was sitting on the couch with Ray. She told them Geoff was in the back. She does not remember now the exact words she used. She walked back the way she had come with Ray following behind her. He was carrying an object wrapped in material. Her mother did not go with them.

Ray was carrying the object with the material around it in his right hand. As they reached Carly's bedroom she stepped in, out of the hallway, but Ray kept going. When he reached the figure in the hallway he told him to get out and turned on an adjacent light. He said something like "Get out, you fucking cunt." She thinks he said that at about the time she saw the light go on. This was when she was hiding in her room behind the door in the triangular space defined in a corner of her room when the door was open. From there she could partially see down the hallway between the hinges of the door.

Ray was shouting at him. She doesn't remember what else he said. He had removed the material from the object he was carrying as they had walked down the hall. It must have been before she turned off into her room or she would not have seen it. He sort of pushed Geoff. She had not seen what was under the material but thought it was a gun. He pushed him over a bit and then just shot him. She heard a thud and then the sound of a slow drip from somewhere, something liquid. She saw little bits of Geoff, like his sleeve, through the hinge gaps. Ray nudged him with his arms, just a little push, and then he shot him. She heard the gun and then a dripping on the floor. From the triangle in her bedroom she waited and heard Ray walk back up the hallway to the front of the house. A car door was opened and a car was started and driven away. She had assumed it was Ray who had driven off. Then she left her bedroom to find her mother.

When Carly reached her mother, Yadwiga did not know that Geoff had been shot. Her mother had told her that she had not heard the gun. Over the next few days Carly spoke about it to many people, including her father, Ricky, who had wanted to know every detail, particularly everything that Ray had done. When it was suggested to her that she could not possibly have seen all that she said she saw from the triangle in her bedroom, Carly disagreed. She knew what she saw and what she heard. Five or ten seconds after Ray had told him to get out of the house, she heard a loud bang. Immediately after the bang came a soft sound and a dripping. She could not remember if she used the word *prowler* when she first saw someone in the driveway, but she did not think she subsequently told her mother and Ray that a guy was inside the back of the house. Carly had seen him clearly by then and, although he had not said hello back to her, she knew who it was, that it was Geoff. She told both her mother and Ray that Geoff was in the house. She did say *guy* sometimes, but not when she knew the person's name. His name was Geoff.

I'm sure it's not you, nothing you've done. You haven't done anything. Her mother probably wouldn't let her. Well, it's a courtroom for

Christ's sake. Her father died. He was killed and this is the trial of his killer. You saw him do it. It's a disaster for them. Well, try to put your-self in her mother's position. They'd be devastated. She has to bring up two little kids on her own all because of what happened . . . what Ray did. Whether it's murder or not probably doesn't make much difference to Amy's mother. Or to Amy. No, not till it's over, and anyway, if any-one rings her, it had better be me, not your mother. Yes, I will but not till after the trial. You did your best, didn't you? Then you should be proud of yourself. I am sure they did. Why shouldn't they believe you? You just said what you saw. Told them about the gun. What you saw from your room. You did see it, you know you did. We've gone over it so often. You've done everything right. Oh, she'll get over it. She didn't see every-thing you saw. You told the truth. She can't not talk to you forever. She will when it's all over, I promise.

Deli Bishop was the owner of Superior Cleaning Services. At the request of the police Victim Liaison Officer, she attended the Quinlan home on Saturday the fifth of March and cleaned the house. She believed that the police had already finished their in-vestigation of the crime scene, otherwise she would not have been allowed to clean. This was the rule at crime scenes, and Su-perior Cleaning specialized in these sorts of cases. Deli Bishop had seen it all: brain, intestine, fetal fragments, bone and soft muscle tissue, all clinging to or embedded in the walls and soft furnishings of the places she had cleaned. They also did office work on a contract basis. They had to, she explained. There was not enough of the other.

It was Deli who found the dark car seat cover with blood on it. She remembers it had a hole in it and she asked the lady of the house, a Mrs. Yadwiga Quinlan, what she ought to do with it.

The police had missed it, she supposed, or else they felt it was unimportant. They always took the things they needed before she was called in, the things they consider important to the case. In the end she had it incinerated. No one seemed to want it and it was filthy.

Lionel Kravitz had taken the oath before. He held the Bible in his right hand as he was asked to do but placed his middle finger within its pages, making it a book with two halves. He was the Psychiatric Registrar at Dandenong Hospital. At around one forty-five a.m. on Saturday the fifth of March, he examined Ray Islington, mostly in the presence of Mr. Islington's solicitor, who kept coming in and out of the room. Dr. Kravitz observed that the patient was manifesting extreme anxiety. Mr. Islington was clearly upset, but the doctor felt constrained in the questions he could ask him. The solicitor had advised the patient not to speak to the doctor about the events that had caused his anxiety.

When his solicitor had left the room, Mr. Islington had told him that the relevant events had happened two nights earlier. He had been driving around in his car ever since. His distress could be traced back to two nights earlier when, while at his girlfriend's house for dinner, he had been alerted to an intruder by her daughter. The intruder had attacked him and a gun wrapped in plastic had been discharged into the intruder. Mr. Islington said he had been horrified. The man had died. Mr. Islington had said that he did not know how this came about and that he had driven around in his car for most of the next two days.

In Dr. Kravitz's opinion the patient, the accused, was very upset but was not what he would describe as acutely psychotic. He was tearful and shaking but this was consistent with severe stress and, all things considered, Dr. Kravitz did not think at that time that Mr. Islington posed a substantial risk to either the medical staff or to the police, who apparently had been called by Mr. Islington's solicitor before he had driven him to the hospital. The doctor had given the distressed man tablets to help him sleep. He said that while he could not attach any specific probability to it, it was possible for shock to give rise to localized memory loss.

Detective Senior Constable Morgan was one of four police officers to escort Ray Islington from the hospital to the police station, and it was he who had asked the bulk of the questions the jury watched on a television monitor, the interrogation having been recorded on videotape. Ray was exhausted, his eyes wide and red streaked. He wanted to cooperate one hundred percent to get to the bottom of this dreadful mess, this dreadful mistake. He brushed his hair back off his forehead with his left hand, wanting to go with these fellows on their inquiry, but needed them to take it easy because he hadn't slept for two days. . . .

The kids had gone to bed and I was on the couch—first sitting, then lying down—with Yadwiga. Carly came out of her bedroom and said there was a prowler outside or something, some guy outside. She was frightened. Yadwiga got up from the couch. So did I but she got up first. Yadwiga was first. She was closest to the edge of the couch so she *had* to get up first. I couldn't get up until she had.

We went down the hall to the back door and into the back garden. Yadwiga was ahead of me and went towards the back garden. I lost sight of her. I went the other way. I couldn't really see anything. It all happened so quickly. Carly was pretty . . . pretty frightened. I went back into the house to her. Yadwiga keeps wood on the porch for the fire and as I came back in I picked up a log or what I thought was a log. I couldn't really tell what it was at that time. It was wrapped in something, some material. I don't know, I just picked it up and when I got to the end of the hall near the kids' rooms, he startled me and we struggled for the wood, or what I thought was wood. I couldn't see. I didn't know it was Geoff. But he struggled with me for the wood. The wrapping was coming off in the struggle. I must've squeezed because, as you know—do you mind if I smoke?—I shot him.

Ray had offered to take Detective Senior Constable Morgan and the corroborating officer to where he thought he had left the car. He couldn't remember exactly where. He had just driven around without any sense of time or of where he was. He knew more or less where he had left it, or thought that he did, but, after driving around for close to forty minutes and still not finding it, they returned to the police station where the interview was continued. Ray was sorry. He had thought he knew where it was. He must've been close to two days without sleep. It had all happened so quickly and Ray was in shock. They had to understand that Geoff was his friend, his and Yadwiga's. He took another sip of coffee and gently slid an unlit cigarette up and down between his fingers so that it made a slight tapping sound on the table. Detective Senior Constable Morgan was offscreen but his voice was clear. That was probably all for now. The camera closed in on Ray, who continued to tap the cigarette. Then he looked up and heard, "You are being charged with murder."

Still angry? Well, you'll just have to give her more time. I know you didn't lie. After the trial she'll be more reasonable, I'm sure of it. No, but when she's upset she's liable to say things she doesn't mean. I was

married to her, I know Yadwiga very well . . . very well. I still love you
and you know that I want us all to be together again.

The Sheriff's Office had arranged a bus to take the jury to
what had been the Quinlan home, but it was late. All the
minibuses used for airport shuttles and senior-citizens excursions
to the casino were unavailable. The jury waited in the jury room,
drinking cups of tea, making small talk about whether or not
they were *morning* people and queuing for the use of the toilet.
When their bus finally arrived it was a long sixty-seater perfect
for interstate trips but less suitable for frequent turns in the narrow, leafy streets and cul-de-sacs Ricky and Yadwiga Quinlan
had once been unable to resist. Position was everything.

It was a small house, smaller than it had sounded over the
previous couple of weeks, and once you had been through it a
couple of times, there was only one thing left to do, and together
in small groups and one or two on their own, each juror walked
the route they had heard described so often. Here was the doorway to the garden where Carly had waited. Here was the lounge
room where Ray and Yadwiga had lain together on the couch.
Next was the hallway where, just outside the boy's room, it happened. And off to one side was Carly's room. Each juror went
into Carly's room, and one by one they put themselves in the triangle that was defined, just as she had said, by her open door and
the corner of her room. Each of them looked through the crack
between the hinged edge of the door and the wall and, adjusting
their positions to approximate Carly's height, they saw the extent of Carly's view of the hall where the deceased had been shot.
When they had finished they were led as a group back on to the
bus by His Honor's Tipstaff. After they left, the Judge and the

Associate came into the house and did exactly as the jury had done, placing themselves at varying heights within Carly's triangle to see what they could see of the hall, and, like each of the jurors, they could see almost nothing.

Now that all the evidence had been called, the Prosecutor stood side-on to the Judge and commenced his address to the jury. He started running through the evidence that had been presented. The reluctant juror felt she would scream if he ran through each witness's evidence again. Was there no one who could stop this colorless man? The blood spattering was consistent with the findings of the postmortem. The angle of the discharge and the manner of firing, with the gun pointing upwards, demonstrated, he suggested, that the firing must have been deliberate. He reminded the jury that Yadwiga Quinlan had testified she did not have a gun in the house. Carly Quinlan had sworn that she had seen Raymond Islington get what had to be a loaded shotgun. It was about a meter long. She had watched him.

The Prosecutor said the presence of the loaded shotgun in Islington's car was consistent with premeditation. Islington would have heard Yadwiga Quinlan say that it was Geoff's car. He would have known when he saw the car that it belonged to Geoff, a man whom he knew and knew to have recently made advances to Yadwiga. Carly had told both of them that it was Geoff who was in the back of the house. She led Islington, who was by then carrying the wrapped object by his right side, down the hall to where the man she had already identified as Geoff was standing unarmed. Islington told the deceased to "Get out . . ." using words which indicated that he knew the deceased's identity. Carly was by this stage in the triangle the jury had observed was formed in her bedroom when the door was open. Looking between the hinges of the door, she had seen Islington remove the material from around the gun. She saw a push and then heard the shot.

You should prefer the evidence of Carly Quinlan above all others, even as against that of Yadwiga, her mother. Carly was an eyewitness. She had not only identified the deceased, she had alerted her mother *and* the accused man as to his identity. She, unlike her mother, has had no relationship with the accused man that might color her view or cloud her memory. Unlike her mother, she did not have any guilt to assuage with respect to the advances of a desperately unhappy man now dead or with respect to the telling of them to a desperately dishonest man now accused. The Prosecutor said the accused man's disingenuous attempt to assist the police to locate his car amounted to a "consciousness of guilt" on the part of the accused, as did the fact that the murder weapon could not be found. He said that the amount of evidence inconsistent with innocence was overwhelming and that the jury should return the verdict "guilty of murder." Then he sat down. The juror with the bra strap wondered why he had not moved more, away from the table and over to the jury like they did on TV. He hadn't really moved his hands much, either. If asked, she would have given him four out of ten.

After a fifteen-minute break, the jury returned to hear the defense counsel address them. He spoke more slowly. Their task, he said, was not an emotional one but an intellectual one. They should put aside any question of whether they liked or disliked any of the witnesses and they should be vigilant against jumping to seemingly attractive conclusions. The main question they had to consider was whether the Crown had proved beyond reasonable doubt that this tragic event was a murder, with all of the elements required by law to constitute murder. It is not sufficient for the Crown to establish that it was *possibly* murder or was *probably* murder. The Crown had to prove all the elements of murder *beyond reasonable doubt* and those words mean exactly that. "Exactly that *what*?" the yellow T-shirt juror said to himself.

The argument, put forward by the Crown—that Ray Islington had carried the gun around with him in his car and that what you are considering here was a *premeditated* killing—is clearly ridiculous, patently nonsense. I know you will see it as nonsense. Carly has told the police she saw the silhouette of a person walking up the drive to the sliding door at the back of the house and then back to his car in the street. This frightened her enough to cause her to seek out her mother and Ray and alert them to the presence of someone she accepts she might have described as a "prowler." Of course, it wasn't a prowler, it was Geoff. Why didn't he announce his appearance? And then, a moment later, why did he not say something to Carly inside the house?

Ray told the police that the instrument he picked up from the log pile on Yadwiga's back porch was wrapped in material of some kind. Carly said this, too, you will remember. She had seen the wrapping around the object as she walked with Ray down the hallway to confront Carly's "prowler." That was the car seat cover which had been left at the scene and was later incinerated by Deli Bishop of Superior Cleaning Services. Had the car seat cover not turned up on the photographs, the Crown would have you believe Ray Islington made *that* up too. "Yes, I bet they *would've* said that," the foreman said, nodding, before realizing that his lips were moving.

Much, the defense counsel continued, has been made by the Prosecutor of Carly's evidence and the store you should place on it. The events surrounding Carly that night were obviously the most traumatic events in her young life, and while nobody is suggesting any dishonesty on Carly's part, not all of her evidence is reliable. You know what I am referring to. This young girl, in trying to be helpful, has gone too far and described things that she just could not have seen. You have all had the chance to see the scope and dimensions of the area where these tragic events took place. You might well have found yourselves in the triangular area created in Carly's bedroom when the door is open. It is not possible, by standing inside that triangle and looking through the gaps between the hinges, to see as much as she says she saw. You know this. It is impossible, and if she has this wrong, what else in her evidence is wrong, mistaken?

This is a murder charge, ladies and gentlemen, and you will want to be very careful in the jury room when considering the weight to be given to the testimony of a distraught little girl. Under normal circumstances we would all want to give her the benefit of the doubt, but remember, the onus is on the Crown to prove their case *beyond* reasonable doubt. The consequences of your decision are about as big as they get. They can't get any bigger for Ray Islington, not when His Honor is wearing the red robes.

Really? How do you know she's visiting him if she's still not talking to you? Well, at least Brian is talking to you. He's a good boy. She'll get over it. Yes, after the trial. If he's found guilty? Of course she'll get over it. You didn't do anything wrong. All you did was tell the truth. Christ! Ray killed him, not you. You saw him do it. Don't be silly! You know you saw him. Come on, Carly. Don't be upset. If they find him guilty we can all be together again.

The critical question, the defense counsel continued, is not where the gun came from or whose gun it was. There is no question that what Ray carried under his arm, as he walked down that hallway to investigate the uninvited presence of the man who had frightened his woman's child, was a gun. The critical question is: What happened at the end of the hallway? Carly has described what she claims to have seen, but you know she did not see it. She could not have seen it. The Prosecutor wants you to accept that Ray's intention was to murder Geoff and that this was premeditated. He invited you to believe that Ray was motivated by revenge and jealousy on account of Geoff's advances towards Yadwiga some two or three weeks before. But you will remember Yadwiga's evidence of Ray's very calm response, gently advising her that perhaps she had been too charitable in her polite rebuffs. And it seems he was right, doesn't it? There is no way one could equate his mild response with the type of response consistent with forming the intention to kill. There was, at that time, some prospect that he would be moving to Bruthen anyway. The relationship would have flickered to its extinguishment. You will remember all this, put it all together and find more than reasonable doubts everywhere you look. Ray only needs you to have one.

The defense counsel paused to clear his throat and take a sip from a glass of water. After the shooting, Ray panicked and ran away. One can imagine him thinking, *How the hell am I going to explain this?* So he ran out of the house barefoot with the gun. What do we really learn from this, ladies and gentlemen? Ray Islington was scared out of his mind. Wouldn't *you* be if you had just shot a family friend by accident with a gun you had not even known existed? When you think about it, this would certainly have been the most nightmarish thing that had ever happened to him. He said as much, you will remember, to Detective Senior Constable Morgan in the videotaped record of interview. He told him that he had not slept for close to forty-eight hours. You will remember Dr. Kravitz, the Psychiatric Registrar who examined Ray at the hospital. Dr. Kravitz told you that Ray was tearful and shaking, consistent with him being in a state of severe stress. Everything adds up, doesn't it? Where are all those brilliant lies the Prosecutor wanted you to find?

You would know from your own lives that when people experience trauma they are most likely, most prone, to act irrationally. He told the police he didn't know where the car was. Was that a lie? The Crown wants you to think it was. But why should he lie about the car? It was only a means for leaving the Quinlan home. He had already told the police that he had shot Geoff and, in panicked horror, driven away in shock. When the police found the car, there was nothing of any forensic value in it. If there had been, you can bet the Prosecutor would have told you about it.

"Yeah. I bet he would have, too," the foreman said, nodding again.

Ray had admitted that his clothes had blood on them, the defense counsel went on. That is because he had been involved in a shooting accident. He told the police about this. Nothing dishonest about it. His clothes had blood on them. Of course they did. These are not the actions of a dishonest man. This is the behavior of an hysterical man, a man made hysterical by the sudden and accidental shooting of his friend.

So, let her visit him. What do you care? Don't be so silly. Anyway, he's not going anywhere for a long time. Because he killed your friend's father. Yeah? Who's going to believe that he found a shotgun in the woodpile and picked it up without knowing what it was? You testified that you saw him get the gun from the boot of his car. Yes, of course they'll believe you. What's the alternative: that Ray squeezed a thin log into poor old Geoff what's-his-name?

The Judge adjourned the court temporarily for the jury to take a break between the end of the defense address and his charge to the jury. The Tipstaff gently guided them into the jury room, but they did not need any guidance by this stage of the trial. They were veterans, knew the system. The reluctant juror took it upon herself to start making the tea. By now she had almost memorized how everyone took their tea. Three sugars for the bra strap, one for the foreman, none for the yellow T-shirt. The Tipstaff closed the door behind him and went back into the court. The television journalists had come down to the fourth court sensing the trial was nearing the thirty-second-grab part of the judicial process. They had come briefly for the prosecution opening and had only now returned, it seemed, to say hello to the Tipstaff. How was he? What does he think? Come on, you always know something, Trevor. But the Tipstaff, who said nothing, was named Bert.

The Associate had been thinking about manslaughter, the critical word the jury had never heard mentioned in court. Neither the Crown nor the defense had mentioned it, and to the Associate, unnecessarily qualified as a lawyer, this was fascinating to say the least. The common law, the law of precedent, regards all unlawful homicides which are not murder as manslaughter. There were two main types of manslaughter, voluntary and involuntary. For an accused person to be found guilty of voluntary manslaughter, there may be the same intention or malice aforethought required for murder, but the presence of some defined and specific mitigating circumstance will reduce the murder to manslaughter. Provocation was one such mitigating circumstance.

The Associate was thinking about Ray Islington and about provocation as a defense to murder. As a student he had rote-learned Devlin J.'s classic definition from *Duffy* (1949) for his criminal law exam: "Provocation is some act, or series of acts, done by the dead man to the accused, which would cause in any reasonable person, and actually causes in the accused, a sudden and temporary loss of self-control, rendering the accused so subject to passion as to make him or her for the moment not master of his mind." What was Geoff's act or series of acts? There was none and Ray was not suggesting that he had lost control.

Involuntary manslaughter, on the other hand, may be characterized broadly as fitting into one of two categories: unlawful-and-dangerous-act manslaughter and reckless or negligent manslaughter. Yadwiga was standing by the dock talking to Ray, who was standing with his feet apart, stretching. Counsel were outside in the courtyard with their instructors, smoking.

The mental state required for a person who had caused the death of another to be found guilty of unlawful-and-dangerous-act manslaughter was merely the intention to commit the unlawful and dangerous act, be that act the brandishing of an unlicensed weapon or assault or some such act with a weapon. The Associate could not see why the Crown was not trying for an unlawful-and-dangerous-act manslaughter conviction in the alternative. The Judge was in his chambers drinking tea when the Associate put this to him.

The Judge was at a loss to explain it. The defense was going for broke. It was clear that they were punting on the jury having trouble as to Ray's intention at the precise moment the gun went off. Perhaps the Crown didn't want to give the jury the easy way out of returning a manslaughter verdict? Murder or nothing.

"But what if it *is* manslaughter?" asked the Associate.

"I can't put manslaughter to the jury if neither the Crown nor the defense has gone on that basis. If I did put it to them and they returned with manslaughter, there'd be an instant appeal."

"On what grounds?"

"Unsafe and unsatisfactory, bias in my charge, something along those lines. There's High Court authority."

"But what if manslaughter is clearly open on the facts?"

"It *is*, but there cannot be two Prosecutors, one fool down there trying for a murder conviction on the basis that it was premeditated and me up on the bench pushing for manslaughter when the Crown hasn't even put it."

"What if they came back with manslaughter all on their own?"

"Well, that would be interesting. That's a different story," said the Judge. "But would *you* have the guts, if you were not a lawyer, to return a verdict that neither of two Counsel nor the Judge had put to you? Come on, we'd better get going. Let's try to avoid an overnighter."

The Judge spoke slowly and with a greater solemnity than any of the jurors had ever heard:

"Murder is committed when a person kills another person by a conscious and voluntary act done with the intention of either killing that person or of inflicting really serious injury upon that person where the act was done without lawful justification or excuse and with the death occurring within a year and a day."

The reluctant juror did not think she could stand another minute of sitting there, impassive, inert, next to these people, the eleven other randomly chosen colleagues of hers, that idiot in the yellow T-shirt. How many yellow T-shirts does he have, or does he wash the same one every night? Who cares anymore? Ray is a shit. Yadwiga is a fool at best. Hamish McPherson still can't get used to being the foreman. It's the highlight of his life. His family are going to have to shoot him when this is all over. He is unbearable. Will it ever be over?

His Honor continued:

"The Crown has to prove that it is not a reasonable possibility that any defense is open on the evidence. There is no dispute that the discharge of the shotgun killed the deceased and I will not deal with that element any further. But the Crown must prove that the discharging of the firearm, if you are satisfied it was done by the accused, was a conscious and voluntary act."

The foreman was leaning forward in his seat. *What does he mean by* if you are satisfied it was done by the accused? *Is that a hint or something? I think he might be trying to tell us something. I'm with you, old boy. I don't know about the others, but I'm with you. I'll have to mention it to them later. Must make a note. I suppose it's part of my role as foreman, that sort of thing. Some of them might have got it, but not all of them. I'm sure the young girl would have missed it, sweet young thing.* Then the Judge's voice came back to him:

"When I speak of a voluntary act which causes death, in the context of this case I am speaking of whether the discharge of the gun was a willed act of the accused. The relevant question is whether the discharge of the gun was a willed act, a voluntary act. If, for example, a person was holding a gun and had no intention of discharging the gun but was bumped by someone else and then, without his exercising any control over his actions, his finger came into contact with the trigger and caused the gun to discharge, then it could not be said that the act causing the death was the voluntary act of the accused man."

The juror with the bra strap wondered. I think I know what he means. It sounds a bit like that night at the beach when that boy drowned. It was hot like it is now and we had barbecued chicken with coleslaw, potato salad, beer and red wine. It was a nighttime beach barbecue to raise money for the surf lifesaver volunteers. I was swimming after everything else, late, with some of the members. Everything happened quickly there as well. There were about four or five of them and me swimming out by the rocks at Sandringham. They were clowning around with me, dunking me and trying to take off my top. It didn't hurt or anything but then they did get a bit rough. There was a sort of tug-of-war over me. I got kicked. Everyone was having fun until one of the boys bumped his head on the rocks. No one knew. No one meant it or anything. They were just clowning around with each other, some of the volunteers. Maybe he was pushed or just slipped? We didn't know. Split his head open. I bumped my head, too, and swallowed water. He drowned right next to us. We didn't know, not at first. Then she heard the Judge again.

"The accused was asked by Detective Senior Constable Morgan: When was the first time that Wednesday night that you acknowledged that it was Geoff inside the house? Answer: While I was struggling with him. Question: Did you make any efforts to have Geoff identify himself? Answer: Well, I—I could when—while it was happening, it—I could see that it was him. I recognized him.

My thoughts were just stopped because I was so—so scared what would be there."

Oh God, no. *He's* not going to go through all the evidence too? the reluctant juror shouted to herself. Murder was becoming completely explicable to her.

"Question: You said earlier that you had your finger on the trigger, is that right? Answer: Well, no. I wasn't aware of it but I must have. I—I can't understand how else it would happen."

The Associate swore in three jury keepers in front of the jury, the Judge's Tipstaff, a Tipstaff attached to another judge and a female permanent jury keeper from the Sheriff's Office. It was their task to keep the jury from having any contact with the outside world until they had returned a verdict. Then the jury was sent into the jury room to commence their deliberations. It was not possible from within the jury room to gain any information via a pocket transistor radio as to the fortunes of Our Sovereign Lady who was racing in the third at Morphettville. The yellow T-shirt was upset. His plans had come to nothing. Let's get this over then. Come on.

But it was not something that was going to be gotten over quickly. The yellow T-shirt insisted Ray was guilty because otherwise he would have fired more than one shot. If there had been a real struggle, there would have been more than one shot. Someone else said that was nonsense. There was a general commotion, someone agreed, voices everywhere. How many shots were there? The foreman asked for quiet and then for a show of hands. All those who thought that there might have been more than one shot were asked to raise their hands. The reluctant juror stood up from the table and got a glass of water.

No, that's normal. The Judge has to go over all the evidence for them. It won't be long now. Well, she'll probably get worse before she gets better. After the verdict, I mean. Well, because your mother isn't over him yet. She'll get over him but it will take a little bit of time. Even for her.

At six o'clock no verdict had been reached and the Judge reconvened the court. The jury was given the option to cease its deliberations for the day, retire to a hotel for the night under the supervision of the three jury keepers and return the next morning, or else to break for a meal and try to reach a decision before nine p.m. After a brief meeting in the privacy of the jury room, the foreman announced that the jury preferred to take a break for a meal and then to continue its deliberations. The Judge said that if the members of the jury wished messages to be passed on to their families, they could write short notes with the relevant names and telephone numbers and his Tipstaff would see to it that they were passed on. Then he adjourned the court. The barristers, solicitors, journalists, family members and onlookers all left hurriedly in search of telephones or personal space to make calls on their mobile telephones. This would be a long day. The yellow T-shirt sent a message to his wife through the Tipstaff. "Not over yet. They're giving us a feed. Probably won't be home tonight at this rate."

Still out! What the hell's taking them so long? No, I don't know. I'm not blaming you, Carly. Well, just because . . . I don't know . . . it's obvious he did it. You told them you saw him do it. I just don't know what's taking them so long. They can't be much longer now. How's your mother? Why not? Is she there? Okay. I get it. Talk about something else till she goes. Anything. I don't mind. How's your brother?

The Associate was last to leave the court. He walked up the back stairs to his office to disrobe and meet up with the Judge for dinner. Maybe Thai this time. He was still thinking about un-lawful-and-dangerous-act manslaughter. The *unlawful* act had to be more than a civil wrong. And, as to its *dangerousness*, it had to be such an act that all sober and reasonable people would in-evitably recognize that such an act must subject the other person to at least the risk of some harm resulting from it, even if it was not serious harm. The judge was on the telephone to his wife. The Associate went back to his office and waited.

The jury did not reach a verdict by nine o'clock. The court was adjourned until the morning, and arrangements were made to transport the jurors to the Roundhouse Motor Inn. The sec-ond Tipstaff and female jury keeper kept the jury quarantined in the motel foyer while the Judge's Tipstaff startled, calmed and explained all, in that order, to the after-hours clerk who had no bookings under either the Department of Justice or the Sheriff's Office. Twelve rooms? At this time? No. *Fifteen* rooms? No doubling up. Okay. Which one's the Sheriff out of all of you, anyway, because I'm feeling a bit "Wild Bill Hickok" myself tonight.

The two Tipstaves waited up together until all the jurors were settled in their rooms. As was so often the case, they soon got talking about their respective eligibilities and entitlements from Veterans Affairs. Only men who had served their country in combat did the government have the effrontery to pay as poorly as the Department of Justice paid its Tipstaves. There was always talk of the Department phasing them out, but it was shrugged off fatalistically by the Judges' men in the heavy gray coats, and with each year the heaviness under their coats made it harder to shrug off. If the Vietcong couldn't finish them, what hope did the Department have? It was time to hit the sack. Got to be awake in time to get these buggers up and running. About to turn in, the second Tipstaff saw his colleague at the drinking fountain with a small bottle of pills.

"Help you sleep, mate?"

"No. Stops me dreaming."

The second Tipstaff lightly touched the firm shoulder of the other old soldier as they passed each other on the way to their rooms at opposite ends of the corridor. Once they had closed their doors, everything was quiet. Only far-off televisions on other floors could be heard mixing with the indiscernible low white hum ever-present in places where people pay to sleep.

A little while later a door opened and the foreman tentatively made his way into the corridor wearing ersatz leather slippers and a pale blue terry-towelling dressing gown.

He walked past five rooms before stopping at the door of the sixth. He stood alone in the corridor and wiped the palms of his hands on the front of his dressing gown. Then, hesitantly, he knocked on the door twice and waited. There was no answer, and with his hands now inside his pockets he turned his back to the door he had just knocked on and surveyed the length of the corridor. It was still empty and, turning back to the door, he knocked again. He was retightening the terry-towelling dressing gown belt when she slowly half-opened the door.

She had her bathrobe hastily draped over one shoulder, but the other, the shoulder farthest from the half-open door, was exposed. It was the first time he had seen her shoulder completely exposed, without the thin cover of a bra strap. It was a hot night. Her hair was dishevelled. He swallowed.

"I'm sorry, my dear. I hope I didn't waken you?"

"No. I was . . . I wasn't asleep yet."

"I just thought I would . . . check in on you . . . see if you were all right. It's so hot and . . . with everything we've seen and heard in the last two weeks and with this . . . decision that you . . . that we all have to make . . . I wouldn't blame you if you were a little upset or were having trouble sleeping. I was having a bit of trouble sleeping and I thought that if I was . . . well, a sweet young thing like you, I might be having trouble as well. It's all a bit upsetting isn't it, eh, especially . . . especially for a sweet young thing like you?"

He moved in towards the door and extended his arm so that his hand might touch the skin of her uncovered shoulder. As she stepped back out of his reach, the door opened further and he was then half inside the room. The bed was unmade and on the floor next to a white bra he noticed with a shudder of revulsion the boldness of a yellow T-shirt.

Between the overtime and a full breakfast of cereal, eggs, bacon, sausage, tomato, toast and coffee, the Tipstaves agreed crime was not too bad. As long as the jury didn't play up on you. It seemed there was more chance of a criminal jury playing up than a civil jury, but then, there were less and less civil juries these days, so it all evened itself out in the end. It was hard to say exactly what it was about murder that made a jury more likely to play up. Perhaps it was the photos. At first they'd all be squeamish, wouldn't touch them, but after a few days you could open the door to the jury room and find any one of them flicking through the photos with one hand and a jam fancy in the other. But this lot was no trouble at all. The Tipstaff had them back in the jury room at court by nine o'clock, all washed, fed and ready for work.

The yellow T-shirt started things off with a rousing exhortation to everyone to find Ray Islington guilty of murder and end their confinement. This was the second day cooped up like animals and it was bloody ridiculous, inhuman. He shot him and the little girl had even seen it, so why not stop the messing around? The foreman asked exactly what it was Carly saw. Wasn't she in her triangle at the time of the shooting? The mention of the triangle started everyone talking at once. Couldn't see a thing from there. Was she lying? Lying or just mistaken? What did it matter? Wrong. Carly was wrong. Wrong in what she *said* happened or wrong in saying she *saw* it happen? Hold on just a minute, you're starting to sound like them out there. This is not hard. You know he did it. Shall we go over it from the beginning? Why don't we? No need to. All those who think we should go over it from the beginning, raise your hands, please. Please.

By ten o'clock the courtroom was beginning to fill. The television crews were the first to arrive. Their reporters had heard, like everyone else in court the previous evening, that the Judge would not be taking a verdict before ten thirty, but it was almost as though the waiting itself added urgency to the event. The crews camped in the street not far from their variously sloganed TV station wagons. Next to the words *Nobody Knows News Better* on the first wagon, a rival crew had fingerprinted in the dust *Than Anybody Else.*

Boom microphones looking like small furry dogs attached to the handles of devices used to remove leaves from swimming pools rested on the footpath. They would remain asleep until they were thrust into someone's face to record how it feels to be free or how it feels that the man who killed your dad has been found guilty. And if there was no verdict in time for the morning news update, they would be raised above the marvellous hair of a young woman to record her announcement that the jury had not returned a verdict yet. Then it would be her turn to get the coffees. They smoked a lot of cigarettes and drank a lot of coffee. It was recognized by the proprietors of the nearby Four Courts Café that a good defense address could make a substantial difference to a day's takings.

By twenty past ten the lawyers had arrived, their cases, books, papers and depositions all neatly piled at each end of the bar table. The accused's solicitor was there for the first time in days, having heard on the news that the jury was out. He had been very busy in the last twelve to eighteen months. Things had really started to take off for him and he was usually unable to be in court on a daily basis when his clients were on trial. A sole practitioner, he had cursed the bureaucrats at the Legal Aid Commission for investigating his habit of charging for instructing in court without actually attending in body. The clients never complained and his business was brisk. To think he had almost gone into real estate!

The dumpy woman sat at one end of the long bench that made up the second back row, just as she had every day. She had brought a straw basket, which she kept close to her. It contained some magazines and, hidden among them, a thermos flask of tea. Her sister, who had come down from Swan Hill to stay for a while, had suggested the tea. A calm and capable woman, it had been a great help to have her stay. She put her up in Amy's room and Amy had slept with her in the big bed. There was room enough. The lawyers all said good morning to her and she nodded just slightly, searching with one hand between the magazines and the thermos for the Sweetex.

In the jury room the discussion continued. The Crown has to prove all the elements of murder beyond reasonable doubt. Everyone agreed. They listened silently to the reluctant juror. She had not spoken for some time, and her earlier silence lent a significance to her words now as she promised the yellow T-shirt they could wrap it up neatly and quickly if he would just give her a chance and listen. Sympathy swung towards her. The idea of giving her a go was enthusiastically received. It was only fair.

"We don't need to be sure of anything. The way the Judge put it, if we have a reasonable doubt about any of the elements of murder, we're not *allowed* to find him guilty and we must go back in there and say 'Not guilty.' Now, the element we keep coming back to is his state of mind, what they've been calling the *intention*: Did he have the intention to kill or cause really serious harm? I wasn't sure yesterday, but your arguments turned me around."

"*My* arguments?" asked the yellow T-shirt.

"Yes. You reminded us that only one shot was fired, and that at the time—the time the shot was fired—no one was there to see it except Carly from her triangle."

"And Carly couldn't see a bloody thing from that triangle," said the yellow T-shirt.

"Exactly. So nobody saw the struggle *or* the firing of the gun. And if we don't know exactly how it occurred, what hope have we got of knowing what his intention was? He might've meant to kill him, but we don't know. None of us knows."

Everyone agreed, even the yellow T-shirt.

"So," said the foreman, "you're saying if we don't know his intention, we've got a reasonable doubt?"

"Yes, and if we have a reasonable doubt, we have to find him not guilty. We have no choice. That's the law, if I've understood the Judge."

"It's wrong. You know it's wrong," said the yellow T-shirt.

"The thing is, they haven't done their job properly, so it's not our fault."

"Who hasn't done their job properly?"

"The Crown. It was you who made me see it."

"You're right about that. He's a lazy bastard, that bloke. You know, I saw him doing the bloody crossword while the Judge was talking to us. What a bastard: makes all that money and sits there doing the crossword."

The foreman asked whether they were all agreed to return a not-guilty verdict. He asked for a show of hands and looked around the room. One by one, everyone had put up their hands except the bra strap and the yellow T-shirt. There was silence.

"Oh, come on! If *he's* not guilty then the Pope's not a Catholic! You all know he bloody did it."

No one said a word. The bra strap looked down at her feet. It seemed they were all waiting for something. The yellow T-shirt stood up and walked to the other end of the table, where he stood for a moment facing the whiteboard.

"Oh, what do I bloody care? Let me out of here, for Godsakes. Okay. I pointed this out yesterday. Count me in. My hand is up. Could've saved us a day. Count again. I'll vote not guilty. I can't stand it any longer."

Another show of hands was called for. It was unanimous this time. The foreman went to knock on the door, the signal to the Tipstaff that they required his assistance. The door opened and the Tipstaff asked if everything was all right. "We're ready," the foreman said and then, quietly, "It was the girl, the young one wouldn't come around." The Tipstaff nodded.

Everyone stood up. The reluctant juror washed out a mug and had a drink of water.

"Like *Twelve Angry Men*," she said to herself.

"Like what?" asked the bra strap, standing near her.

"I was just thinking of that movie, *Twelve Angry Men.*"

"Yeah, with Jane Fonda."

The Tipstaff had seen it before and felt a knot in his stomach. The interval between the jury's knock and the announcement of the verdict in any murder trial is a highly charged time. Even impartial cogs in the wheel cannot help but feel anxious. It does not matter how many times you have experienced it, there is always a hollowing of your being in the time between the knock and the verdict, he explained to one of the Protective Services officers, who nodded in agreement.

The jury takes its place and everyone studies their faces for some indication of the result.

"Mr. Foreman, has the jury agreed upon its verdict? How say you: do you find the accused guilty or not guilty of murder?" The Associate's voice has a slight quiver in its clipped precision. Everyone in the room is, for the merest instant, on trial themselves. Nothing can save you.

"Not guilty."

"And that is the verdict of all of you?"

Some of the jurors nod, some smile. The bra strap takes the arm of the reluctant juror. She rests her head on the woman's shoulder. The yellow T-shirt looks away. Yadwiga is smiling through her tears. The defendant's solicitor has his back to the Judge with this thumb up to Ray, but Ray does not see. He has his head in his hands. The Judge begins to thank the jury for their attention and their diligence. He reminds them of their importance to the legal system and to the community. Senior and junior counsel for the defense are beaming. The informant is seated behind the Prosecutor. He says nothing as he watches the jury file out of the court into the jury room.

A little later on there will be an uncomfortable moment in the alley at the back of the court. Taxis will arrive to take the jurors home. Some of the jurors will be waiting, belongings in hand, as Ray Islington talks to his lawyer. None of them will look at Ray Islington except for the yellow T-shirt. He will prop himself up against the wall of the court until the newly free man has to look at him. The yellow T-shirt wants to say something. He is going to, is about to, when he feels the firm hand of His Honor's Tipstaff on the small of his back and hears, just quietly, "Move along, my friend. Show's over, thank you." But in that time there is just time for the bra strap to smile at Carly and whisper something to her as she and her mother push by.

I don't know. I wasn't expecting it, that's all. No one was expecting it. Because he did it, so you would have thought they'd find him guilty of something. Should've been murder, for Christ's sake. I'm not shouting. Now, come on. No one's blaming you. Well, I'm not. When did you talk to one of the jurors? I don't believe it. She couldn't have said that. You must've misunderstood her. Let me get this straight. She said they acquitted Ray because they didn't believe you could've seen him do it? But you did see him. Yes, you did. You told me you saw him. No, I did not. How can you say I put you up to it? I didn't put you up to anything. I just wanted you to tell them what you'd told me. No, I did not make it up. Don't you start blaming me.

Don't worry about your mother. Well, she shouldn't be. No, there's nothing to be afraid of. He wouldn't dare. Carly, he wouldn't dare. Because he knows if he does, he'll have me to answer to. Yes, well, I'll come over, then, won't I? Of course you can come here, but not right now. I need some time to think. Get a few things organized. Soon, I promise. Very soon. Business. Just some business, that's all. No you're not. You're my big girl, aren't you? You're not scared. No, you're not.

The dumpy woman is an "early bird." If your car is in the car park before nine thirty in the morning, you are an "early bird." She could stay in the city all day without spending another cent on parking. It occurs to her that perhaps never before has she parked the car in the city with hours on her own to do with as she pleased. No responsibilities, no children, no husband. Geoff had been her husband, a shy husband. She walks outside through the Lonsdale Street door of the Court. She sees Yadwiga and Ray surrounded by journalists, photographers and television crews and crosses the road quickly. She walks up William Street to the Flagstaff Gardens. There had been a clock outside the station. She had used it to determine whether or not she was going to be late for Court. It was gone now. There was gravel where it had been. She still has her watch but it is unreliable. He had bought it for her birthday once.

The Flagstaff Gardens feel smaller from within than they look on the outside. It is a city block of green amid the gray. Who else comes here? Office workers? Homeless people? Geoff used to take the children to the park near their home when they were small: nothing so elaborate as this. It was more of a reserve than a garden. She tries to remember its name. It has a sports oval. The Ludstone Reserve. She could see the sign with its name in her mind. They were so young then. She hopes they will remember those times at the Ludstone Reserve. Who was Ludstone? Perhaps she could have gone with them? Why hadn't she gone to the Ludstone Reserve with Geoff and the children?

Having sat in the gardens for the best part of an hour, she walks all the way down William Street to Bourke Street, to the mall. Myer is having a sale of sheets and towels. She had not been there for some time. The second floor across Little Bourke Street has sewing machines along with the sheets and towels. Not everything has been reduced, only the stock in the bargain displays. She had loved him. Was it really true that he had gone to Yadwiga like that?

From linen and haberdashery she goes all the way to millinery. Most of the hats seem stupid to her, but one catches her eye. It is a crushed green velvet with something thinly embroidered, something like faint flowers against soft grass. Flowers from a distance. But she has no need for a hat. He has been buried almost a year. The place has changed. She did not get into the city very much—not as often as the people around her. They even browse faster than she can.

She stays in the store for hours. So many people ask to help her, but what can any of them do? She goes into almost every department and subdepartment: crockery, earthen cookware, china, glass, silver, white goods, computers and cosmetics on the ground floor and out into the street. The buskers are packing up. It is almost dark.

As an "early bird," her car is near the entrance. "Good night, missus," a Lebanese boy calls from inside the booth. She had smiled at him every day she had parked there. Sometimes she had taken the train. She does not have to go straight home tonight. It is strange to her. She feels nothing, keeps expecting him home. She can't wait to tell him that Ray got off. She sees it with her own eyes. "Well," he might say, "these things happen."

The supermarket near home stays open twenty-four hours now. She could get her shopping over and done with at night, leaving more time for herself on the weekend. More time to take care of herself, rest up, meet a shy man and start a family with him, have him hold her in the middle of the night when the wind is howling and the light over the Ludstone Reserve sign is shaking in sympathy with every other light in the city.

She parks the car in the supermarket car park. It is surprisingly busy for this time of night, but then, she has never shopped at this time before. The big receiving depot opens onto the car park. Its corrugated iron doors are wide open and a huge delivery van is being unloaded. Newspapers fly around her. Ray Islington's face and the headline I DIDN'T MEAN TO SHOOT MY FRIEND take up the front page of the tabloid.

In the supermarket a kilogram of polyunsaturated mayonnaise is selling for three dollars fifty. This week's special in the meat department is barbecue steak, four dollars fifty a kilogram. The specials are important now. How long can she accept money from her sister? The dog might have to go. But Amy will be heartbroken. She thinks of her daughter. Her sister should have picked her up from the psychologist by now.

In one aisle a young man begins unpacking bananas, in another aisle it is toilet paper, another, Glad Bake nonstick cooking paper, Chum dog food of the hearty stew variety, quick-frozen peas and scrub-free bathroom cleaner. Blades in Stanley knives are changed when it becomes too hard to cut the packing. It is getting late but the stock from the receiving depot keeps coming. The price guns shoot out the price rapaciously, in a succession of conscious and voluntary acts, and the young men scream old love songs down the fluorescent-lit aisles as they stack the shelves. *Don't pull your love out on me baby / If you do then I think that maybe / I'll just lay me down and cry for a hundred years . . .* And from the depths of the receiving depot and the fresh produce deliveries comes a sound most of the night fillers cannot hear. Those few that can hear it mistake it for something mechanized, in need of servicing. It is a sound like nothing these young men have ever heard, and not one of them would be able to guess its origins by just listening. A soft woman lies facedown in the almost dark of the receiving depot on a bed of cos lettuce leaves and discarded tabloid killers, wheezing, coughing, choking on the dust and debris of no-name-brand packaging and a life marked down, drastically reduced.

GOOD MORNING, AGAIN IN THE TIME OF THE DINOSAUR YOUR NIECE'S SPEECH NIGHT THE REASONS I WON'T BE COMING MANSLAUGHTER **THE** *HONG KONG FIR* **DOCTRINE** I WAS ONLY IN A CHILDISH WAY CONNECTED TO THE ESTABLISHED ORDER SPITALNIC'S LAST YEAR A TALE IN TWO CITIES

A momentary loss of muscular control and now you don't speak. Now you do not speak. Not to me. Others may hear you and I may overhear that they have heard you and then try to warm myself on this. But ever since that loss of control, my loss, my first loss, I can only imagine the sound of your voice.

Of all the ebbs and flows in feelings and in circumstance, of all the possible endings, this one, the one we are living now, was unimaginable. Yet, in the middle of the night, night after night, ever since this version of the end, since this too-real ending began, I imagine you imagining that it was deliberate on my part. I imagine you bringing to bear on this that mode of thought, that cast of mind, which I have always championed, promoted, propagated, the one that is mine, the only thing I have left.

At night in the dark I lie awake, imagining you sifting the evidence against me to determine whether this development which weighs you down more and more with each day, a development we had more than once talked of, dreamed of, hoped for, but never planned—this onetime dream which you now must see as a heavy and hateful burden—I imagine you trying to decide whether or not it is the result of a conscious and voluntary act on my part. And because of the soundness of your mind and because, if we except the odd principle here or doctrine there, I taught you so well, you will have to conclude that I deliberately made you pregnant. If I were you I would find the same way. And yet, it is not so.

I can only conclude that you think it was deliberate; otherwise, why would you not speak to me? Why don't you speak? Say anything. You always have. You have always felt free to say anything, sometimes apologizing later. In truth there were so many things I wanted you to say that you would never say, not even on request. There were other things I'd rather you had not said. I would take anything now. Tell me that he knows, knows everything. Tell me he is on his way around here. Just speak to me. Tell me it's all my fault, that I have ruined everything for you, that you no longer care for me. Or tell me something I don't know.

I used to call you when I knew you were unavailable just to hear your voice on the machine. In my mind I would replay the voice you use with your children. I have always loved hearing it. I have heard your children singing. I do not think that they will sing to me. You look at them, then at yourself, and have to blame someone, as though it were one of them whose laughter, whose future was being extinguished.

The guilt is not new. For more than two years now you have looked at your husband with sorrowful eyes. Responsible in large part for his position in the firm, for whatever success he has achieved, you have dreaded being responsible for the shell of a man he promises to be should you ever leave him. And you will leave him. Not as we had planned, not for a long time, not for me.

Your children love him, as they should, and their love for him occasionally makes you wish I had never been born. You do not love him as you have loved me. But nor can you ever hate him. He is pathetic, which you struggle not to see, but he is well-meaning, even kind at times. Why should you hate him? You have no reason to. As the father of your children, he must always have top billing in your dramatis personae whereas I can be killed off in an instant. A warrant for my execution was drafted at the moment of this conception. But when I die this last time—and I died every time you closed a car door without me, stayed out late for drinks at work, hung up the phone, left my home in a cab or got undressed in front of him—when I die this time, I leave a child behind.

None of this could have been imagined: not two weeks ago when it happened, nor fourteen years ago before I had even gone to the bar, back when I was still masquerading as a member of the Law Faculty, and you were doing an even worse impersonation of a law student. Your husband was a slightly better student than you, though you have long since been a better lawyer. He plods along diligently enough, at least until recently, but you take the problem apart, queen of the defense and counterclaim. Your letters of demand have always amused me. You manufacture causes of action where there are none. But the secret to besting you in litigation is simply to outlast you. I don't think your opponents realize how quickly you get bored. You own to a thoroughness and diligence you do not possess. You never did.

I learned this fourteen years ago when marking your exam

papers. I should have failed you, but I felt sure some spineless toady of the Subdean would have second-marked you to at least a pass, especially when he realized that you were who you were. When this dawned on me, I didn't fail you, either. Instead I laughed out loud when, by referring to a *deeming* provision as a *demon* provision, you demonstrated that you had not read any of the texts or cases and were relying solely on your own scrappy lecture notes, or maybe Tom's.

You thought I didn't remember. But I remember everything, or at least I used to. That's why they brief me. I was never sure why you did. Tom only began briefing me because you told him to. He has never really forgiven me for not giving him a credit. He was lucky I didn't fail him. It was you who stopped me. Not anything you said, but even then you had so caught my attention that I could not in good conscience fail your boyfriend, as he was then. I could never have satisfied myself that it was really his answers that failed him and not the recurring images I had of his hand in the back pocket of your jeans. Anyway, he wasn't such a bad student and isn't such a bad husband. How many women would not trade places with you? Still so very attractive, looking younger than your years, with two beautiful children, a partner at a prestigious law firm, and married to another partner about whom the worst you can say is that after all these years he has become too much like a brother.

But I cry out loud for you into the brittle nighttime air in my twelfth-floor apartment, so low no one can hear me, so high I can't get over it. Nobody knows any of this and it's been this way for two years or more. I have wanted to tell everybody but I have no one to tell. My colleagues, those distended alimentary canals in three-piece suits, would not understand. Weak, bigoted and sanctimonious, their tolerance is exhausted by a few intoxicated weeks in shorts and T-shirts patronizing the people in Southeast Asia they will not accept as immigrants. They glide around their leafy suburbs in four-wheel drives and vote for the codification of social inequality when it is marketed to them as freedom. Nor can I tell my friends, the friends I grew up with. They *would* understand. And so I cannot tell them, either.

We were foolish not to take proper precautions, not to take any precautions. Foolish, negligent and unlucky. Those morning-after pills have a ninety-five percent success rate. I checked, not because I didn't believe that you had taken them but simply because I'm, well, me. That's what they pay me for. One of the best around. So how could I let this happen? Yes, *let* it happen, not *make* it happen. Do you really think that I thought you would leave him if I made you pregnant? You would leave *me*. And you have.

I have been alone before but now it will be worse. I am hungry for you, for your voice, your touch, your hand on my face. It is as real as anything I have ever experienced, and nothing—no sleep, no conversation, no idea or image—can hold this hunger at bay, not even for a moment. You are with me as I dress, as I go through the motions, becoming by day again a suited man with suitably qualified opinions recommending for or against some or other suit just to kill time in the hope that the hunger will dissipate, in the hope that I may feel some slight diminution in the need I have to be with you. I have never been sure that you knew quite how much I loved you.

I loved the smallest things about you, things you did not recognize in yourself, your little-girl's grin, your embarrassment in the face of my recognition of it. While you may call it arrogance,

I really did want to assuage your smallest sadness, your slightest irritation. That is how it was that not only did I listen to all your concerns but I offered solutions, I tried to fix everything. This annoyed you.

I bought presents for your children. This could annoy you too. They were inappropriate, too old or too young for them; but worse than this, they were my attempt to come into your home. I wanted your children to take pleasure or comfort from something I had bought for them. But the presents made you angry because the children were not mine. They never would be. They were your husband's, and my gifts brought your guilt right to your door, and inside, into their bedrooms.

There is a certain beach I cannot pass anymore. Near the city, we walked on it together only once, but that hour or two so contained what I have always wanted that the sight of it now even from the car splits my chest till the salt stings like a fresh wound every time. You remember the time I speak of. I watched the wind push your hair away from your shoulders.

I want to hold you. It has never been like this. Yes, I have ached for you many times over the years, at my desk, at the supermarket, at home on the couch, in bed alone at four in the morning; but now, this time, I can no longer tell you about it because you do not speak to me. You do not speak because I made love to you and I stayed too long inside you. You think it was a ploy to have you leave him. I had no such ploy in mind. I would never try to trap you, much as I need you.

How many men need you? I could list them: clients, colleagues, junior and senior to you, plus the many I do not know about. I often list them, especially the ones I don't know about. I know how men look at you. I have seen them. But how many of them know the sound of you as your blood stirs and you cry out, how many know the touch of your hand, of your tongue, how many know the damp feel of you when you are ready to consume someone who really knows how to say your name, how many know the taste of you?

I always knew that I could never compete with the mistakes you made over ten years ago: the mistake of marrying a man whom even at the time you were almost tired of and then having children with him, cementing your place beside him with them, loving them as you do and with them loving him. Your life became so full with work, with the children, cocktail parties and the every now and then flirting with fidelity that kept me hanging on. You suspected that I always knew you could not bring yourself to leave him and so we always changed the subject. This is why you think I have done this deliberately. You feel your body changing and now you do not speak.

But I hear you in the middle of the night. You come to me and won't let me sleep. I put out my hand to touch the side of the bed that you have known. The sheets are cold. I will grow old in them. I have been alone before, but this is worse because now I have you to remember and nothing like you to look forward to. Even when I had you I cried for you, just looking at you. Do you remember? In one of those stolen moments I looked at you on the bed in a country hotel and was overcome with the strength of my feeling for you. You didn't say anything, you just put your hand to my cheek.

You would make me laugh and then express a child's dismay at the power of it, your power. But your power was always greater than that and still is. I am distracted. I cannot concentrate. I cannot work. I can barely pretend to work. I am panicking. I long to see you but we do not even speak. Longing to see you is not new to me. I have spent far more time waiting for you than you have spent waiting for me. Whenever you have said that you will call me after a certain time, each minute between that time and your call was felt twice: once as anyone would feel the minute and once again imagining that you have left me. It is my problem; it is not your fault. It is the foolish way I have loved you for years now.

Your occasional cruelty did not help. This was not a matter of my loving you all the more for keeping me on my toes. As well documented as this strategy might be, it has not worked on me since I was an adolescent. No, I loved you in spite of the things you would say or do every now and then. I loved you when you hated yourself most. On the eve of a rare planned weekend alone together, you went out drinking with a client, first at a nightclub, then at his hotel. You came to my home late the next morning looking blue and sick, telling me it was "business," he was a business associate, an important client, telling me it was okay because other people saw it, other people were there, not telling me that you had been with him in his hotel room till six in the morning.

What did I do when you came to me this way? I took you in and put you to bed. I gave you black tea with honey and lemon, an analgesic and Berocca. I closed the curtains and whispered to you. You were tired but did not want to sleep, you did not want me to go. So I lay down on the bed by your side. I was deeply hurt but I swallowed it all. Should I have kicked you out? You half expected me to. If I had, or if I had been more that way, would you have left your husband by now? I don't know. Possibly, possibly not.

But if I had been more that sort of man, I would have been a different person. You have said that it was this quality of under-standing or the *way* I tried to love you that you had never known before. It helped you to love me. When you told me this I was greatly relieved, because I often thought you didn't understand it: *She doesn't get it.* I wanted to create an atmosphere of calm around you, to love you unconditionally, not only like a lover but like the very best parent, forgiving, gentle, knowing your weaknesses, trying to understand the core of you. I cared for you that much. And now you do not speak.

You do not speak and there is no one I can tell. Nobody knows. For your sake and, I suppose, for mine, we have told no one. So now I sit here alone, while in your house you make grilled cheese on toast for your children, your husband watches television and inside you something of ours lives. Not yet a child, nothing yet showing. You knew straightaway, certainly by the next morning. You felt as you had with your other two.

"I always know," you said on the phone in that last conversa-tion. And you did. I didn't think you could know—not so soon. What were the chances? People try and try, but not us. We made it in one. What will you do now? You wanted another anyway, but if you keep it and tell Tom the child is his, you will be pun-ishing me for the rest of my life. There will be a son or daughter I will see glimpses of, snapshots pulled out at the firm's Christ-mas drinks, if I am still invited. I will be one of a number of people with a drink in their hand making a semicircle, admiring photographs of your sweet children, except that in my case one of them will be mine. Nothing I have done or could ever do would warrant such cruelty to any of us, to me, to Tom, or to our child.

I do not think you will keep it even though part of you wants to. Part of me wants you to. I say it although, at first blush, it appears an admission against self-interest. I have gone over it many times. You must know that I have. Why did I not pull out? If only I had. How could I have been so stupid? Perhaps you will never believe this but, that last time, after you had climaxed, I felt so free, so relaxed, so full of how good it was to love you, to know your body intimately, to know you wanted to spend the rest of your life with me, that I forgot that I was not free at all. I let myself go. It is not freedom when it is forbidden, when it is stolen, when it comes hardly ever between the hours of *x* and *y*. I did not forget for long but it was long enough, and now you do not speak.

You do not speak, and I, with so much work, so many colleagues, such responsibilities, such a fine reputation, I am paralyzed. I am afraid to return any calls lest someone hear the panic in my voice. I am afraid to go to court for the smallest application because I might see you, perhaps in another court, through the glass or talking with clients or other lawyers. I could not bear for you not to speak to me. I feel now as if I shall never be able to bear it. The thought of it terrifies me. I am not breathing well. I cannot sleep. I cannot live without being in touch with you.

This will not die for me. Having known you as I have, I will always want to know how you are, what you are doing. This will not dissipate for me. But you, who are so much more skilled in the art of putting up walls, you will have managed some distance already. One day I will find myself talking to you again and the tone of your voice will be light, matter-of-fact, with barely a hint of unfriendliness, and I will know that I am dead to you. If it is on the telephone I will want to slam it down. If it is in person I will want to run. In public you will come as close to ignoring me as you can without arousing suspicion that I ever meant anything to you. I can see it now and so can you. You are a survivor, you have told me. I thought I was too. I am not sure anymore.

Alone, in private, you will not always be so safe. Before, and even after you leave him, perhaps even when you are with someone else, or with the one after that, you will find the little notes I sent you. They were always inadequate. I knew that. They were not the love letters you wanted. I was too afraid of being caught to write a proper love letter. This is it now: you are holding it in your hand. But those little notes, you will look at them once or twice in the next ten years before finally throwing them out. No one will ever mention me to you, at least not in the context of the man you wanted to marry, to have children and grow old with. You will look at those notes a little wistfully and think of me. The thought will last until another thought which you prefer replaces it. We will hear many things about each other. Mostly they will be untrue. They will hurt.

I have friends. You don't know them, couldn't know them. Most of them I have mentioned. They're not lawyers. I have known them for over forty years. We grew up together, stayed over at each other's houses as children. We used to get up in the middle of the night at each other's parents' houses, go into the kitchen and eat our parents' jam out of the jar with teaspoons, in the dark. We grew up doing this. They got married, became architects, doctors, businesspeople. I became an "uncle" to their children.

I would arrive early at dinner parties and play with their children, watch the kids crawl all over their parents while the parents humored me, feigning interest in some case I was involved in which had been reported in the papers. The children, shiny hair, ready for bed, would be allowed to stay up a little later than usual. Wrapped in their dressing gowns, they would take tiny slippered steps around and around the room offering hors d'oeuvres to the guests, to their parents' friends.

"Thank you," I would say with exaggerated gratitude, perhaps interrupting some anecdote which was never really funny and which irked me even as I told it. Eventually the children would kiss the guests good night, one by one. I would ask my friends if I might read the younger children a story or tuck them into bed. I am their "uncle." I would read to them, thinking of your children, thinking of you. A mouse, a train, a cat; do your children know this one?

I would read them stories until they were sleepy and then I would turn out the light. On my way back to the adults, I might hear one of the older children in another bedroom whisper to their father, my old friend.

"Is Uncle gay?"

"What?"

"Is Uncle gay?"

"No, he's not gay."

"Then why doesn't he have any children?"

"Shhh! He'll hear you. He doesn't have any children. Go to sleep now."

"Why?"

"Because. It's late, past your bedtime."

"No, why doesn't he have any children?"

"He's . . . he's a very successful lawyer. He's very smart. You should try to be like him when you grow up. He gets into the newspapers. Now go to sleep."

My friend might catch me in the hall and put his hand on my shoulder on our way back to the dinner guests.

You do not know these people. I had always hoped that one day you would. They don't know you, either, but I have at times insinuated your name into conversation, albeit in a professional context. They wouldn't remember my doing it, but I have heard myself. I have longed to tell them about you, to tell them how I feel about you, to bring you to their houses, for your children to play with their children. Your children. I have never even met them.

You might not even like these people. We have stood beside each other at our parents' funerals. They have let me sleep on their couches, drunk, wearing nothing but their bathrobes. I have woken up in the middle of the night on their couches thinking of you, asleep naked, beside your husband. Or perhaps awake. Perhaps it was his turn, for the sake of convention, for the sake of appearances, to allay any suspicion. Perhaps he is having you now.

There are friends who have older children. Two of them are old enough to be studying law. I watched these kids grow up. Now and then I am asked to their law schools to give guest lectures. If I have time I go and stand there in front of the students. They make me feel old and so I talk to them about old cases, old principles of law, principles they'll forget or never use. But they ask me questions because something or other might just turn up in one of their exams. And you know how I love to give advice.

At one of these guest lectures some smart-arse kid drops a Latin maxim which I translate along the lines of *Equity says keep your hands where I can see them.* Nobody laughs. Someone asks about *Restitution.* Can you imagine that? You wouldn't want to know about that *now.* Someone wants to know the difference between rescission and repudiation. I tell them it all depends on whether your brief is to enforce the contract or to get out of it.

Some of them laugh—hardly any. They sit there dumbly, type-A serious bastards already, shitting themselves about where they're going to find work. They're right to be scared. But some of them, a handful, will find work with you and one or two young men will fantasize about you while the young women will either be afraid of you or else want to be you.

Questions come from everywhere, anywhere, ranging all over the syllabus. Someone asks me to go over the *Hong Kong Fir* doctrine. By *go over* they mean teach from scratch because they either didn't understand it, skipped the lecture or haven't read the case. You missed my tutorial on the *Hong Kong Fir* doctrine, didn't you? You sure screwed that up in the exam.

I always meant to explain it to you. When two parties agree to contract with one another and then the first party breaches the contract, how does the second party know whether it has to continue fulfilling its contractual obligations, being entitled only to damages, or whether, in addition, it can treat the first party's breach as putting the contract at an end? Before the *Hong Kong Fir* case the courts divided contractual terms into *conditions* and *warranties. Conditions* were said to be those terms which go to the essence of a contract, whereas a *warranty* was only incidental to the contract. Accordingly, if the first party breached only a *warranty*, the second party was entitled only to damages. But if the first party breached a *condition*, then, in addition, the second party could treat the contract as being at an end.

The problem was that the distinction between a *condition* and a *warranty* was an artificial one. It wasn't always easy to determine in advance which terms actually went to the heart of an agreement, which terms were merely deemed as such or which terms were merely incidental to the main purpose of the agreement. The court in the *Hong Kong Fir* case said, in effect, stop wasting time over the question of whether a term is a *condition* or a *warranty*. Instead, look at the effect of the breach of that term. If a breach of the term so goes to the root of the contract that it makes further performance impossible, makes the whole contract frustrated, the innocent party may treat the contract as at an end.

If you could have given me something along those lines back then, some version of that, you would have passed the question. If you could have illustrated it with an example, you would have passed with honors. Look at the effect of the breach. You have an agreement with two men. One is a formalized agreement reduced to writing. The other is not. The other is with me. Forget the terminology. Look at the effect of breach. You will not see it all. You will not see what is happening to me. No one will. No one knows. It will be for all the world as though we never happened.

You have never been hurt before, never had a relationship end before you were ready, never failed to have any man you have wanted, any job you have wanted. You do not know what it is just to shut down, to walk around dead inside your clothes. You will eventually convince yourself that this never happened, that *I* never happened. Then only I will know. But if only I know, did it still happen?

I cannot sleep, think, read. Where are you now? I kiss you though you're not here. I am so used to waiting for you, so good at it that I cannot stop. You will, sooner or later, get on with things, but I will go on waiting, my breathing interrupted, my step faltering when I think it is you in the street until one day it is you and you do not stop but look right through me.

But what shall I do now, right now? Think, sweetheart,

think. You who had wanted me for the rest of your days, think about me, think about me now. What should I do? What will I do? Sit in the living room and stare at the ageing fruit in the bowl? Go to my study? You know it, all that wood, all those books. Is this the reward for loving not wisely but too well? Can you see it, sweetheart? Shall I go to my study to lose myself in yet another brief, another pleading? By an agreement dated years ago I, the plaintiff, agreed to love you unconditionally in return for an offer of the rest of your life. The terms of the contract were partly oral, partly implied and partly imagined. It has been breached in a way that makes its further performance impossible. I am entitled to treat it as at an end. But I am unable. There is damage.

GOOD MORNING, AGAIN IN THE TIME OF THE DINOSAUR YOUR NIECE'S SPEECH NIGHT THE REASONS I WON'T BE COMING MANSLAUGHTER THE *HONG KONG FIR* DOCTRINE **I WAS ONLY IN A CHILDISH WAY CONNECTED TO THE ESTABLISHED ORDER** SPITALNIC'S LAST YEAR A TALE IN TWO CITIES

M adeline, my wife, never used to wear a watch. She does now, I am told. For a long time, in a very inexact way, I had kept time for her. There was the time before we were married and the time after. There was the time before I was hospitalized and the time after. There was the time she needed me and the time after. And there is now.

I am not well and I make no bones about it. It is largely a psychological disorder, but only the most obvious of its manifestations have ever led me to hospital. These flights of fancy, as Madeline initially wished them to be known, are actually psychotic episodes. But these are just its most extreme symptoms. It is more than the sum of these. It is there all the time and no one knows what it is, a disease so new, so rare, that they haven't developed a classification for it. They had one briefly but the condition mutated beyond human understanding, beyond recognition. My work is said to compound the malady. I am, by profession, a poet.

When I cry I suck on my front teeth and purse my lips involuntarily as though in anticipation of an onslaught of kisses. I never realized that I did this, never even suspected it. It is a mannerism just short of a tick and it belongs to me. There is a rhythm to it and I rock slightly in time with the pursing of my lips. I do this all in time. This rhythm is a matter of instinct with me. I am a poet.

How does that happen? In spite of everything, how does one become a poet? The term has become derogatory. How did *that* happen? It all happened before Madeline's father died. These days people assume, if ever they give it any thought, that poets must be inept, glassy-eyed people who, tyrannized by their own private internal anarchy, ramblingly conjure instant affect. But that, of course, is a stereotype. And it all starts way before this.

You are born. You remember nothing of it but get told at selected intervals that yours was a traumatic birth. The nature of the trauma does not really matter. What matters is that you are told about it at an early age. It quickly assumes a tremendous significance in your own private mythology. You visualize it in gray or sepia as a scene from a prewar newsreel. As you grow up you use it to explain otherwise inexplicable and unjust events. It is why you cannot perform certain tasks as well as other people, or at all. It is why your mother was this or that way with you.

You read, not just well, but powerfully.

You do just well enough at school for your distraction from what other people are interested in to be encouraged once, briefly, by a sympathetic teacher who, by the time you timorously graduate, has left the school and cannot be reached.

You read more.

You get a clerical job and study literature and history or philosophy, classics or art history at night. At work you meet an attractive young woman from the country. You flatter her. She flatters you. You write a poem about her. You tell her it is your first but it is not. It is actually just the first poem you have ever shown anyone. She is your first, the first to see it. But the poem is not your first. The others, the earlier ones, were naïve, derivative and masterfully bad. This one, too, is bad, but you show it to her because otherwise, without it, in its absence, you are a clerk. It works and you are a poet.

You spend time together. You take each other to art galleries and museums. You teach her and then recite in unison the opening to "The Love Song of J. Alfred Prufrock" by T. S. Eliot:

Let us go then, you and I,
When the evening is spread out against the sky

You get promoted. There are more art galleries. She gets promoted. There are more museums. You drink strong coffee, almost professionally, in the inner city area. She encourages you to submit the poem about her for publication. She tells you she has never met anyone who wrote poetry. You suspect that it is just that she has never met anyone who admitted it. You think everyone writes poetry. The poem about her is published. You share a kind of delight.

You meet other people who have published poetry. You take her to their poetry readings. The two of you drink coffee with them after their readings. You get promoted again. She knits you a jumper. You meet her parents during a weekend at their cattle farm in the country. One still night you tell her about your traumatic birth. You get married.

You are married. She gets promoted. You write a volume containing many poems. Two of them are published. She gets promoted. There are more museums. She gets pregnant. You write some poems about it. She takes maternity leave but not before being promoted again. A child is born. In many senses he is yours. Andy. You write *Poems for Andy.*

Andy grows to learn Christmas carols, and when he is old enough to sing them, you change the lyrics outrageously. You change their meaning. You take away their meaning. Rudolph the red-nosed reindeer had a very shiny *name*. It is a game. It delights him. It is the last time you remember delighting him. She gets promoted.

You take him to museums. You write a poem about museums, about taking your son to museums, about the ways in which museums record time. You used to go there with your wife. Later she sends you there with her son. He continues growing. "What are you feeding him?" colleagues ask at work Christmas parties. Too big for your knee, you recite to him across a room: *Twinkle twinkle little bat! How I wonder what you're at! Up above the world you fly, Like a tea tray in the sky.* Too big for Lewis Carroll, there is so little in him that resembles you. Your parents die. It affects you more than certain acquaintances think it should. She gets promoted.

Your son grows. *Up, up and away!* He plays different games. He grows more like his mother, at least more like her than like you. They share a certain closeness you attribute to the famed bond between mothers and sons and also to your traumatic birth. She tells you she does not want any more children. You write a poem about this. It is published in *Meanjin*. It is anthologized. The anthology becomes a prescribed text for secondary students.

Of the six years your son spends at secondary school, fifty minutes are devoted to poetry. The anthology is for a moment in your son's hands. One book between two. It is an austerity measure. He does not see you waiting in the table of contents. They read Kipling. At work you are made redundant. Still not old, you read ever more. She gets promoted.

Your wife's father dies and bequeaths her the farm. She resigns with a large payout. Your son leaves home. You and she return to her roots to run a cattle farm. She tells you it might be good for you. You are so pleased to hear that she wants it to be good for you that you do not question the move. You know nothing about farming or cattle but you can write poetry anywhere, if indeed you can write it at all. You picture a new rural phase with rural themes. Wordsworth meets Ted Hughes and Les Murray. You aim to keep in touch with the literary community through the membership of committees. You plan to be a literary agitator. You will write angry but witty pieces denouncing government funding cuts to the Arts. "Your Tiny Handout Is Frozen."

The year that Madeline and I moved to Mansfield was the year that Andy and one of his friends bought a four-wheel drive to take around Australia. He was by then already a big and practical young man, good with his hands. All the girls liked him. He had not wanted to go on to university. He did not have any plans for the year after the four-wheel-drive trip. He told me this quietly as we shared a cup of tea on the verandah the day he drove up to Mansfield to say good-bye. It was, I thought, a defining moment in his development, and it occurred to me that it should have been acknowledged with some sort of going-away party. But we were new to the area and, other than the people Madeline knew from her youth, we did not know anyone to invite. He would have hated the idea anyway. He spoke quietly in a low, soothing, anxiety-free voice. He did not read. I thought that maybe he would when he got older. He could do everything else. He had declined several offers to play a number of sports at a professional level. Madeline and I were so proud of him, so proud of his balance. I suspect that he already thought I was mad.

Mansfield was settled in the 1870s and soon became home to families of Irish and Scots settlers. Madeline's family, of Scottish descent, had been there for generations. "The best ones had packed up and left," she had always been told. They were farming people. Madeline had been the first to move down to Melbourne, but her father's death and my unemployment convinced her that it was time to return. Her childhood, or what I knew of it, had not been an unhappy one. The whole Shire, and not just her father's property, was full of memories for her, memories, and roads not taken.

By the early nineteenth century the first European explorers had found the soil to be rich. There was an abundance of grass, excellent for grazing cattle or sheep. (Our neighbor grazed sheep.) But even so there was initially some reluctance to settle it. Perhaps it was the influential opinion of the then Surveyor-General of New South Wales, who described much of the region as "utterly useless for every purpose of civilized man." Madeline said time stands still in Mansfield. Her family was born and died there, so it had not stood still for them. Something I refrained from pointing out. Andy and I had only been there once.

Madeline's father had employed a young, newly married

neighbor of his to assist him with the running of the farm, and on our arrival Madeline and I immediately appointed him manager of the farm. Her father had needed only his physical assistance, but I needed a full-time tutor. His name was Neil Mahoney. In his early thirties, he was the youngest of a large family, large enough to spare him from working his parents' property. His wife was almost ten years younger than him and, within a year of his becoming our manager, was expecting their second child. Madeline had heard that it had been difficult for Neil to find a wife because the Mahoneys had too many sons for their acreage. It was said they would overgraze. Two older Mahoney boys had left Mansfield for Melbourne only to return, having been unable either to find or hold on to jobs. Now they were both married and, together with Neil's father and an older sister's husband, they all worked the Mahoney farm.

Neil was patient with me, patient in his explanations and his demonstrations. In return I was honest with him. I told him I was a poet who had tried to support himself and his family as a clerk. I was also an occasional essayist, I told him. (This was not completely untrue. I had written one unpublished essay titled "Critical Theory as a Metaphor for Illness.") I tried to be unafraid of my mistakes or at least faithful to them. I had never been a farmer before and was not meant to know the things he was teaching me. But despite this I still had to fight the feeling that he thought I was a fool. He watched me.

It was not anything that he said, but I felt a little uncomfortable with him. It was an unease that never really disappeared completely. Each time I felt uncomfortable in my role as a farmer, I would force myself to write something, even if it was just a letter to a newspaper. I composed verse in my head while examining the fences with Neil or hay feeding the cattle during winter. I learned that, despite the rain, it was too cold and dark in the winter for the grass to grow. We needed the grass to grow to feed the cattle to support ourselves. Neil worried about the weather and the grass all the time, but I never did. After all, if the grass did not grow, no one could fairly blame me. Madeline could not blame me. I did not think she could blame me.

She found in me something to blame when I returned from the town one day with three kittens. They were a gift for her. I had bought them from the younger sister of the bored and sullen teenage girl with scrambled-egg hair who worked at the Welcome Mart. Where the older girl at the Welcome Mart had made a weapon of her adolescence, the younger girl had not yet given up on adults and would talk with them in the street. She would even offer them her kittens for sale.

"People don't keep kittens in the country—not here," Madeline told me when I surprised her with them in a canvas bag the young girl had thrown in at no extra cost.

I thought she might warm to them if I left her alone with them. In the shed I found Neil cleaning a rifle. He seemed to know what he was doing, yet again. I knocked tentatively in order not to surprise him.

"Is that your gun, Neil?"

"No, it's yours. It was your father-in-law's."

"What do we need a gun for?"

"For killing things." He looked up at me.

"Like what?"

"Animals that need to be put down . . . cattle . . . all sorts of things. You just never know."

There was so much I did not know. What I knew was of no

use to the people around me. Perhaps it was of no use to anyone. And I did not really know it. It was more that I had heard it. Lines, words, snatches of poems, came to me and then from me. I was merely a conduit for them. What did they have to do with me? Mostly they were not even my lines. I could be in a field and suddenly I would be unable to rid myself of Eliot or Wordsworth or Shakespeare. Increasingly, however, it was something from the Russian poet, Osip Mandelstam. His lines, more than any, got me through the day. They hummed to me. Eventually I could not get rid of them.

If you are *voluntary*, they let you keep your own clothes. This was the most obvious difference between the first and the second time. Another was that I did not know how I got there the first time. I was there when I woke up. I was lying on a bed with tubular steel railing around it. My pajamas, the sheets and the pillow cases were a standard blue, all with a Department of Health logo on them. The bed next to me was unmade. The mattress was covered in vinyl and had brass eyelets over which there was a thin metal gauze. Two beds down from me a man lay on his front, trying to fit all of his face on the Department of Health logo on his pillowcase. He wore blue pajamas too. We were not *voluntary*.

I tried to remember how I got there but could not. I had been in the car with Madeline. She was driving. It was a long drive. We were going to Lake Eildon. The kittens slept huddled together in the backseat. Madeline turned off the radio after we had driven a short distance. I noticed she was not in her usual sloppy slacks but was instead wearing a dress. I remember she was wearing a brooch.

"Why do you have your good clothes on?"

She shrugged and kept her eyes on the road.

"I had an uncle who used to tell us, 'Always wear your worst clothes.'"

"Why?" she asked without looking at me, still with her eyes on the road.

"You have more of them. 'Don't be tempted into wearing your best clothes,' he'd say. 'Save them for a better occasion. If ever you find yourself wearing your best clothes, it means you've admitted to yourself that it's never going to get any better than this.' They buried him in his best clothes."

"That's not true," Madeline said, both hands on the wheel.

"No, it is. I had an uncle and . . . he's . . . he's dead now. . . . But it's like the title of that book by Yevtushenko, prose, not poetry, *Don't Die Before Your Death.* Yevtushenko's telling us to wear our best clothes before it's too late. He's got a remarkable spirit, that man. I met him, you know, in Melbourne."

"I know."

"Few years ago now. Told a great story. Well, more than one, but this one concerned a poor Russian peasant who tried to save what little money he had by training his horse to eat less and less each week. With every week the peasant fed his horse a little less than the previous week.

"One day, his neighbor noticed him putting a piece of string around the horse's stomach.

"'What are you doing?' he asked the poor peasant.

"'I am training my horse not to eat so much, to work on less and less food.'

"'That's madness! Both of you will come to a sorry end,' the neighbor replied.

"'You think so. Look at this,' the peasant said, removing the string from around the horse. 'This is where the two sides of the string used to meet around his waist, and now—look!' he said, letting the surplus string dangle in the breeze before adding with pride, 'And he still works!'

"The peasant continued cutting back his horse's food. Each week the peasant boasted to his neighbor about the savings he had made on his horse's food that week, and each week the neighbor continued to warn him of his, the horse's and his family's imminent demise if the peasant persisted in his folly. One day, the peasant approached the neighbor with more string than ever suspended from his sausage fingers dangling in the breeze. He cried out triumphantly to his neighbor, 'Still working, and this week I gave him *no* food!'

"With the money he had saved on the horse's feed, he drank throughout the night, celebrating. When he woke the next morning, the horse was dead. Two weeks later the Revolution came to the village where the peasant lived, horseless, with his family beside his neighbor and his family and their healthy horse. When the revolutionaries got to the peasant's house, they found him shouting at his wife, a knife in the hand where once the string had been, his children cowering in the corner. They had first seen the neighbor next door with his wife, children and his horse, and now they saw poverty and desperation in the peasant's home.

"'Did the bourgeois kulak next door reduce you to this, Comrade?' they asked the peasant.

"'Yes,' the frightened peasant answered. 'Yes, he always mocked me, said I was crazy and that I would have a miserable end.'

"The neighbor was immediately arrested for being a bourgeois kulak, dragged out of his house and shot in front of his wife and children. Immediately after the execution the peasant was given his dead neighbor's horse.

"The peasant was of course overjoyed, falling over himself to praise the revolutionaries. He quickly had his children singing revolutionary songs and before too long was himself a member of the Party. Such was his zeal and his genuine peasant origins that he was taken to the capital and paraded as a fine example of the modern citizen, an agrarian peasant who had seen the virtue of the Revolution.

"He became well known throughout the Party and was rewarded with higher and higher appointments until finally he was appointed commissar in charge of literature. One of his duties was the allocation of grants and stipends to poets and prose writers. It was said that for years he could be heard exclaiming in drunken exaltation down the corridors, 'Still working, and this week I gave him nothing!'"

Madeline had her eyes on the road. The trees were rushing past. We were nearing the lake.

"That's not true," she said.

"Well, it's a story but—"

"Yevtushenko never told you that story."

"No, well, he didn't tell it directly to me but—"

"How can you lie like that?"

"Oh, Maddy . . . It's a . . . it's a story."

"You lie to yourself."

"Maddy, let's not argue."

But we did. She did. She shouted at me in an increasingly shrill voice. She sounded hysterical. I heard her but could not make out her words. It reminded me of birds in the country first thing in the morning. She drove faster and shouted louder till neither of us could see the trees for the wood. There was not a trace of the young woman for whom I had written that poem so long ago. The person in the driver's seat would have been unrecognizable to that young woman. We had come so far, too far and I, wanting to go back, began reciting:

"Let us go then, you and I
When the evening is spread out against the sky"

But she did not join in as she once had.

"Let us go then, you and I . . ."

"Shut up."
I began repeating it.

"Let us go then, you and I . . ."

Nothing.

"Let us go then, you and I . . ."

She stopped the car abruptly so that it jerked forward after the engine had stopped. We were as close to the lake as the car could go. Madeline leant over to the backseat, opened the mouth of the empty canvas bag with an outward stretch of one hand and scooped up the kittens with her other hand. She moved so quickly. The side of her body touched my face. I could suddenly smell the perfume she used to wear so long ago. She was wearing it again. She handed me the canvas bag with the kittens inside and reached over me to unlock the passenger door. Then she spoke.

"So go, then."

"What?"

"Put them out of our misery." She pointed to the lake.

"In the lake?"

"Drown them."

"Oh no, no, Maddy. I can't."

"It's best," she said, leaning over me and opening the door. "I can't keep them and they won't survive out here."

"I can't. Maddy, I can't."

The kittens mewed from inside the bag.

"Will you go!" she shouted, pushing me out of the car.

I fell out of the car, standing only to trip over a fallen branch. The kittens spilled out of the bag, scurrying in different directions. I tried to catch them, grabbing hold of one at the expense of the other two, going after another and losing the first. Madeline shouted something but I could not make it out. Very quickly I had lost all three kittens. They ran and I ran. I ran and ran. Towards the lake. I heard the car pull away. The kittens were gone and so was Madeline. All I could hear was the sound of myself: my breathing, running, heaving. There was dirt in my mouth. I had fallen, cut my leg, a ridiculous man facedown in the dirt beside Lake Eildon, crying to myself.

Let us go then, you and I,
When the evening is spread out against the sky
Like a patient etherised upon a table.

The sweet features of my personal failings, once just hinted at, had grown too pronounced for her.

Was she crying, too, in the car? Now I am sure that she was not. But, waking tranquilized in someone else's pajamas in the permanently makeshift psych ward of that tiny hospital, I still had not realized, despite what had just happened, the extent of her contempt for me.

From the outside the building is spacious; yet, from the inside, the walls creep up on you. They crept up on me. So did Hugh Brasnett. Hugh's bed was two away from mine. He was the young man, not much older than Andy, whom I had seen earlier lying on his front trying to fit his face on the Department of Health logo on the pillowcase.

"Who is Mandelstam?"

"What?"

"Who is Mandelstam?" he repeated.

"Mandelstam was a Russian poet. Why do you ask me that?"

"*Was?* Is he dead?"

"Yes. Why?"

"You were calling for him."

"When?"

"Before. When you came in. Before they gave you a shot."

"Who gave me a shot?"

"She did," Hugh said, pointing at a young woman I had to lean forward to see out of the doorway. Her name was Sarah. She was a nurse and I learned later the younger sister of Neil Mahoney's wife. If a field mouse could be an attractive young woman, it would look like Sarah.

"He's awake now," Hugh called.

She put down whatever she was carrying and came to sit down on my bed.

"How're you feeling?"

"Okay. A little—"

"Confused?"

"Well, yes, but I was going to say . . . embarrassed."

"Who's Mandelstam?" Hugh interrupted.

"You're Madeline's husband, aren't you?"

"Yes."

"My brother-in-law, Neil, is her manager."

"*Her* manager?"

"I'm sorry. I thought . . . Wasn't it Madeline's family's property?"

"Yes. That it was. That it is."

"Who the fuck was Mandelstam?"

Hugh was so bored that interrupting us seemed the best thing on offer. So I found myself in the psych ward of a tiny rural hospital telling a disturbed but not unintelligent young country boy about the life and times of Osip Mandelstam. And Sarah, whom I had expected to leave us, stayed where she was and listened.

"Osip Emilievich Mandelstam was born in Russia, of Jewish parents, in the last decade of the nineteenth century. Educated in St. Petersburg, he had the misfortune of being unable to do anything at all with himself except write some of the finest poetry his country and perhaps the world has ever known."

"Why is that a misfortune?" Hugh asked.

"Because Mandelstam was writing in a place that valued poetry so much that a poet could be arrested for a single poem.

Many lesser poets were arrested, exiled and sometimes killed for their writing, even the ones who made a religion of attempting to curry favor with the regime. And Mandelstam was temperamentally incapable of this sort of thing.

> "I was only in a childish way connected to the
>   established order;
> I was terrified of oysters and glanced distrustfully at
>   guardsmen;
> And not a grain of my soul owes anything to that world
>   of power,
> However much I was tortured trying to be some-
>   one else."

"That was beautiful," Sarah said.

"How do you remember it?" asked Hugh.

"I'm . . . a poet," I said, and then, turning to Sarah, "If you're Neil's sister-in-law, you would probably know that I'm not a farmer." Sarah smiled uncomfortably.

"We've never had a poet here, have we, Hugh?"

"Really," I said, looking around at the blue, pink and green pastels surrounding me. "That *is* surprising."

"What happened to Mandelstam?" Hugh asked.

"He recited a certain poem, an epigram, privately, in front of five people whom he must have regarded as his friends, and the rest is, as they say, history."

"What happened?"

"It is said he was in Pasternak's apartment, Boris Pasternak, who wrote *Doctor Zhivago.* He was there one night. Mandelstam, bravely or foolishly, depending on your point of view, recited a very short poem which sealed his fate. It's hard to believe he didn't know the danger he was putting himself into, and yet, if he did know, it is even harder to understand why he did it. But one night, in May 1934 I think it was, after he had been laughing and talking for hours with his wife and their friend, the poet Anna Akhmatova, and an irritating translator, a pesky hanger-on, there came a knock at the front door of the Mandelstams' apartment. It was by then one o'clock in the morning, and before opening the door his wife announced quietly, 'They've come for Osip.' They had been expecting this.

"The men of the secret police always wore the same civilian overcoats so that people were never in any doubt as to who they were. Perhaps this was the intention. That night there was no doubt who they were. There were no introductions, not even a cursory check to see if this was the Mandelstams' apartment. With a practiced skill they quickly went past his wife without touching her, and suddenly Mandelstam's tiny apartment was filled with men in overcoats checking their identity papers and efficiently frisking them for concealed weapons.

"Of course, Mandelstam had no weapons. He was a poet. He only had words, and after showing him a search warrant the secret police went tearing through their drawers, looking for Mandelstam's words. One of the policemen took time out from the search to advise the civilians not to smoke so much, producing a box of hard candy from the pocket of his uniform trousers and offering them some.

"The search continued all night. The secret police, the NKVD, as they were called, made two piles of Mandelstam's papers, one on a chair, one on the floor. When the translator, like a frightened primary-school student, asked permission to go to the toilet, they contemptuously let him go home. Without any particular malice they kept walking over the papers they threw on the floor. The sun had already risen by the time they left the apartment. They took only forty or so sheets of paper—and Mandelstam—with them."

"Why were they contemptuous of the translator?" Hugh asked.

"He was an informer sent there to make sure the other three didn't destroy any manuscripts before the knock on the door. The NKVD always had contempt for their stooges."

"But . . . who was Nadia?" Sarah asked in the voice of a child, as if embarrassed by her need to know.

"Nadia? I didn't say anything about Nadia."

"You did before," Hugh said. "When you were out of it."

"Who was Nadia?" Sarah repeated.

"Nadia is the name Mandelstam called his wife, Nadezhda. What did I say about her?"

The two of them looked at each other.

"What kind of woman was Nadia?" Sarah asked.

My mouth was dry. This impromptu lecture on Russian literature was even more bizarre than the events leading up to my hospitalization. I thought for a long while about Mandelstam's Nadia.

"Her every thought was about him. If not for her, we would not know him. She saved his manuscripts. She wrote letters to him when he was imprisoned, letters she knew he had little chance of receiving. But she wrote them anyway. She would have known they were beating him, starving him, freezing him, but still she wrote to him. She wrote, *You came to me every night in my sleep, and I kept asking what had happened, but you did not reply.* That was in the last letter she ever wrote to him."

None of us spoke. It was left to someone else to break the silence.

From another room someone looking for assistance called, "Excuse me." Sarah stood and straightened herself up before leaving the room.

"Do you think . . . you're Mandelstam? Is that it?" Hugh asked.

"No. I don't think I'm Mandelstam. That would be too easy for them, Hugh. I'm not Mandelstam. I don't think I have his talent, his feeling for language. I don't live in his times. I don't have his life. I don't have his . . ."

Sarah came back in. There was someone to see me. It was Andy. He took a couple of tentative steps. I watched him see me there for the first time. He moved his sunglasses and car keys from one hand to the other.

"This is my son, Andy."

Hugh looked at Andy and Andy looked at Hugh. I wondered what was uppermost in my son's mind. Was it the humiliation of seeing his father in a psychiatric ward? Or was he thinking that Hugh and I had already had a conversation that transcended any he and I had ever had? If he was thinking this, he was right. But whatever he was thinking, he nodded politely to Hugh, told me he would be waiting at reception and then left me to change back into my dirt-ridden clothes in front of Hugh.

Nadezhda Mandelstam wrote that so many of her contemporaries, whether they had been imprisoned themselves or not, were extremely well "prison-trained." They knew instinctively how to seize what she called "the last chance of being heard." Hugh went back to the Department of Health logo on his pillow until I had my pants on, but then, when he turned his attention back to me,

I could see that he was sad, sadder than he had been throughout his introduction to Mandelstam.

"I think I might like to be a poet. What do you think?" he asked me quietly.

"I think you're well on your way," I said as we shook hands. As I walked out I heard him begin the poet's business of keeping himself company: "I was only in a childish way connected to the established order." He said it quietly. There was no one else there.

Sarah and Andy were deep in conversation as they walked towards the gates, and I, not wanting to add to the wretchedness of the circumstances of their meeting, lagged behind them. A slightly older, slightly attractive, slightly qualified young field mouse of a woman had to explain to a strong and unpretentious young man from out of town that she did not really understand what his father was doing in the dirt beside Lake Eildon or why he cried without shame in between lengthy monologues about a Russian poet and his wife. All she could tell him is that his father could go. Andy and I said good-bye to her. Then he turned and thanked her. When he put his hand on my back, new tears came to me, small ones suggesting that I might be all right. He still had the four-wheel drive and he opened the door for me.

"Are you right to go, then, Dad?"

"'Let us go then, you and I . . .'"

Neil had taught me to drive a tractor. Both of us did our best. In spring, early summer and early autumn we waited for rain. He taught me to mend a fence as well as anyone, but my stretches did not always hold firm. Occasionally cattle would stray. Once Neil had found two of the cows in the shed at the back of our house. He had been repairing something for Madeline. I don't know what it was. Things around the house used to break. She would discover them and he would fix them, all without my knowing. She would talk to him about finances, the farm's, his, and ours. Sometimes I would come in and they would be going over the books with a cup of tea or a beer in summer.

It was nothing, he said, but I could sense that he pitied me. I knew he was double-checking everything I did. As uncomfortable as we were around each other, I could not fault his effort around the property. He could not have taken greater care of everything if it had all been his.

After a while I got used to him checking my work. I got used to working on my own too. Sometimes I would see him in the distance and wave. Perhaps he was shortsighted, or else it was just that men on the land did not wave, just as men on the land did not have pet names for particular cows. There was one we had for a time, one with a long, angular face, that seemed a little aloof. I called her Garbo. It did not catch on.

Andy had built a wooden partition in the shed and was living there. I suspected this bothered Neil, who would have felt his access to the shed somewhat restricted by Andy's presence. He liked to be up early and would often start in the shed, cleaning things. I never knew exactly what he was cleaning. The tractor, the pitchforks, the saws. Once Andy saw him cleaning the gun. I heard them talking. Andy had stumbled out of bed on hearing him.

"You gotta do that?"

"I'm sorry if I woke you. Got to keep things clean."

"You gotta do that now?"

"We'll be seeing some foals pretty soon. Foaling season is when things have to be put down, the ones that won't make it."

I started to wonder if I did not actually create more work for Neil, given that he had to check everything I was doing. Some days I would quit soon after lunch and spend the rest of the afternoon reading on the verandah. Andy had made me a chair out of some wood we had lying around. He had stripped it, sanded it, sealed it and then tacked a padded leather pouch on the seat and another at the back. He put some springs on the back legs so that it rocked or tilted a little. Then he painted all the wood pastel blue. I had become a man colored pastel blue. The color made it ugly but I could only thank him. It was very comfortable. It became my chair.

Andy liked doing things with his hands. He was good with them. He started restoring secondhand furniture at O'Meara's in town, and before long they were even selling new chairs, tables and cabinets that Andy had made. Sarah had put him in touch with O'Meara. They had started seeing each other. She would visit him occasionally in the shed. I would hear the car. More often he visited her, It must have been difficult for her to come to our place, given the circumstances in which she had met me. And I would see her again in similar circumstances.

Instructions can be given in many ways: as advice, as suggestions, as orders. Even orders can be given in more than one way. I did not own the land that Neil and I worked. I did not work properly the land my wife owned, and I seemed incapable, through any exertion, of earning my wife's respect. Whether or not poetry, the writing of it, was an activity capable of squeezing even the barest regard from Madeline, I was not the poet to do it. Somehow Neil knew all of this and he gave me instructions accordingly. After a while he spoke to me as I had once heard him speak to one of his children, in sharp, matter-of-fact barks.

Very early on, in the days when we still took our breaks together, I had made the mistake, while searching for something to
say, of commenting on the beauty of a bluish flower that grew
confidently in clumps by the front gate. It was our enemy, he told
me. It was Patterson's Curse. It was a weed. We had to eradicate
it. If the cows ate it they would spread it through their manure
and get sick themselves. I thought it was pretty, but apparently
it would take over the grass if we let it. We could get rid of it by
hand where it grew in little clumps by the gate or the house but
if it was in the open, we had to use a tractor.

Together and separately we had cut grass, leaving it to dry
and become hay, which we either fed to our cattle in winter or
else sold at the market. As with most other jobs, Neil had shown
me how to make hay and how to sell it. Sometimes we would do
it together and other times separately, on our own. From early
on, though, I noticed that he almost always wanted me to take
the hay to market on my own. At first I did not think too much
about it, but then I realized why he was sending me there alone.
He was ashamed to be working another man's land, at his age.
His family and personal circumstances were known throughout
the area, and as hard as it was for him to work someone else's
land, it was unbearable for him to be *seen* doing it. Later I realized it was more than just this. The indignity was that much
greater for him if he was seen driving in, unloading and selling
the hay with me.

So I was alone with my hay in the market the day a cattle
farmer, a neighbor, found some tiny bluey-purple petals among
my bales. There were not many, but there did not need to be. It
was a disgrace. Word of it spread like fire, and each telling
pinned me tighter to the disgrace. Everybody heard. "Deliber-

ate," some said. "A fool" was the verdict of others. How slowly the people in town moved along the main street, until I came near them. I heard whispers in the aisle of the Welcome Mart. The scrambled-egg hair girl at the checkout looked up at me. In the time we had been living there she had dug herself deeply into her adolescence. She showed no sign of leaving.

"How can I help *you?*" she asked me rhetorically, focusing all her boredom and contempt somewhere below my eyes, between my chest and my belt buckle. The man in the stockfeed and merchandise center grimaced when he saw me walk through the door. It was bad enough to be found writhing in the dirt near Lake Eildon, but now it was widely thought that I had tried to sell hay laced with Patterson's Curse to my competitors, to my neighbors. In the way of small towns and large offices, no explicit allegations were made to my face, so there was no right of reply, no one to whom I could direct an apology. It was not possible to explain that it was not deliberate, that it might not have been me. When I told Neil what had happened, he said that he already knew. He sniffed and looked at his hands. That was all he said.

He was not there when some men came to the house to talk about it. They said I should be prohibited from selling at the market. It was not clear whether they meant hay or everything. This was their view irrespective of whether the Patterson's Curse had been deliberate or an accident. They would not stay for a cup of tea or a beer. They would not sit down. Andy was out with Sarah. There was just Madeline and me.

I had ruined everything for her. I could not be trusted, not even to work. She feared that we would not be able to make a living even if we were able to coax life from the sullen earth her father had left her. In disgrace with fortune and men's eyes, I felt her shoe hit me in the back of the neck without warning. It was nine days after the men had come and still she would not speak to me. But she spoke to Neil. I heard her.

"I've got to do something."

I was outside. It was quiet but I did not hear a response. They did not know I was there.

When I cry I suck on my front teeth and purse my lips involuntarily as though in anticipation of an onslaught of kisses. That was the way Hugh Brasnett described it. He was still there. He had not left. His father, a thickset man, was the town butcher. Everyone knew him and therefore knew what had happened to his son Hugh. There was no incentive for Hugh to recover. If he left the hospital he would need to leave town in order to start again. He was still an *involuntary*, but this time I was a *voluntary*.

"Tell me again about Mandelstam," Hugh demanded. He was so happy to have me back. At first I thought it was simply because he was bored, but after a few days I could see that he was often engaged in something, even busy. He flirted with some of the female patients, regardless of age, over the smorgasbords of watery tuna and stale bread. He traded successfully in tobacco and marijuana.

"It's five dollars a joint here," he explained, and when I said nothing he added, "Look, I don't set the price . . . and . . . and it's not my fault. Myself, I don't smoke. That shit does nothing for me."

He kept an interested eye on the transient female patients and slept with quite a few of them, sometimes in our room, sometimes in theirs or else in the bathroom. The woman he kept coming back to was a quiet older woman, about my age. She was really quite pretty. He seemed to regard sleeping with her merely as an extension of his friendship with her. One night they were in our room. I had the covers over my head but I could still hear them.

"You take me to another place . . . to another time," she whispered, "but I have a son about your age. He doesn't want to see me."

Sarah was less delighted to see me. Still sympathetic, the meeting of her personal and her professional lives clearly made her uncomfortable. Though we acknowledged the connection, I was much too ashamed to exploit her love for my son. This time I was embarrassed for her, for her having to work there, for her seeing me see her having to interact with the other patients. There was little room for dignity. Within a few days she asked me privately whether there was anything I would like Andy to bring me. I made a list of books and got them ten days later. She brought them, not Andy. He did not visit this time.

"What are you reading? Is it Mandelstam?" Hugh asked. "Does it have the poem that got him into trouble?"

"They all got him into trouble, but I know the one you mean. The one about Stalin?"

"Yes, the one they were looking for the night of the knock at the door, the night the men in overcoats came . . . when he was with his wife and that pain-in-the-arse translator and Akhmatova."

Hugh remembered everything I had told him about Mandelstam's arrest in 1934. He seemed to take pride in remembering.

"When did he write it?"

"About six months before his arrest."

"Find it, will you. Read it to me."

"We live, deaf to the land beneath us,
Ten steps away no one hears our speeches,
But where there's so much as half a conversation
The Kremlin's mountaineer will get his mention.
His fingers are fat as grubs
And the words, final as lead weights, fall from his lips,
His cockroach whiskers leer
And his boot tops gleam.
Around him a rabble of thin-necked bosses—
fawning half-men for him to play with.
They whinny, purr or whine
As he prates and points a finger,
One by one forging his laws, to be flung
Like horseshoes at the head, the eye or the groin.
And every killing is a treat
For the broad-chested Ossete."

"He sounds like my father, fingers fat as grubs. What's an Ossete?"

"An Ossete is a person from Ossetia, which is just above Georgia in the former Soviet Union. Stalin was supposed to have come from Georgia, but there were rumors that he was part Ossetian. I'd imagine the rumors were meant to cast doubt on his ethnic origins and parentage. For Mandelstam it was probably a way of naming him without naming him while reminding the reader or the listener how hateful he was."

"Who, Stalin?"

"Yes. How hateful Stalin was."

"And that was the poem they came looking for six months later?"

"Yes, I think so."

Hugh sat up against the bed head and spoke quietly, almost reverentially. It was as though he knew his words could hurt me but he had to say them anyway.

"It's not just his poetry, is it? I mean, it's not just what he wrote that makes you . . . *feel* him so much." There was a gentleness to his voice.

"What do you mean?"

"You want to *be* him, don't you?"

I smiled. "That's crazy, Hugh."

"Well, maybe, but . . . that's why you're here."

"I don't know why you say that."

"He's like a . . . role model for you."

"Mandelstam? Mandelstam . . . suffered quite incredibly. His life was miserable. Separated from his wife, he lived in poverty in an insane and brutal time, in an insane and brutal place. His work was banned. Why . . . why would I want to be him?"

"Because you're a poet. I have heard you. When you came in, that night. I heard you."

"Oh, come on, Hugh. Is this some sort of a game, telling me things I've said in a delirium, because if it is, it's beneath you. It's pretty . . . facile."

"Calm down, will you. I'm not trying to be offensive."

"No . . . but when did you gain this sudden expertise in poetry, Russian history and psychoanalysis?"

"But you *do*."

"Do what?"

"You do want to . . . *be* him. He was a great poet, a true original, and he was . . . deeply loved . . . so deeply loved . . . by his wife. You need him to . . . help get you through."

When I cry I suck on my front teeth and purse my lips as though in anticipation of an onslaught of kisses. Hugh continued.

"It's okay, you know. I understand it. See, you're not really crazy. It's just how you get through. You're . . . only in a childish way connected to the established order."

The nurses liked to have us out of bed. They kept a book in which they recorded our responses to their instructions, whether we were cooperative, how willing we were to take a shower. A doctor would occasionally read the book and this was called treatment.

I liked to think that I was a good influence on Hugh. I never balked at getting up, taking a shower or cleaning up the ward: the cleaners did not have to touch our area. In all the time I was there, Hugh did not give them any trouble, either, until the end.

We were playing chess in the dayroom. The television was on in the corner. The screen showed some very good-looking people in a hospital setting, some of them patients, some of them staff, all of them tanned. Apart from the sound from the TV, the room—the ward, as it was called—was fairly quiet. It was at this point that Hugh was distracted, not by the television but by a nearby conversation. A young man had come in to see Hugh's friend, the older woman. The young man, who I later learned was her son, held in his fist a tiny bunch of flowers, which she took from him apprehensively. Hugh watched as she brushed hair out of the young man's eyes. I tried to renew his interest in the game but could not, particularly once he had heard his own name.

The woman mentioned Hugh's name a few times and the young man looked in our direction. Then his voice started to get louder. As its volume increased, so did the overall tension in the room. In the television hospital a man and a woman were hugging. But in our ward the young man was shouting at Hugh's friend. She pulled her dressing gown tighter around her, just as ashamed as he said he was.

"No, it's not like that." She smiled.

But it was, and it wasn't, like that.

"You're fucking sick, you know that? You really are." It was already too late to say anything. Hugh stood up, knocking over the chessboard. A pawn fell in my lap. Everyone watched as Hugh approached the shouting young man.

"Stop talking to her like that."

They pushed one another. One of the nurses ran off to call for assistance. No one from the staff was on hand to see Hugh get punched in the face, on the side of his jaw. Some of the patients moved in to get a closer look. The quiet older woman had torn her gown trying to come between them. Hugh was laying into her son's face with a maniacal speed by the time he was outnumbered by hospital staff.

I felt a hand on my shoulder as I sat there without moving.

"Just stay there. Don't get involved."

It was Sarah. I listened to her and watched them overpower Hugh. The woman was shouting at him. He had battered her son. A doctor, two nurses and a maintenance man held him. He was twisting, trying to break free, trying to make them see that he was defending the woman's honor. He was trying to convince them that he was still "the funny guy, the joker, the good normal guy" of the ward. But his protests became increasingly frenzied, hysterical and futile as he twisted and thrashed his legs about with everyone watching. A procession of patients accompanied him and his captors, some cheering him on, some shouting abuse, others just watching, fascinated by his pain or pleased that this was happening to someone else. There were not enough staff on hand to keep the patients away. They all saw how he kicked and struggled as the nurses pulled his pants down and gave him a shot. It was terrifying to see it, to see his anger, to see my young friend's transformation, his degradation. His inability to distinguish between his status in the ward and that of any visitor would have made the apparent arbitrariness of their intervention all the more intolerable. Why did they not constrain the other man? Why did they not give him a chance to explain that this was not a psychotic episode? This was a fight, well-intentioned, even gallant.

Sarah's hand stayed on my shoulder. No one saw me weep. Hugh was taken to a padded cell in the isolation wing. I had done nothing at all while this was going on. The next morning one of the doctors approached me and suggested that I was ready to rejoin my family, that I should leave that day. It was thought that I was better.

Having dressed, shaved and packed, I waited in the room all day for Hugh to come back. But he did not. One of the nurses asked me if I wanted to call home to arrange to be picked up. I said that I would make my own way home. The walk would take me an hour or so, but I felt I needed it. Before leaving, I wrote Hugh a note. I did not refer to the events of the previous day but instead reminded him that in Mandelstam's time people used to copy out poems as gifts for each other. The gift was all the more valuable if the publication of the poem was proscribed. Then I wrote out the one he liked most, his favorite, thanked him and wished him luck. The note, I knew, would do nothing for him. *I was only in a childish way connected to the established order.*

By not even trying to help him during the disturbance, I had demonstrated that I was ready to join the outside world. This was the world Sarah would have me rejoin. It contained my son, whom she loved. I could imagine the way they talked to each other, the way she loved him in spite of the embarrassment that was his father, the way they promised to take each other away from all that smacked of their parents' generation. If I had done nothing else for him, I had brought them to each other. Now she brought me back to him. And I *had* done nothing else for him. That he had grown up solid as a tree, strong, uncomplicated and good with his hands, all of it had nothing to do with me.

The fruit was falling from the trees by the side of the road. Sometimes it rolled away, far from the trees. I walked into town. It was almost deserted at that time of day. The dogs were asleep on the steps of the public library. The hairdresser was closed. Through the window of the butcher shop I saw a man hosing down drip trays and wondered if it was Hugh's father. Fat pink sausages hung in the window like Stalin's fingers. The man looked up at me with suspicion. His face was the face of a tyrant. Hugh had fought him just as he had fought what he perceived as injustice a day earlier. His father had so often sworn at him, demeaned him, hit him. When Hugh had fought back, the local police made a deal with the butcher and Hugh became a local involuntary patient.

A couple of Harley-Davidsons were parked on the grassy median strip in the center of the main street opposite the hotel. The bank and even the bakery were closed. It was night by then. The streetlights had come on and I walked home knowing that when I left the precincts of the town I would be walking in the dark. There I was under a streetlight, moths overhead, looking at my reflection in O'Meara's Furniture, where Andy worked. By changing my position and orientation I could manipulate my reflection into chairs my son had built or helped restore. I wished so much that I could have given him something. When I cry I suck on my front teeth and purse my lips involuntarily as though in anticipation of an onslaught of kisses. I saw it in the window. I sat on my pastel blue chair, the one Andy had made for me. When I moved away, it remained in the window. It was for sale.

The last thing you see as you leave town is a blue and white sign, *Feeling the hurt? Call Lifeline on 13 1114.* After that it was dark. I walked home in that dark to the sound of things I did not understand. Nature conducts so much of its commerce at night. A real poet would have understood the semiotics of the nocturnal whisperings that were all around me. In the trees something was waking up. In the long grass something was eating, something was drinking from a dam, something was mating wildly, something was killing. With only the blue light of the moon I saw none of it and heard very little but the sound of my shoes on the road. I thought of Mandelstam, of his poetry, in spite of the danger that waited for me when I thought of him. Verses came into my head as I walked with my pack on my back, verses seemingly at random. True poets, both of us: he for his writing, me for my remembering. I was hoping there was something heroic even in just memorizing his work. Like a narcotic, Mandelstam's words had a dangerously soothing effect on me, and I breathed them in and took strength from them as I walked.

I've many years to live before I'm a patriarch.
I'm at an age that commands little respect.
They swear at me behind my back,

in the senseless, pointless language of tram fights.
"You bastard!" Well, I apologise,
but deep down I don't change at all.

When you think of your connection with the world
you can't believe it. It is nonsense. . . .

There is a little light at the gate to show the number of our
property. Other than that, there was no light between the gate
and the house. I unslipped the chain on the gate and there, at my
feet, was some Patterson's Curse. I left it untouched and quietly
closed the gate. The lights of our neighbor's home looked like
fireflies in the distance. From the house I could hear music.
Someone was playing my old Louis Armstrong: "Lyin' to Myself," it might have been. The light was on in the shed and I saw
the back of Andy's car. Was he getting a taste for Satchmo? Was
he inside dancing with his mother? We had danced, the three of
us, to my jazz records when he was a little boy.

I stood on the verandah and looked in through the lounge
room window to where the music was coming from. Madeline's
shoes were at almost perfect right angles to each other. Magazines were in several piles, unstraightened, probably unread.
Something made me continue peering through the windows before coming in. I wanted to catch a glimpse of the way things
were without me. I thought of what she might say when she saw
me for the first time, and it made me want to delay everything. I
stepped off the balcony and back onto the front drive. For a moment I thought of turning back.

I went to the shed and put my pack down at the door. A radio played softly and I knocked before entering.

"Yeah?" I heard him say in a voice I had somehow given him. I entered without answering. He had been varnishing something but stopped when he saw me. He looked as though he had seen a ghost.

"Dad?"

I said nothing. I did not know what to say to him.

"Dad."

It felt good just to hear the word. He put the brush down on some old newspaper and came over to me. We looked at each other and then he hugged me.

"What are you making?"

"How are you feeling, Dad?"

"I'm fine."

"Does Mum know you're here?"

"No . . . no, I saw your light on and just thought I'd . . ."

I wondered what I would need to do just to be able to see him every day, with his permission, day after day, without bothering him. I would be quiet. He need not know I was there. I could promise not to be mad again.

"I'll take your pack. Let's go inside."

We should never have gone inside, or at least, I should have gone by myself. We heard the trumpet solo from the lounge room. Andy called out. Her shoes remained untouched. We walked down the hall. I went first, reluctantly, feeling an eerie nonspecific need to grab him by the hand and lead him away or else to shelter him. On my own they might have missed me altogether and I could have walked away without them knowing I knew. As it was, she looked over me and straight at Andy.

The bedroom door was open. It all looked unplanned. She was sitting on the bed in her slip, facing us. He was kneeling and had his head between her thighs. Andy dropped my pack. Madeline called out our son's name. I backed into Andy, instinctively trying to push him away as though it was not too late, as though he had not already seen them. She stood up. Neil looked over his shoulder.

"You fucking pig," Andy called.

"Andy!"

"For Christ's sake," Neil said.

Andy lunged at Neil but could not get past me. He tried again and got a little farther but, in doing so, pushed me into the room.

"Andy, take it easy," I called from under him.

He stood up. Madeline and I were trying to keep him away from Neil. The trumpets played.

"You filthy fucking pig," shouted Andy.

"Listen, son," shouted Neil over the top of the music, "you don't make anything better . . . calling . . . carrying on—"

"You're fucking vermin, Mahoney."

Madeline was crying. I felt her tears on my face. Andy and Neil had pushed the two of us together as we tried to keep them apart.

"Vermin. Fucking snake . . . in the fucking grass," Andy shouted in a voice I had never heard as he ran down the hall and out the back door towards the shed. I stood and looked at them. No one had said my name. Should I have tried to hit him on Andy's behalf? Should I have hit her? Should I have tried to shake her? What was so wrong with me that I could not share my son's rage, the rage he felt for both our sakes?

"Oh, what the fuck are you staring at, you lunatic?" Neil said as he brushed past me, putting on his shirt.

"When did you . . . get out? Nobody . . . said anything," Madeline asked, looking at me for the first time.

"I was . . . a *voluntary.* I could leave whenever I liked."

Neil was buttoning himself up in the lounge room. His shoes were beside hers but I had not seen them. Madeline followed him and I followed her.

"It's not what you think," she said.

"Madeline, how can it not be what he thinks," said Neil, irritated, hurriedly putting on his shoes.

"Shut up," she shouted at him.

"He knows what he saw," Neil said, now standing with both shoes on. "He's not an idiot, Madeline," he said as the screen door slammed and Andy came down the hall, his feet slapping the linoleum.

"Just a poet," I said as Andy came back into the room filled with the rage of youth and some just for me. His mother saw it first.

"Andy, put it away," she said as he pushed her to one side.

"Are you mad?" shouted Neil.

"Andy, no," I called, and reached for him, pushing him off balance.

The first shot went into the wall.

"Andy, it's not worth it."

Neil knocked over the upright lamp.

"Someone's got to fight back, Dad," and he shot him twice in the chest. The sound rang out over the valley and over our lives.

Neil Mahoney seemed to jump in the air. It was as though he was bouncing between planes of air. Madeline shouted his name. She shouted hysterically, her voice high and mad like that of a bird in the country first thing in the morning. Neil lay on the floor by the wall. His blood was leaving him for a pool on the floor beside him. Seeing her go over to him increased Andy's fury.

"Get away from him," he shouted at her.

I grabbed at the gun. I had lost her years ago. Suddenly I could see that so clearly.

"Andy, give it to me."

He did not resist for very long. Madeline was kneeling beside Neil, crying, saliva and mucus forming bubbles at her mouth. The music was still on.

"You've killed him, Andy," Madeline said.

"No, he's not dead."

"Yes he is, Andy. He's dead. Come and see."

Andy walked slowly towards the body but I stood in front of him, blocking his way, still holding the rifle.

Now the night was real to me. I stood with a gun in one hand, the other blocking my son's approach to the man his mother, yet again, cradled in her lap, the man he had just shot. Andy was breathing heavily. I pushed him back with my body and he obeyed. The two of them looked at me. I looked for any trace of myself in him and they looked at me as if for the first time. There I was, his father, her husband. I looked at her semi-nakedness, at the outlines of her breasts above Neil's slumped body, for any trace of the shy girl for whom I had written that poem all those years ago. How quickly all this had happened. How quickly everyone had gone mad.

Though none of this could be undone, I knew what to do with a clarity and certainty I had never known before. I turned off the music while they stayed still.

"I want you to listen to me, both of you," I said. And they listened. They did as I instructed and stayed just where they were while I went to the laundry and got a towel. I took it back to them so they could see what I was doing, all the time holding the gun. With the towel I wiped it down several times, thoroughly, including the trigger. Then I put my hands all over it.

"Andy, you left here before I got home. *I* found your mother. *I* got the gun and *I* did this. Get in your car and go. No one will doubt me on this."

"Dad, no!"

"Andy, get in the car."

"Dad, you can't do this."

"Andy, the sooner you go the better. Go to Sarah's, anywhere. One of us . . . your mother will call an ambulance about five minutes after you've gone."

"Dad, I can't let you—"

"Listen to your father, Andy," Madeline said.

"But, Dad . . ." He was crying.

"Just go! Get the hell away from here."

We heard him start the car. Madeline was still on the floor.

"Look at the clock."

"Why?"

"I want you to take note of the time and call an ambulance in five minutes."

"Give him five minutes. Tell them Neil's already dead. Then they won't hurry."

I put the gun down and covered his torso with the towel. These were the longest minutes. They were the minutes in which years came to a head. Madeline moved away from Neil's body and sat down next to me. Her gaze kept shifting from the clock to me to the wall where Neil lay slumped and then back to me. They were the minutes when we could have talked, outside the veil of her dissatisfaction and outside my sense of failure, for the first time in years. They were the minutes when the two young people that had fallen for each other more than twenty years earlier could have met in their older bodies and, together, grappled towards an explanation.

I say this because in those minutes she looked at me as she had not been able to for years, without contempt and without rancor. I was the person she had loved nearly twenty years ago. In those minutes I was not a failed clerk nor a quixotic poet. I was not mad. I was her old lover, her long-lost friend, who had not intended to be a man incapable of living up to his promise. Most of all I was the father of her son and I was saving his life.

There was a time after his first arrest when Mandelstam became convinced that his executioners were going to come for him at a particular time of the day, and each day, at that time, he waited for them fearfully. When Nadezhda managed to find out that the time he expected them to come was six o'clock in the evening, she took to surreptitiously moving the hands of the clock every day, telling him, "You said six, but it's already a quarter past seven." Madeline never used to wear a watch. She does now, I am told.

I waited for her to count the minutes, and when she had called for an ambulance, I took my pack which was unopened and walked out of the house down the path to our gatepost, past the clumps of Patterson's Curse and back into the night. I took the road and kept walking. A long while later I heard the ambulance in the distance. I thought only briefly about what lay in store for me, and when I did I was not too troubled by it. A man who shoots someone is far better understood than a man who is racked by a hopeless addiction to the music in words.

And in the dark, by the side of the road, I realized it was really other people's words that I heard, not my own. I had made the mistake of thinking that because I could hear, but really hear, Mandelstam's words, I was myself a poet. It was an easy mistake to make, since real poets say that poetry begins, like music, as phrases played inexplicably in a person's head. It was just that in my case they were Mandelstam's phrases. But I heard them, and not faintly, either. I heard them clearly, unequivocally, when I was trying to do other things. I heard them when I was trying to be a clerk, a farmer, a poet, a husband and a father. And I hear them now when I need them most. I am thus still only in a childish way connected to the established order. Perhaps this is a crime.

GOOD MORNING, AGAIN IN THE TIME OF
THE DINOSAUR YOUR NIECE'S SPEECH
NIGHT THE REASONS I WON'T BE COMING
MANSLAUGHTER THE *HONG KONG FIR*
DOCTRINE I WAS ONLY IN A CHILDISH WAY
CONNECTED TO THE ESTABLISHED ORDER
SPITALNIC'S LAST YEAR A TALE IN TWO CITIES

Spitalnic lay in the hospital bed. It was night now, and the reassuring sounds of human activity were scarce. All visitors had come and gone. Even the night nurse had said good night to him. The next time he would speak to anyone would be in the morning when they woke him to prepare him for surgery.

This was the time of night, and indeed of one's life, when reminiscences, fantasies and fears invade the mind, wreak havoc with it and unbalance one's usual, if only superficial, equilibrium. He could not sleep. His entire lower body was hot while the torso was cold. Each limb took on a life of its own. His feet told him to get out of bed. His face begged to be washed. His genitals mocked him with recurring itches that could not be satisfied or prevented. Spitalnic was afraid to scratch lest one of the night nurses creep in thinking him asleep, only to find him seemingly arousing himself.

At twenty, Spitalnic, a sometime bon vivant, had enjoyed a

better-than-average sex life. His love life, however, had been less spectacular, and in the last twelve months both had been cause for concern. The things that had gone wrong had been small individually, trivial and sometimes even laughable. But collectively the events of the last twelve months had left the undergraduate Spitalnic lonely, more reserved and possessing a deep moroseness that belied his often jovial exterior.

This twelve-month period had begun with his girlfriend of two years leaving him on the day of an exam. When questioned, Spitalnic would concede that he had been in the process of falling out of love with her, but she wasn't to know this. Celia had large warm green eyes and thick mousy-brown hair. The memory of her smile could now reduce Spitalnic to tears, and often did. But the biggest thing in her favor, from Spitalnic's point of view, was her love of Spitalnic.

She would read the books he recommended. She adopted his taste in films, drama, music, politics, and was coming around to accepting for herself the high moral code Spitalnic set for himself and others. But she did not come around sufficiently. She began seeing another boy while still involved with Spitalnic. The other boy offered excitement. Spitalnic offered security. For a while she was torn. A body needs both excitement and security, even if the two are almost diametrically opposed. She deceived herself that the relationship with the other boy was purely platonic and that it would only upset Spitalnic unnecessarily were he to be aware of the extent of her intimacy with the other boy. This period of self-deception ended abruptly when the boy grabbed her and kissed her unexpectedly one day on campus. She wanted him to and she let him.

There was a three-week period between the beginning of Celia's physical relationship with the other boy and her finishing with Spitalnic. During this time she grew cold and sullen. She spoke in a monotone and affected an attitude at best of indifference, at worst of impatience. She kissed Spitalnic as one kisses an elderly aunt at a family gathering. None of this was lost on Spitalnic despite his being absorbed in preparations for the end-of-year exams.

Celia, too, knew what she was doing and hated herself for it. She resented Spitalnic, who looked so pathetic trying to comfort what he saw as a manifestation of study-related anxiety with demonstrations of his affection. She hated herself for this too.

Her double life, her guilt, her pity for Spitalnic and her anger at herself for letting such a situation arise at so crucial a time in the student calendar led her to break it off suddenly. She did it over the phone with tears and a feeling that her throat had contracted beyond the point where she could continue to breathe. But she did continue to breathe. It was the morning of Spitalnic's economics exam. He was stunned and said nothing. She hung up. Spitalnic failed the exam.

"Relationships begin and end every other day, especially where young people are concerned," his parents volunteered. They shared a fear of Spitalnic's penchant for self-indulgence, despite sharing so little else that their divorce in the year of Spitalnic's bar mitzvah seemed close to inevitable and their marriage close to unbelievable.

Spitalnic's father, an academic philosopher, was the son of a rabbi, his mother the daughter of a clothing manufacturer. She married Spitalnic's father to spite her parents and to get away from them. She was seventeen then. She was forty-two when the divorce came through on the ninth day of the Hebrew month of Av. Spitalnic had lived three years with each parent since their divorce by the time Celia had finished with him.

The end of his relationship with Celia and his failing of the exam had a disastrous effect on Spitalnic. He lost interest in his appearance. He would not shave for weeks at a time. His hair was unkempt. He stopped eating regularly. His father accused him of inflicting anorexia on himself and they fought bitterly over this. He swore viciously at his mother and resurrected previously contentious issues from her married life that they had agreed not to discuss.

This all changed quite abruptly when Spitalnic found somebody new, somebody with the potential to restore his self-respect. He met her at a party to which his friends had talked him into coming. Alison was an aspiring journalist who had recently moved from another state in order to further her career. She had short black hair and pale skin that contrasted with her deep blue eyes. She was two years his senior.

They were introduced in a crowd and never given an opportunity to speak alone. Spitalnic took mental notes of their conversation, clutching at any sentence, phrase or glance that could be construed as a sign of interest.

It was, of course, impossible under the circumstances to get her phone number; but, remembering where she worked, he was, after some little research, able to contact her. Their first private meeting was arranged after a brief yet friendly telephone conversation. It was a dinner engagement.

Spitalnic, surprised at the ease with which he found her place, arrived early and so waited in the car until he was five minutes late. He was nervous on entering and his mouth was dry, but when he saw her in the doorway he knew that his apprehension had to be overcome. She was, after all, quite beautiful. Her voice was loud and warm. She offered him a drink and this almost threw him. No girl he had taken out previously had offered him a predinner drink, and he did not know what he should answer. He declined the offer after consideration.

The restaurant he chose served French cuisine. The waiters called him sir, which embarrassed him. The conversation flowed easily even before they had been served with wine. Alison was ambitious, vivacious and likely to succeed as a journalist. He thought that if she could put at least two words together, her looks and personality would do the rest. She was politically active, left of center. Spitalnic, too, was left of center but was certainly not politically active. Spitalnic did not feel comfortable as a member of any organization or committee. The prospect unsettled him. He was not a joiner.

Alison argued that the best way to bring the Left back around to the side of the Jews was to get involved at the grassroots level, to infiltrate. She spoke convincingly and with enthusiasm. Spitalnic suggested that her words would not seem out of place in a passage from *The Protocols of the Elders of Zion*. Alison laughed and sipped her wine.

As a student, she had organized a counterdemonstration against a National Action demonstration. She had contacted the mainstream press and television stations and generally organized sufficient support to outnumber the fascists. It had been a major success. She was then nineteen.

After dinner they drove to the city to browse in a bookshop that closed at midnight. They discussed fiction with that combination of heartfelt sincerity and genuine one-upmanship that would have amused an observing third party. She was impressed with the breadth of his reading and he was heartened by this. He bought her two books, inscribed them in the shop and regretted it immediately.

"You have to rush things!" he heard his father say. "Are you trying to bribe her?"

Maybe he was. Spitalnic hoped it wasn't obvious. She thanked him and he was embarrassed. Was this a form of prostitution? he wondered. Two books for a cup of coffee in her lounge room and a good-night kiss upon which to ponder.

But she was not a party to this contract. Spitalnic did get a cup of coffee and finally a peck on the cheek, but between these two events Alison had entirely deprived him of his initial hopes. He was informed that her life was too hectic to give a relationship any sort of a chance and that, in fact, at this stage of her career, she did not really regret that this was so. Furthermore, she had recently extricated herself from a relationship with a person only twelve months younger than her and *that* age difference had proved too big an obstacle. The boy was far too immature. Not that she was suggesting that Spitalnic was too immature. Did he understand that? What had he understood?

Spitalnic had switched off almost immediately after the spiel had started. He felt the same numbness he had felt when Celia spoke to him over the phone on the day of his Economics exam. This time it was less justified. How could he really be hurt? He had only seen her twice. He had already, midway through dinner, recognized her as the beautiful and ambitious owner of a potentially lethal *pisk*. But he had not expected to be wounded by it so soon.

Alison kept talking. Spitalnic looked through the steam em-

anating from the coffee mug at the novels he had bought her and
held back a tear that would be born in the car on the way home,
but which was conceived with Celia weeks ago.

At the door of her house Alison told him that she still wanted
to see him, to keep next Saturday night free and that she would
call him during the week. Then came the peck on the cheek.

With one day left before the commencement of the new university year, Spitalnic had only one summer Sunday afternoon completely to himself that did not need to be shared with the tools
of Keynesian or neoclassical economics. He had seen, advertised
in the Yiddish paper, the opening of a museum to commemorate
the Holocaust. Having failed in attempts to persuade his friends
to go to the opening, he went alone. There was already a large
crowd when he got there and he was forced to walk a consider-
able distance from his car to the museum. Police were patrolling
the adjacent streets in large numbers. Was there nowadays a
large police presence at the opening of all museums, or only those
commemorating the slaughter of Jews? he wondered.

Spitalnic had no choice but to stand at the back, almost in
the street. There was a crowd of maybe three hundred packed in
between the platform in the courtyard of the museum and the
street. Most of the three hundred were elderly European Jews,
most likely survivors. The sun was hot and the sky was bare.
With the highly visible police presence, the nearby railway lines
and the high density of perspiring Jewish bodies within a
barbed-wire periphery, Spitalnic wondered if anyone else had
noted the similarity of the surroundings to those of the events
they were commemorating.

On the raised platform at the front of the courtyard sat eight dignitaries from various Jewish organizations and a politician from each of the major parties. All of the speeches, other than those by the politicians, were in Yiddish. Survivors of the Holocaust were being told the importance of Remembering in a language only they could understand. *They* were not likely to forget, so why weren't they using English? Spitalnic mused.

The politicians used different terms and expressions to convey that they regretted the Holocaust; that the larger community is indebted to the local Jewish community for so many things that to mention one in particular would be to trivialize the Jewish community's outstanding contributions in the areas of . . . ; that their Party is committed simultaneously to assimilation and to the maintenance of distinct ethnic identities; and that the tragedy of this current generation is its failure to remember what it is that future generations should never forget. Each politician received generous applause from an audience that had, almost to a person, not understood the words, let alone the meaning behind this verbiage. But they were not applauding the speeches, nor even the speakers. They were applauding the country in which gentiles courted Jewish votes; they were applauding the fact that today they could move freely on either side of the barbed-wire fence. They were applauding because they had survived Hitler.

Spitalnic had paid the entrance fee, although by standing in the street he had not actually entered the museum. There was a mini-trestle at the entrance where one could buy programs. A fleshy woman in her sixties sat behind the trestle selling the programs. She had been listening to the Yiddish speakers and had not noticed the acute shortage of programs with which she was now suddenly faced. She called out to a tired-looking man whose concentration camp number showed below the right sleeve of his short-sleeved shirt. From the woman's mouth came a high-pitched whisper full of inappropriate panic.

"Mietek, get more from the car. We've run out!"

The man could not make out her words but recognized the tone. He had to make his way from deep within the crowd. He began with "Excuse me" but soon took to pushing and prodding his way towards the entrance. He was visibly perspiring, but those around were oblivious to his exertions despite the fact that the speeches were now in English and therefore harder for them to understand.

"Mietek, get more from the car—and hurry!"

Spitalnic, being at the head of the queue for the booklets, saw the little man turn one hundred and eighty degrees one way, see no path ahead, and turn one hundred and eighty degrees back. There were numerous beads of perspiration on the man's head now. He was level with Spitalnic when he began to gasp for breath. His legs gave way like ice under the hot sun. His body slapped the pavement and Spitalnic caught his head. The woman rushed out from behind the trestle to where Spitalnic held the gasping man's head.

"Mietek, what's wrong? Get a doctor!"

The word *doctor* rippled through the immediate layers of the crowd. A young officious-looking man made his way brusquely to where Spitalnic held the gasping head, now partially screened from the sun by the little man's numbered forearm. The doctor undid the buttons of the man's short-sleeved shirt and started thumping on the man's chest. He told Spitalnic to place the man's head on the ground with the face pointing up and ordered the woman to call for an ambulance. The woman immediately delegated her authority.

"Call an ambulance for Mr. Hillel—and hurry!"

The opening of the Holocaust Center proceeded in ignorance of the events taking place on the street side in the barbed-wire periphery. Mietek Hillel died as the wheels of the ambulance came to a stop outside the museum. The body was placed on a stretcher, put inside the ambulance and shunted quietly away with few people at the opening being any the wiser. The Nazis had finally got Mr. Hillel, and Spitalnic looked for somewhere to wash his hands.

The university year began without the least shame for its inauspiciousness. Alison did not call as she had promised, nor did Spitalnic expect her to (although *hope* is something altogether different). The lecturers repeated the nagging demands they had made the previous years. Spitalnic settled down to his courses without much procrastination. He referred to the economics course, which he had failed and was forced to take a second time, as "the bastard," the illegitimate and unwanted child of Celia's new relationship. Since neither "the bastard" nor Spitalnic had any connection with Celia now, Spitalnic was forced to be its sole guardian. He had driven to her house with a gift for her birthday but she was out. She never called to thank him.

Spitalnic spent the first six weeks of university mostly in the company of Reuben, his friend of seven years. They had gone through secondary school together. Reuben had seen Spitalnic put on weight during his parents' divorce and lose it and his virginity at sixteen. Spitalnic had seen Reuben stop growing and gain admission to the law school. Lunch with Reuben was the best part of each day. If it was sunny, they would eat outside; if not, they would eat in the "caf," the culinary institution where the reputations of the socially mobile students were made, discussed and embellished. Reuben was equally disenchanted with university life. One had to be either a wealthy establishment socialite or a Marxist of sorts from an alternative establishment in order to walk straight into any prefabricated social circle. Since both he and Spitalnic were Jews, they were indigenous to neither establishment. There were Jewish students on campus willing to sell their birthrights for a place within one or other of the establishments, but they were not two of them.

Their circle of friends included anybody, regardless of race, sex or faculty, who possessed a clearly recognizable ounce of sincerity. It was a small circle. Spitalnic introduced people he liked to Reuben, and the favor was reciprocated. Within a few months their circle had widened a little. Spitalnic had introduced Reuben to Greg, a short boy with straight black hair who proudly admitted to having no religion but whose nose (it was said) had made him the frequent target of anti-Semitic jibes and thus an honorary Jew. Greg was a third-year arts student majoring in politics with leftist leanings, but, as Spitalnic was fond of saying, he was no *meshuggener.*

Reuben brought Sandy into their circle. She was a blond girl with slight features and a cherub's smile. A second-year science student, she did not look old enough to have gone through secondary school. Spitalnic took to her immediately, but not in a ro-

mantic way, for this would have seemed almost immoral or sacri-
legious. Her smile, her laugh, her seemingly unlimited good nature, made her the object of Spitalnic's paternal attentions.

At first she was intimidated by him. His sense of humor seemed
to her offbeat if not at times sick. He made obscure references to
things she had never heard of. Was he laughing at her? Was she expected to know of these things? What did these people see in such
a little girl? But it was not long before she warmed to Spitalnic. As
the weeks and then months progressed, they became closer. Spitalnic would do little things for her. He would often buy her lunch.
If the group was laughing and he saw she was sad, he would change
places and sit next to her, give her his lunch, his coat and scarf in
winter. The others affectionately referred to him as her grandfather.
Spitalnic laughed at this with the rest. But when the laughing was
over, he wondered about his relationship with Sandy. He did sin-
cerely love this little girl, but he was not in love with her. What
Spitalnic felt for Sandy was unique in his emotional experience and
he could not explain it. She, too, loved him, but was not in love
with him. She had a boyfriend studying pharmacy whom she had
been seeing for close to a year. She was in love with him although
they fought a lot.

Indeed, all the members of the lunchtime circle fought inter-
mittently with those with whom they were in love, "since that is
the wont of those of such an irrational state of mind," and Spitalnic thought all the members of the circle possessed such a state
of mind. By and large their partners were not associated with
the university, and so the meeting of the lunchtime circle was a
lighthearted event, a communal midday sigh of relief, free from
the complexities, uncertainties and melodrama associated with
daily romantic interplay. All those present at lunch could hug

and hit, kiss, fight and make love at other times. All except Reuben and his friend Spitalnic.

Enrolled in one of Spitalnic's tutorials was a girl with shoulder-length snow-white hair. She wore heavy eyeliner. Spitalnic was aware she was not beautiful but he was attracted to her nonetheless. She had a certain scent that mesmerized him. He thought of this as a standard feature nature issues as compensation to those women who are almost beautiful. Spitalnic looked forward to these tutorials and was disappointed when the girl missed them, as she often did. But he knew she would attend on the day she was due to read her tutorial paper. It was a poorly researched paper riddled with grammatical errors, read in a voice embarrassed by its own frailty. Spitalnic made sure he was the last to leave the room and he complimented her on her paper before asking her to have coffee with him. She accepted.

Over coffee he found her friendly and more self-assured than he had expected. She was a political animal, left of center and disappointed with the mainstream. What was the mainstream and how did one enroll in it? Spitalnic wondered to himself. Her name was Christine. She liked old movies and jazz and lived around the corner from Spitalnic's mother, and that was enough for him. He ask her out three days later.

Over a period of five weeks, Spitalnic saw Christine on three occasions outside of university. On each occasion he was too busy being witty, concerned, compassionate, humble, pensive, vivacious and, sometimes, solemn to notice that she was never any of these. From the time he invited her out to the time he left his mother's house to pick her up, he lived in fear of her regular phone calls to cancel or postpone their engagement. These inevitably came with excuses so lame that they fell on Spitalnic with a heaviness that caused a tightness in his chest. But by the next morning he had always found a way to justify her behavior, to forgive her and even to feel sympathy for her because she was so tired or had left an assignment so late. Perhaps he could help her with her studies or help her better organize her time? Could he make such suggestions without seeming condescending? She had already ribbed him for being too conscientious and much too concerned with academic success.

A physical relationship of small proportions had developed by the end of their third encounter. Spitalnic was reluctant to begin it, not because he was not strongly attracted to her, but so that he could offer his lack of forwardness as proof of the sincerity of his feelings. And it was for this reason that he was content not to hurry things. But what were his feelings for her? By the end of the third night, buoyed with the lust of their trivial frolic and intoxicated by the prospect of a semipermanent relationship, Spitalnic had completely forgotten about Christine herself, about who she really was. He was besotted with the hope that his nagging loneliness, Celia's other abandoned child, "the bastard's" sibling, was about to die.

Their fourth nocturnal meeting was scheduled two weeks after the victorious third. When Spitalnic arrived at Christine's house she was barefoot in torn overalls, her hair disheveled. Her natural scent struggled against his aftershave and eventually overpowered it. Spitalnic wondered at the chemistry of such a scent. He wanted to make love to her then and there on her living room floor. Christine told him that she was frantic. It was Saturday night and she had a three-thousand-word assignment worth forty percent due in on Monday that she had, for various reasons, not been able to begin. Did he know that the midyear exams were only three weeks away? She was very sorry, but there was no way she could go out with him that night at all. She would be working through the night.

What could Spitalnic say to this? He was very disappointed, but by the time he turned the key in the front door of his mother's house his thoughts had reached sympathy, the final stage in their regular evolutionary process. He went inside and watched television. He imagined Christine at home in her bedroom at her desk. He knew the difficulty of writing essays under the pressure of time. How desperate she must have felt to have left the decision to the very last moment. Spitalnic felt obliged to reassure her that he understood, that it made no difference to *them.*

At eleven o'clock, brandishing a box of chocolates, Spitalnic knocked on Christine's door. Her roommate opened it and invited him in. She inquired about the box of chocolates. Spitalnic told her they were for Christine. She expressed surprise at this. By now Spitalnic and the roommate were standing in the lounge room. From there they heard the sound of a key turning in the front door. They were both silent. Christine's laugh was followed by the voice of a man insisting that he was not drunk.

Christine walked from the front door through the darkened passage into the lounge room following by the now silent male. She no longer wore overalls but a navy cotton skirt with a white blouse unbuttoned sufficiently to reveal her cleavage. Her face stiffened when she saw Spitalnic. She did not see the box of chocolates that lay on the table beside him. The roommate looked at the floor. Time slowed for Spitalnic; it almost stopped. Even as he lived it, he knew this was one of those scenes you never forget. There was even time for it to trigger other scenes without missing a frame of the present. He remembered the time when, at the age of about three, his parents told him to go into his grandmother's bedroom to unwrap a present they had left there for him. He emerged triumphantly holding the toy to find his parents gone and his grandmother holding a suitcase that was already too familiar to him.

Christine's scent argued against everything that Spitalnic saw. He glanced fleetingly at the male behind him and then stared at the wall behind her shoulder. There was a painful silence. Finally, Spitalnic said that he had come to see if she was all right. Christine said that she was, to which Spitalnic replied, "Good" and "Good night, then." He walked past Christine and her friend through the darkened passage to the front door. The roommate followed him to the door where she said good-bye with vicarious sheepishness.

The night air was cold but Spitalnic's face was hot. In the rearview mirror of his car he saw that his face was red. His ears felt particularly warm. He started his car and hoped that his mother would be asleep by the time he got home. He did not want to tell her what had happened. He did not want to tell anyone about it, not even Reuben. He tried to see the night in perspective even as he drove home. He had to get home quickly and quietly. Even if it stormed, the next day had to be better than that night. By then whatever he felt would have been caused by something that had happened in the past. He had to go to sleep as soon as he got home. The sooner he ended the day, the better. Spitalnic wanted to cry. Was there anyone who, with full knowledge of everything that had taken place, would be able to explain Christine's behavior? Spitalnic felt sure that an explanation would significantly diminish the pain he was feeling. For a moment he considered driving to Reuben's house. Would Reuben be awake? Would he be home? Spitalnic remembered that Reuben was out for the second time with a young woman he had met at an art gallery. It was at her exhibition. Reuben had suddenly developed a keen interest in art. Reuben would not be home. The best thing Spitalnic could do would be to go to bed.

He approached a set of traffic lights as they turned red. He slowed his car to a stop behind the first car in the inside lane. There was a sudden thud accompanied by the tinkle of broken glass. Spitalnic felt his upper body jerk forward and then backwards suddenly as his car was pushed from behind into the car in front. The offending car accelerated past both Spitalnic's car and the car in front of it almost invisibly as the lights turned green. Once past the two damaged cars, it abruptly turned back to face the direction from where it had come and disappeared down a side street. Spitalnic thought of chasing it but heard his father's warning against driving in anger. Anyway, there was a stream of traffic going the other way. He drove past the intersection and pulled over to the curb as soon as it was safe. His neck hurt and he wanted to vomit.

He saw the lights of a car parked behind him go out and a man step out of it and walk towards him. It was the driver of the car into which he had been pushed. Spitalnic got out of his car.

"Did you get his number?" the man asked.

Spitalnic told the man that he had not even seen what type of car it was. The man swore. Spitalnic was afraid that the man would find him somehow responsible. He knew that he was not at all responsible, but perhaps that did not matter. He had not been responsible for anything that had happened to him since the day of his exam when Celia had left him. Spitalnic felt he would lose any argument with the man until such a time as the weakness in his knees disappeared and he could stand without leaning against his car.

But the man was not angry with Spitalnic at all. They were comrades, innocent victims. They were citizens with rights that had just been violated. Their rights had been violated together. The man checked the damage to Spitalnic's car and said sympathetically, "Christ, you got done pretty bad!"

He then suggested that the two of them go over to the nearby service station and report the accident to the police. Spitalnic loved this man who had suffered himself and yet could still be sympathetic. This man would understand everything. While the man was on the phone, Spitalnic even considered telling him what had happened with Christine. This man would know why she had behaved the way she had. He was the type of man you would want beside you in the trenches.

The man got off the telephone and told Spitalnic that the police had said there was nothing they could do without the number plate of the car or a description of it. Spitalnic pretended to be disappointed but really he did not care. They exchanged details and the man drove off. Spitalnic surveyed the damage to his car and then drove home in an uncertain state of consciousness. He crawled into bed and wept silently into his pillow until the day finally ended for him.

Reuben, it seemed, had struck a deal with the artist. Some combination of physical appearance, common interest and previous experience had led each of them to agree to share more time with each other than with anyone else and for one's concerns to be the other's concerns. After a certain unspecified period of time, they would tell each other that they were in love. Around this time outside observers would begin to take it for granted. At some stage during all this they would tell themselves. The deal entailed an exclusive and healthy sex life, with options on an increase in their self-esteem.

Reuben was happy and he told the lunchtime circle, including Spitalnic, all about Sara the artist, now the reason for Reuben's life itself. Everyone was happy for Reuben, even Spitalnic, although he knew Reuben's relationship would accentuate his own loneliness. He was now the only unattached person in the circle and his best friend's newfound happiness would be nourished with the hours that they used to share. Reuben was the only person in the circle who Spitalnic had seen outside university, and now even his extracurricular time was taken. But still Spitalnic rejoiced in his friend's good fortune, along with Greg and Sandy and everyone else. He was ashamed of his silent and secret mourning and managed to hide it from everyone but Sandy, who saw the sadness that gnawed at his insides and occasionally surfaced in his eyes.

With the loss of Reuben as an independent being now firmly entrenched in his irrational state of mind, the lunchtime circle increased in value for Spitalnic. But he was not the only one to bask in the joys of simple friendship. There developed, among those of the circle, a closeness, a caring akin to that in only the most fortunate of families. Many times the discussion would turn to a problem someone was having with their family or with their partner. Advice was given. Questions were asked. Solutions were sought. Someone would comment that one of the others was not looking well and everyone would offer an opinion. Reuben, Greg and some of the others would discuss a film they had seen while Spitalnic would tell Sandy about the Jewish New Year, about the symbolism behind the eating of the apple and honey. She asked whether Jews exchanged New Year cards and how to write *Happy New Year* in Hebrew.

Spitalnic made his way to the "caf" to eat lunch with his friends. He had developed a stiffness in his neck and a dull ache in his lower back since the car accident. He sighed to himself a deep sigh that he had never been taught. It seemed to him that with every day and every new ache he felt more and more a *shtetl* Jew.

Reuben and Greg were not there yet when Spitalnic arrived, although he was twenty minutes late. Sandy had no idea where either of them was. She thought that perhaps it was the Jewish New Year and that they were not coming in. She knew it was any day now but thought Spitalnic had said Thursday. Spitalnic told her that she was right, that Rosh Hashanah was on Thursday, but that this would not explain Greg's absence since he was not Jewish. Sandy said she was glad she had not missed the Jewish New Year because she had something for him. She took an envelope out of her basket and handed it to him. It had his name on it. Spitalnic opened the envelope to find a red card shaped like an apple with drops of honey drawn on it and *Happy New Year* written on it in Hebrew and then again in English on the inside. Sandy asked if she had written the Hebrew correctly. Spitalnic, still looking at the card with his eyes shining, hugged her and said that she had. She said she had had the idea weeks ago when he told her about the New Year and that she had kept the scrap of paper on which he had written *Happy New Year* in Hebrew.

Greg appeared, out of breath, and sat down. Spitalnic showed him Sandy's card but he was uninterested. He had come from the library and had passed Reuben running to the car park to drive home. He had told Greg that his grandmother had died and to get Spitalnic to call him that night.

The funeral was the next day. Spitalnic went to his morning lectures before picking up Sara and driving to the cemetery. The night before when they had been at Reuben's house, Sara had intimated that she would not be coming to the funeral. Reuben said nothing but clearly wished that she would come. Spitalnic attempted to persuade her to come in a broken conversation that would start whenever Reuben left the room to make coffee or check on his mother, and would stop when he reentered the room. She said she had never come into contact with genuine mourning before and was afraid of it. She never wanted to go to a funeral until it was her own family that was mourning. She would feel out of place. Where would she stand?

In stops and starts Spitalnic tried to convince her that she ought to come. He explained that funerals were always unpleasant but that this was something she would have to endure for Reuben. He would need her there. If he needed her and she loved him, she would come. It was simple.

She did come. She stood with Spitalnic at the back of the crowd that had gathered in the heat at the grave of Reuben's mother's mother. Reuben, standing at the mouth of the grave, took over the hugging of his mother while his father recited Kaddish when instructed by the rabbi. Tears formed in the eyes of Reuben and his sister as they saw their grandmother's coffin lowered into the grave and their mother's response to it. Spitalnic moved to the edge of the grave to take a shovel with which to cover the coffin with soil. With the first clump of earth that hit the pine box, Reuben's mother shrieked, but as the mound got higher her cries became muffled sobs. When the service was over, people filed past the grave, stopping to speak with Reuben's parents before heading to their cars in the cemetery car park. Sara embraced Reuben and they both cried. After she had hugged Reuben's mother, she stood between her and Reuben as the people filed by.

Spitalnic was the last to leave the cemetery. Reuben and his family had left to make sure they were home when people called to pay their respects. Reuben had driven Sara back to his house. They were both pleased she had come. Spitalnic walked back to the car park, removing the hair clips that had kept his yarmulke in place. His car was now the only one there. As he made his way to the driver's door he saw dents on the front bumper bar and grille. The right headlight was smashed. Someone had driven into his newly repaired car in the cemetery car park. There was no one else around now. Leaning against the roof of his car, Spitalnic looked out into a sea of graves, the sun's reflection on the marble slabs blinding him. Spitalnic put his yarmulke in the pocket of his suit.

It was his father's turn to have the evening meal of Rosh Hashanah with Spitalnic. His mother would eat with her family. Spitalnic was not born an only child. He had had a brother five years older than him. His brother was born with a hole in his heart, and within a year of his birth Spitalnic's parents had been told that he would require surgery before he turned ten.

If they did not risk the operation he would be confined to a wheelchair and then to a bed until he died before his twenty-first birthday. For the first four years of Spitalnic's life, he was shunted from relative to relative while his parents took his brother around the country and overseas in search of heart specialists who could offer more optimistic prognoses. When Spitalnic was in his fifth year, his brother died while undergoing surgery. His mother had a nervous breakdown in the same year. There was a history of heart conditions on his mother's side of the family. Spitalnic himself was born with a slight murmur that was monitored regularly.

The table was set for two when Spitalnic arrived at his father's place to cook the New Year evening meal. He roasted a chicken, made a salad and put out two pieces of gefilte fish that he had bought on his way home from university. He opened a jar of honey and cut some apples into pieces in order that his father and he would have a sweet year. The two men drank wine with their meal and afterwards broke into song. They sat alone in the kitchen, the philosopher and the student, humming snatches of Hebrew melodies Spitalnic's grandfather had taught his father. These two atheists always ended their pseudoreligious occasions slightly drunk with teary but silent embraces and two white candles still burning. Spitalnic's father missed his son desperately. Nonetheless, he never said anything to get Spitalnic to leave his mother and move back with him. The child had become the parent, trying to weigh up the conflicting needs of his two emotional dependents. Who needed him more? This Rosh Hashanah was no different from others they had spent together. By the end of the night the men were hugging and crying while the white candles burned.

The final examinations were approaching and Spitalnic found himself going out less and studying more. He had exhausted his list of potential female companions. Weekends and week nights he studied. When he lost concentration he would read or go to sleep. His lower back and neck still troubled him. The various physiotherapists he had seen had provided him with only temporary relief. His sadness made him quiet almost always except at lunchtime with his group of friends. These hours became the highlight of his days. He looked forward to them now more than the other members of the circle did. Those were the only times he smiled or laughed. At his mother's house he was bathed in the anxiety she felt for him and his health and in her despair at her own loneliness. With his father he became almost paralyzed with guilt as he saw the longing in his father's eyes, always belittling whatever troubles faced him or Spitalnic, always clinging to every moment he could get with his son. Lunchtime at university was a temporary respite from his parents, from his studies and from the loneliness that often consumed him like an ulcer eating away at his insides.

At least there was Sandy's smile. There would be Greg's jokes, Reuben's concern, a spontaneous hug from Sandy. It was not long before Spitalnic realized that more than Reuben or Greg or anyone else, it was Sandy's time he longed for. If she was late his heart would sink. The smell of her hair had registered in his mind. He tried to recall it when he was alone. Her laugh, her optimism, her innocence—he craved them all. One night at his desk he admitted to himself that he had fallen in love with her. Immediately upon the admission he felt sick. It was a love he knew she did not return. It was born out of his misery and suckled on his loneliness. He felt it could not be aborted without losing himself as well. It was hurting him and yet it seemed to be the only thing sustaining him. He was ashamed of himself and yet could not begin the process of talking himself out of it. Was there a chance of her returning his feelings? Alone at his desk he went through the evidence. Look at her, so genuinely warm, warmer to him than to anyone else in the circle. Celia had left him after two years; maybe Sandy would leave her boyfriend? She seemed to enjoy Spitalnic's company as much as he enjoyed hers. Maybe she was in love with him but had not yet realized it? After all, Spitalnic himself had only just realized it and he was alone. Would it take such a miracle? Miracles happen.

From this time on, it became difficult, almost impossible, for him to concentrate on his work. He would analyze the day's conversations with Sandy, compare them with previous conversations. He took heart when she fought with her boyfriend, and then reproached himself for it. In his waking hours he grappled with "the bastard" and tormented himself with contemplation of Sandy. Soon this contemplation extended into his sleeping hours until there were fewer and fewer of them. He realized that this was no way to kill "the bastard," nor was it helping anything with Sandy. His exams were three weeks away. If he didn't reach some sort of equilibrium, no matter how low, he was certain to fail. He had to tell Sandy how he felt. Not just for his own sake but for hers. Spitalnic felt he was deceiving her. She had trusted him and invested genuine warmth, all the time thinking it was a platonic exchange. But Spitalnic had idealized what they had, made more of it, and allowed himself to jeopardize what they really did have. But no matter what she would say, he felt he had to end this situation of debilitating uncertainty.

It was the last Monday of the academic year. Most of the lunchtime circle did not come in. Only Reuben, Spitalnic and Sandy were there. Spitalnic was quiet but the other two did not seem to notice. When Reuben left to go to the library, Spitalnic asked Sandy to walk with him outside. They walked through the less populated part of the campus. It was a warm day. He had not yet looked in her eyes. He wondered whether she would detect his nervousness. His palms were moist as he asked her to sit down. They were alone, leaning against a tree facing the same way. Spitalnic wondered now whether he would go through with it.

Looking out into an open stretch of grass, he told her that he had something important to tell. He took a breath, still staring out into the distance, and she said nothing. He told her that, without meaning to or even realizing it, he had fallen in love with her. He said that he knew she was attached, that their relationship had been platonic up until then and he had never wished for more. He said that gradually he found himself thinking of her to the exclusion of everything else and cursing all his living hours other than the few he spent with her. He now looked at the ground and told her that he did not expect anything by telling her this but, if he was in love with her, he thought she should know.

There was a silence. Spitalnic's mouth was dry. He continued to look at the ground as she looked out into the distance. Then she turned to him and their eyes met. She fixed a hard stare so uncharacteristic that it frightened Spitalnic and would forever remain in his catalogue of disturbing memories. Then she spoke. She was in love with her boyfriend and did not want to leave him. For a brief moment Spitalnic thought he loved him too. She said that she loved Spitalnic but that she was not in love with him. She suggested that Spitalnic was not in love with her, either, but only thought he was. Then she looked at the ground again. She was visibly upset. She said people had been talking about the two of them, asking if there was anything in it. She had scorned their suggestions. Can't two people of different gender spend some time together without there following a torrent of wild insinuations? She had assured people that, while Spitalnic may have become one of her closest friends, they had remained only friends, the way they had both wanted it. Spitalnic had wanted more. The chorus of insinuations had only expressed the things he had wanted to say. Sandy felt foolish and even a little betrayed. It had happened before that males had attempted to get close to her under the guise of Plato-approved affections, only to spoil it with confessions of romantic love. But never had any male friend been as close to her as Spitalnic.

Spitalnic was engulfed in shame. What if she was right? What if he was not in love with her? Had he just killed a friendship that had become so dear to him? Sandy was now late for a lecture. Spitalnic walked her to her lecture theatre in silence. The door to the theatre could only be reached by a flight of stairs. She ran up the stairs. She was crying. At the top of the stairs she turned before opening the door and said good-bye.

It rained almost continuously during the period set aside by the university for students to study for their final exams. Spitalnic sat in isolation in his mother's house poring over the notes he had made for "the bastard" in much the same way as his grandfather would have studied the Talmud. He remained unshaven during this period and had difficulty sleeping. He thought of Sandy and wondered how she would be thinking of him. He was nervous about sitting for "the bastard." His hatred of it had reached the point where the sight of his notes sickened him. He felt he knew less about the subject than he did the first time he had studied it. Problems arose that never used to exist. He speculated on his fate were he to fail it again. Would the university throw him out for having failed it twice even if he passed his other subjects? And what if he did not pass his other subjects? What would he do if he left university unqualified? What could he do? Red sores developed on his scalp. Their irritation could only be relieved by scratching, which made his scalp bleed. His neck and back pain was exacerbated by sitting at his desk all day. His face was white except for the stubble that grew and no matter how many times he washed his face he could not wash away the tiredness that stemmed from his lack of sleep. How it rained.

He fasted on the day he was due to be examined on "the bastard," not for religious reasons but to avoid being disturbed during the exam. He looked over his notes for a while in the morning and then lay down. He was determined to relax. This was his last exam. He was not overly concerned about the others. It was this one that stood between him and the rest of his life. He drove slowly to the exam. He had plenty of time.

The corridor leading to the exam hall was crowded. People were pushing up against each other. There was a nervous desire to get into the hall as early as possible, almost as if the earlier one sat down the better one would do. Spitalnic stood in the middle of a sea of people. He did not recognize any of the faces around him. He looked at his watch. He was early and so was everyone else. He felt a bead of sweat glide around the crevices of his rib cage. He was reminded of the line in Oscar Wilde's *Ballad of Reading Gaol* in which every day is described as being like a year in which each day is long. For Spitalnic each minute was such a day.

Finally the doors were opened. Spitalnic sat second from the front on the extreme left of the hall that could seat five hundred and was filled to capacity. There was a seemingly innumerable number of rows and three hours and fifteen minutes between him and the door. Nothing he could do now would increase his knowledge. The best he could do was to keep calm and answer the questions as efficiently as possible. One of the legs of the desk at which he sat was shorter than the others. He tried to gain the attention of one of the invigilators to help him rectify the problem but was unsuccessful. His desk wobbled. He took the watch his father had given him off his wrist and placed it on the desk. It was not synchronous with the clock on the wall. This would involve him in a calculation to rectify the disparity each time he looked at either the clock or his watch.

Upon the first reading of the questions, Spitalnic felt that he was unable to answer all but one, but after rereading them a few times he felt the shape of passable answers forming in his mind. Reading time was over and it was time to write. Spitalnic sat with his pen poised above the page for half a minute before etching the first words on the paper that he felt would determine the future course of his life. He wrote quickly, frenetically, pressing hard on the page and holding his breath between sentences.

After an hour his neck was stiff and sore. He massaged it as vigorously as he could with one hand. The back of his head throbbed. Nausea burrowed in his stomach and clutched at his throat. The questions themselves were not going too badly, but Spitalnic was not sure that he could last the distance. Forty minutes later he became aware of the rapidity of his heartbeat. He took several deep breaths to slow it down but it didn't help. He had a sudden fear that he had answered the first question incorrectly, that he had failed to mention an important concept that was relevant to the topic. His pulse quickened. He stopped answering the question he was in the middle of answering and turned back to the first question. Certainly there was no mention of the concept, but was it relevant? He had to decide immediately. He was wasting valuable time. And what of the second question? It was only by chance that he thought of checking the first question. Perhaps the second question was deficient?

He began to consider how crucial the result of this exam was to his life. If he passed he would qualify for a degree. This would enable him to go on and do a postgraduate degree. And that, he knew, was a necessary although not a sufficient condition for a secure and adequately paid job; adequate, that is, to satisfy the mother of his children, whoever she would be. His children—how vulnerable they appeared in his mind. He would make sure that their parents were never divorced. He would make sure that they would never have to sit an exam like this.

Everything depended on how things went for him now. He no longer had any idea of how he was going. He had no faith in his previous answers. He turned back to the third question and resumed writing. His mouth was dry and he felt giddy and weak. Again he tried to recapture his breath and again was unsuccessful. He noticed he was heaving. It grew increasingly audible. Several people around him looked up from their papers and stared at him briefly. He tried to soften his breathing but was unable. The words on his page were blurred. He had difficulty writing. This difficulty increased until he had lost all dexterity in his digits and could not write at all. Spitalnic was afraid. Now he could not breathe at all. He was certain he would die within a few minutes.

He managed to raise his arm slightly and attract the attention of one of the invigilators. Seeing he was in distress, she came with a plastic cup of water. Spitalnic shook his head and mouthed the word *doctor*. The woman alerted two male invigilators, who helped Spitalnic from his chair and grabbed him, one man under each arm. They led him across the front of the hall past each row of desks, his legs dragging along the floor like rubber. He attempted to shelter his face like a criminal from the four hundred and ninety-nine other students in the hall.

It was not a heart attack. One general practitioner and two specialists told him it was not. They said it was a nervous reaction to the strain of the exam. Nonetheless they recommended that his heart be tested. It was tested many times. It was monitored on an ECG. It was listened to. It was even photographed. His pulse was taken before and after situations of physical stress. Finally it was decided that the hole in his heart, which had grown bigger as he had grown, would have to be closed. No one, not his parents nor the physicians nor even Spitalnic himself, ever talked about the consequences of not having the hole closed.

His mother became very silent after the day the fourth cardiologist had recommended surgery. She smoked more heavily, as heavily as she had when her first son had been hospitalized. It made Spitalnic cough. His father spoke loudly and convincingly about what a routine operation it was now and how the quality of Spitalnic's life would improve. Spitalnic knew that he was just as afraid as his mother. What he did not know was that his father, the logical positivist, the atheist who destroyed with ease the first cause and teleological arguments for the existence of God, was crying in a synagogue on his way home from work on the nights he did not spend with his son.

Reuben and Sara visited Spitalnic the night before he was due to be operated on. They brought chocolates, which he was not allowed to eat. He was not allowed to eat anything. They did not stay long. Spitalnic watched television for a while and then read but could concentrate on neither. Where was Sandy? Where was Celia now?

Spitalnic lay in the hospital bed. It was night now and the reassuring sounds of human activity were scarce. All visitors, including his parents, had come and gone. Even the night nurses had said good night to him. The next time he would speak to anyone would be in the morning when they woke him to prepare him for surgery.

GOOD MORNING, AGAIN IN THE TIME OF THE DINOSAUR YOUR NIECE'S SPEECH NIGHT THE REASONS I WON'T BE COMING MANSLAUGHTER THE *HONG KONG FIR* DOCTRINE I WAS ONLY IN A CHILDISH WAY CONNECTED TO THE ESTABLISHED ORDER SPITALNIC'S LAST YEAR **A TALE IN TWO CITIES**

1. Moscow

Where we came from you woke up early and bribed the coming day to be kind to you. Without this you were certainly done for. We could rely on that. But we could not rely on that anymore, not here. In Australia the days were not corrupt. There was no certainty.

I didn't know about the rest of my family, but sitting there I realized that I had taken the waiting with me. Waiting is Russian. Russians know how to wait. It is learnt in queues from an early age. We queued for everything, often without knowing why. I remember as a very small child walking in a street in Moscow with my mother. We came upon a queue. It stretched way down the street, and from where we stood at the back, my mother could not see the shop into which it headed. We joined it immediately and asked the people in front what they were queueing for. They weren't sure but thought it was for children's socks. No one this far back could be sure. My mother left me to keep our spot while she scouted up ahead to verify the socks rumor. I started our waiting, looking down at my cold, cold feet. They were wet from snow and my galoshes kept coming off, a perennial problem with me then. I stood there listening to the people in front without really understanding what they were saying. I was five.

Eventually my mother came back. Yes, it seemed there were socks at the end of the queue. She resumed her spot next to me and we waited, all rugged up, moving only occasionally, almost imperceptibly while she told me stories. They were children's stories, classics, fairy stories and impromptu stories based on people in the queue and surrounding streets. Why was that old man limping? Was it a real limp? What did I think would make him laugh at the end of a hard day of limping?

I was still waiting. This particular day it was in the back of the bookshop in which I worked. I waited for the time when I did not have work there. I catalogued, stacked and sold books. The shame of it was that I loved books. They were my world but when your world was reduced to units, stocks, labels, ISBN numbers and price tags, it was time to move on. That day I also waited for something else, something for which I had never waited before. No one knew about it and I hoped he would be discreet when he called. It was part of his job to be discreet, just as sitting toward the back of the bookshop was part of mine. I had told him to call me there, not at home. I didn't want my parents to know I'd engaged a private investigator.

What kind of person became a private investigator? What kind of person resorted to that special blend of pragmatism and discretion that was the unspoken and unwritten warranty of the private investigator? Most of what we knew about them came from Dashiell Hammett and Raymond Chandler. Did they really speak in that slightly colorful but nonetheless direct monotone that made neither a virtue nor a vice of their amorality? How would this one sound? I wondered.

I first became aware of her by way of an uncertain voice on my answering machine, a voice with unusually perfect English for one so coated in Russian. She was anxiously succinct. She left her name, Rose Gamarkin, and asked me to call her on a number she gave. How did she hear of me? It doesn't matter. People with desperation in their voices always seem to know how to find me. All I know is she needs help, or thinks she does.

He got that right.

He might not even give his real name. I didn't know. I'd have to wait. I'd waited about an hour and a half with my mother that other day long ago. That's how she tells it. I wouldn't know exactly. I wasn't so good with time. When we got to the head of the queue, we found there were still socks left, good-quality ones from Germany. My mother bought a few pairs. They were adult socks. She made me wear them anyway.

I have an unfortunate habit of laughing when I'm nervous. I don't quite know why. Perhaps it has something to do with the circumstances of my upbringing. Perhaps it is the fault of my parents, although, at twenty-eight, I am almost past the stage where you blame everything on your parents. I say *stage* and not *age* because some people come late to the realization that everything is their parents' fault. You can only hope it comes early enough to be rejected for the simplistic explanation it usually is, that it comes while your parents are still young, or at least while they are still sentient enough to forgive you for forgiving them so late, and still capable of loving you when their conviction has been overturned.

Whatever its origins, I laugh when I am nervous and it has been this way since I was at least six or seven. I remember being taught as early as that never to repeat a joke outside the apartment. When I look at small children today, it amazes me that my parents trusted my brother and me not to repeat anything they discussed. But then, Russian children learned different skills, and Russian Jewish children learned certain other skills again, the learning of which takes away some of the freedom of childhood but can also save a life.

Everyone but the drunks and my mother knew to shut up in public. Strangely, she was never afraid of anything. If ever she was called a "dirty Jew" in the street, she would smile and say, "A Jew, yes, that's right." She knew very little about being Jewish, but it gave her some small satisfaction to show pride in the face of anti-Semitism, especially in its crude street manifestations. She was not often confronted in the street—not as often as my father, who had earned a slight limp from it. This was not so much because she did not look Jewish (whatever that means; she certainly did not look Russian) but because she was beautiful. Even the drunks who kept vigil at the entrances of the metro stations were a little taken aback by this proud and striking woman. They say I look like her; she has dark wide eyes, pale skin and black hair, but I certainly do not have her strength. I don't carry myself like she does. There is too much of my father in me. Even though I am a woman, I have always felt my brother is more obviously her child.

My mother could never be relied upon to hide her hatred of the regime, whoever the leader. She lost both her parents when she was four. Her father was a general in the army—no mean feat for a Jew—but she never spoke about this with any particular pride. To stand out is to court disaster. He became a victim of Stalin's paranoia and was killed in the purges of 1937. Her mother was also killed, for being his wife. I am named Rose after her, Roza in Russian. My mother was hidden by her much older half-brother. She grew up knowing she was a Jew but not knowing what this meant except to people who were not Jewish. She was actually more the archetypical Russian heroine in her demeanor. A colleague at her work once had to fill in her nationality for her on a form. Although they did not know each other well, they had become friendly. He knew she was a Jew but out of genuine friendship offered to put her parents down as Russian. He whispered his offer sympathetically, but she became enraged.

"Why do this?" she shouted in a voice the whole office could hear. He could see the rage building up in her to the point of tears and tried to placate her, explaining softly that things might be easier for her with Russian parents, which indeed they would have been. But she whispered to her colleague in that white fury so familiar to me that she did not need things any easier. It must have been because of the depth of his fondness for her that he persisted in trying to get her to see reason, his reason, even at risk to himself. *He* would have been the one responsible for the deliberate falsification, not her. But he did not know her well enough and never got to know her any better, which was probably just as well for him. So what if she was beautiful? This was a woman who danced and sang in the Red Square when Stalin's death was announced. (She was very nearly assaulted.) To end the discussion, she stood on her chair and shouted again for all the office to hear, "Write down that I'm a Jew!"

From an early age I became adept at walking from place to place looking at the ground. Nobody in Russia looks anyone else on the street in the eye, but with one of my hands firmly in the grip of my mother's clasp, no one had a better reason than me not to look up at what was coming. Anything could have happened. Besides, if I had looked up I would probably have just laughed. Even today, if there is someone in the room with me here when this private investigator calls, I will probably laugh. I even laughed in Lenin's tomb.

I was eight or nine and it was to be a very special day for us, part of the rites of the Young Pioneers. There was nothing special about being a Young Pioneer. Every child of that age was a Pioneer, but not every group of Young Pioneers got to visit Lenin's tomb. Someone had to have known someone or owed someone for this to have happened. What a waste of a favor! We were taken by bus for maybe half an hour from school to Red Square. Everyone was excited, even me. I didn't know what to expect. I remember we were all singing "Lenin Loves Me" on the bus. About twenty years later I heard the same tune coming out of a Sunday school here in Melbourne. This time children were singing "Jesus Loves Me."

This was the day we were given our red ties. It signified a certain coming-of-age. First, at six or so, you were a Young October, and then at seven or eight a Young Pioneer. Like everywhere else there was a queue. Lenin's tomb was the regime's sanctioned place of pilgrimage. Looking back now, I find it hard to believe people actually thought they could find salvation by coming there, but it seems that that's what they thought. People from all over the country, old men and women, tourists and us, this day's little children, all of us waiting, then climbing underground down the many stairs. There was the smell of sweat, everybody's sweat mixed with breath. The air that came in with us lived and died a life that was not ours. It was not really air but we breathed it anyway. By the time we got into the tunnel leading to the tomb, no one was excited anymore. Many of us were scared. We were made to keep moving, probably because so many people wanted to see him but also perhaps to prevent anyone looking too long.

The chamber containing the body was dark except for the blue light that shone in a stream over him. There was an unfamiliar smell, presumably of embalming fluid. It wrestled with the body odor and the ersatz air. I thought this had to be a preliminary tomb, the body perhaps of one of his lieutenants. I knew his face so well. This was not him. This was a shrivelled nothing, a head with garish makeup and two big hands protruding from under a blanket. No syphilitic mutant rotting in the spring thaw could look this ghastly. Everyone hurried past as fast as they could and up the stairs on the other side, desperate for some street air. The creature we had seen was not the revolutionary father we had been promised. We were not inspired. For most of us it was our first dead body and we were just frightened. Many of the girls were sick, vomiting on the ground near the exit to the tomb. Not me, though. My stomach was too strong. It must have been a bizarre sight, all these children staggering around in each other's vomit outside the most sacred site in the whole of the USSR, crying, bewildered, disappointed. I laughed.

The Egyptians perfected embalming thousands of years ago, but they apparently took the secret with them. The Russians certainly did not have it. This was not the Lenin I knew so well from my father's plaster molds. My father worked for the Ministry of Culture. It was by the fervor of his public adulation there of Lenin and Brezhnev that he had got me enrolled in my school. It was a special school, privileged. We learned English from the age of seven and were taught up to four of our subjects in English. We had computers, big and slow, but we had them in the seventies, the halcyon days of Comrade Brezhnev, whom we had to thank for everything. It was a model school. Foreigners were frequently escorted around the grounds and classrooms. We would greet them in English, just briefly.

The Ministry of Culture was responsible for distributing the sculptures and statues, and eventually an enormous statue of Lenin stood proudly and firmly outside my school, a testament to my father's desire for me to attend there. He always wanted me to be fluent in English. My school was just about the only sanctioned place for this and, in addition to a more or less benign internal regime, its general academic standard was excellent. It took my father more than two years to get me in. I wasn't supposed to go there because we lived in another district. We lived in the Arbat district till I was five or six, and at first I went to the local primary school. I thought it was fine, but my father had other plans. He has always had other plans. So with Lenin firmly ensconced in the foreground, I started this new school, one of the most prestigious true Communism had to offer. It was part of my father's plan to prepare me for a life outside the Soviet Union.

Most of the students were Jewish, their parents having done everything they could to get their children in there, and almost all the language teachers were Jews. The school did what it could to dispel the impression that it was a Jewish school, but it was largely in vain. Every teacher kept a roll which listed the nationality of each student next to his name. We never knew why they needed our nationalities and no one ever asked. Anyone thought to look really Jewish was "Armenian" and we got on with our work, stopping only to be shown off, like landlocked dolphins, to hard-currency foreign dignatories. There was a certain irony to this, the foreigners coming along to see us being groomed, since many of us went on to work for the Ministry of Foreign Affairs, where, if we were not translators, we either spied or defected. A lot of people in Foreign Affairs were "Armenian."

I was always in awe of my father's determination, literally in awe, a combination of reverence and fear. What was I afraid of? My mother said it would save us or kill him. He was very strong, not tall, thick hands and hairy, everywhere but on his head. When Pavel, my younger brother, was little, he would often watch my father dry himself after a shower, not saying anything, just watching through the gap in the door. Pavel used to have his father's physical strength. Maybe he still has it.

There were four of us in the two-bedroom apartment. We were lucky to have it. My mother and father kept their respective apartments for years after we were born. They were not married. My surname, Gamarkin, is my mother's maiden name. Our father didn't want to get married until they had secured adequate accommodation. Married couples had to give up one of their apartments and live in the other one, even though it might be a one-bedroom apartment meant for a single person. If you wanted a bigger one, you went on a waiting list. If you had children they waited with you. When I was five or six and Pavel was one or two, we left the Arbat and moved into the larger apartment in Novie Cheremushky. The mixture of working class and intelligentsia in the area made for interesting neighbors. The apartments were relatively new, built in the Khrushchev era. But they were falling apart. The plaster inside was flaking, but between each wall of flaking plaster we had more space, two rooms plus a kitchen and bathroom. My mother did our laundry in the bathroom or else sent it out. This was quite common. At that time no one had washing machines.

My father was an economist, at least by training. He had studied economics at university with his usual foresight and with no intention of teaching or working as an economist. Most of the people with whom he had studied became directors of stores. This was the equivalent in the West of a managing director of a small department store, and one could live relatively well doing this. But to be successful in this job you had to steal. Directors were given quotas that could not be filled by legal means. For example, a director might be ordered to sell a certain number of radios whether he had them to sell or not. You have to be quite an economist to do this. In order to get enough radios, the director would have to buy them on the black market. Sometimes he would have to pay the militia, the police, to get them for him or else pay them not to see him get them for himself. Perhaps he had some surplus coats to exchange? Otherwise all payments would have to be made in black money, money which officially he never had but which was in reality the only means by which he kept himself going.

A store director meets people, makes contacts, learns how things can be obtained and takes delivery of a batch of radios to fill his quota of radios to be sold. What if they're defective? He'll clean them up a little. What if they're still obviously inadequate for performing all the tasks expected of a radio? He cannot complain to his suppliers that the radios are defective. He's lucky to have them. There are no warranties to sue on. To whom can he complain? He will have to get them fixed, again with black money. It can't show up on the books. Will he get a refund because the goods are faulty? Will he get credit from the supplier? They're not dealing in radios anymore. How much are they worth in stockings, vodka, toothpaste, refrigerators or compressors? With no refunds and no credit, still the director must pay in full and on time. Otherwise there might be an anonymous call to Internal Affairs. Questions might be asked. What were they worth? Up to twenty-five years. "Certainly," my father said, "store directors can make a lot of black money, but can they sleep at night?" My father was already a light sleeper.

He maintained ties with his economist colleagues but chose not to work as an economist. He claimed that, nonetheless, he was able to get anybody anything. By day he worked at the Ministry of Culture and at night he kept up with his economics. Early on he was sent to the Moscow Planetarium. A stubborn pragmatist with one foot planted firmly on the ground and the other ready to make a move at the hint of an opportunity presenting itself, each day he showed everyone the stars. He was taken under the wing of one of the lecturers at the Planetarium, a renowned astronomer and alcoholic. Often my father would cover for him, even at times delivering his lectures. The astronomer got my father a job as a bookkeeper. He had him promoted to a certain otherwise unachievable level and advised him to join the Party, which my father did. I was always surprised he hadn't done it earlier. Sometime not long after the middle of the century, he met my mother. She says that she fell in love. She was never sure about him.

I don't blame her uncertainty, this orphan with rich dark eyes, curves that would outlast the regime, white skin like silk, full round breasts and a mouth intolerant of stupidity. There was a danger about her with her mane of black hair. And she was Jewish. If she needed him at all, she hated herself for it and tried never to let it show. So what if he was a Jew, this barber-shop baritone stamp-collecting Party member with a limp, economist to the stars from the Ministry of Culture. She could see his mind working. This was no arse-kissing apparatchik. But although she could see his mind working, could see it in his eyes and could see the way he saw her in his eyes, she was never sure that he loved her. This man could get anybody anything. How, then, could he let her go by? He was not about to. She was never sure if this was love or whether it even permitted love.

I had often wondered but never asked whether she had, at that time, any picture of their coming life together or of the life she wanted them to have. What exactly did she think she was getting herself into? But perhaps I was being unfair. Implicit in these questions was the assumption that all that had happened could be traced, step by step, to flaws in my father: that our situation was all his fault. Was he connected to crisis as inevitably as one pole of a magnet to the other? Tempting as this assumption was, I did not succumb to it. Pavel had. He looked for easy explanations and solutions. That was why I was waiting for some news from a private investigator, news for which I was paying in more ways than one, news I was dreading. It was hard enough pretending to be calm at work; it was almost impossible at home in front of my mother. I was sure she suspected something.

But what was she thinking, then, when they got together? She knew from an early age that she was not born under some lucky star but under an oppressive, too often murderous red one. Unlike my father, she was never much impressed by stars of any kind. She was fond of a line by Pushkin's friend Anton Delvig: *The nearer to heaven, the colder it gets.* But the converse is not true. Her feet never left the ground anymore and still I had trouble keeping my mother warm.

They worked by day and studied at night. She studied Russian literature. He was transferred from the Planetarium to the Ministry itself, where he was put in charge of organizing exhibitions and performances coming to and from the Soviet Union. Transportation, insurance, propaganda, it was all up to him. At first she worked as an editor for a naval magazine that was distributed to ships in the various fleets, but later, through his position, my father got her a job as an archivist in a fine-art gallery and museum not far from his office. A jealous man, he later got her an office within the Ministry building directly opposite his office. She divided her working day between the gallery and the office, both of which were about two minutes from my father's apartment. (This was unheard-of. It was not uncommon for Russians to travel two hours to work and two hours back.) By the time Pavel and I were at school, she was able to come and go during the school holidays on the pretext that she was working at home preparing a catalogue. Of course, we never let her do any work.

My father's direct superior was a half Jewish and half German Russian and one of the greatest anti-Semites my father had ever encountered. He never admitted that he was half Jewish and he brought his son up to be virulently anti-Semitic. There would have been nothing wrong with this for a Russian teenager except that the boy had the misfortune of frequently being mistaken for a Jew and beaten up for it. More so than Pavel or I or any of the "Armenians" at school with me, this boy looked the way Russians liked their Jews to look.

Although my father's superior hated my father for his Jewishness and his education (he himself was not educated), he was in the uncomfortable position of relying on my father's contacts. Short, with thick-rimmed glasses and an ever-spreading behind, he looked to his coworkers like a fleshy malevolent triangle with bad breath. An ignorant and paranoid man, he liked to bully and intimidate those around and particularly those below him. A good Party man, he ingratiated himself with his superiors by crediting to himself the achievements of others.

Behind his back, people referred to him as Burzhuiki (pot-bellied stove) No. 1 but his name was Zwier, an uncomfortably German-Jewish sounding name. (His wife was Burzhuiki No. 2, and she was the only person outside the Party of whom he was afraid.) Being half German and half Jewish was about the worst combination you could be in Russia in the middle decade of this century, and it took some extensive betrayals for Zwier to live as well as he did. In the early fifties, during the purges, he was recruited by the KGB and assigned to befriend various Jews in the Party and the bureaucracy to find something for which they could be tried. In the Ministry of Culture he gave vague or impossible orders which he would later deny in fits of rage during which his breath and saliva intermingled to form a previously unknown toxic substance that flew from his mouth or hung like string from his lips. This was the man to whom my father had to report every day.

Every day this man kept pushing my father closer and closer to the edge, to the border either of the country or of his sanity. I could not count the number of times my father came home furious, telling my mother to start tomorrow, to get the papers. "We're leaving!" She would always listen to him, occasionally joining in his denunciation of all the liars and criminals, from

Zwier and everyone in the Ministry to Brezhnev himself, and all the way back to Stalin, before returning to the preparation of dinner. Pavel and I knew to keep away from him at those times.

Then my father would quieten and unwind by the radio, listening to the BBC or the Free Voice of Europe. By the time dinner was on the table, it would be okay to talk to him, gently, and by the end of the night the four of us would be in bed, listening to my mother as she read aloud to us Bulgakov, Solzhenitsyn. We knew never to say anything about it, just as we knew never to repeat any jokes they told each other.

This was a common pattern for years. They were always talking about leaving, and every time he told her to start making the applications, he meant it at the time. But then she would calm him and the cycle would start again. Emigrating meant applying to live in Israel. The authorities would not have even pretended to consider any applications my parents might have made to live somewhere else. So whenever they talked about leaving, it was for Israel. My parents were not particularly fervent Zionists. In Russia it was hard to be. The official media equated Zionism with Fascism. *Pravda* forever carried anti-Zionist cartoons. Even in 1967 during the Six-Day War, the news reports were anti-Israeli. My parents and all the Jews they knew were convinced Israel was going to be destroyed. When my father heard on the radio that Israel had won the war, he went out drinking in the streets like the Russians he hated. My mother waited up all night for him, thinking he had been arrested. She always thought this if he were at all late, which was funny, because she was the one with the dangerous mouth. He was a master of talking to himself under his breath.

After 1967 there was for a while, despite the propaganda, a tiny, barely perceptible defiant spring in the step of many of the

Jews my parents knew. I had a cousin, a star pupil, a physicist who joined an underground Hebrew class. At twenty-three he was risking everything but said he didn't care. He and his new wife were going to Israel. Not long after they joined, the class was infiltrated and they were exposed. That was it. They became *otkazniks*, refuseniks. He started to organize demonstrations. Initially his friends and family gave them moral support, but after a while it became dangerous even to meet with them. My father spoke highly of him. Although he never attended any of my cousin's demonstrations, he met with him often. My cousin was told he would not be permitted to leave the country for at least ten years because he was a physicist. His parents were devastated and eventually his young wife committed suicide.

One day my father came home slightly later than usual. There was blood oozing from his lip and his nose. He had been coming out of the metro station, having made a trip to see my cousin after a terrible day at work, when a couple of drunks had called him a "dirty Jew." He answered them back and a fight broke out on the street. Most people ignored it, some watched and a couple joined in. My father was furious. There were tears in his eyes. My mother, who had until then assumed that he had been arrested, gave him a vodka and began to clean him up. He started again. "Tomorrow, first thing, get the papers. We're leaving. Really. I mean it. This time we're leaving."

We were all in shock at the blood on his face and the tears between his words. Pavel became frightened. My mother was worried that the neighbors would hear him. She asked me to turn the radio on. He sat down, his puffing becoming slower and slower, and listened to the Voice of America. Pavel and I sat on the floor and watched him stare far beyond his bloodied shoes while she wiped his face and gently rocked him like a baby.

The next day no one said anything about it. We got up and dressed and had breakfast. They talked to Pavel and me as though nothing had happened. We went to school and they went to work. At night my father came home on time, with no problems on the way home. Work had not been as bad as it could be. My mother had already started in the kitchen. He sat down, and after he had poured himself a drink, she told him in a quiet voice that she had done it. She had initiated an application for an exit visa. He heard her and knew that was it, there was no turning back. His career was ruined. His contacts were useless, everything he had cultivated. He would be expelled from the Party. He put his hands behind his head and leaned the chair back at an angle, balancing between the table and the cupboards. I think he was relieved. He took a deep breath and held on to it for a while before exhaling. I watched him lean forward and look at his hands. He then got up and hugged my mother fiercely before going to bed. This was the beginning and he knew he would need to be rested for what was coming.

When my parents told their Jewish friends they were going to try to leave Russia, the friends were astounded. Surely it would be worse in Israel. Hadn't my parents heard of the Russian Jews starving in the streets there? I remember a friend of my father's sitting in our apartment listening to my parents' announcement. From the inside pocket of his jacket he pulled out a metal shape and, calling me over, asked me if I knew what it was. When I said that I didn't, he laughed and turned his attention back to my father. "What are you doing this for?" he asked. "She does not even know what a Star of David looks like."

Three days later I was called into the Principal's office. I had not mentioned it to anyone but the Principal knew, and I knew immediately that he knew. He spoke in a kindly tone. Behind him Lenin and Brezhnev hung on the wall, staring out way beyond us. What was all this about? Had my parents talked this over with me? I told him they hadn't, which was strictly true, since all the discussions over the years about leaving—when, if, how and where to—had all been between my parents. We watched, listened—how could we not?—and sometimes asked questions, but we were never consulted.

The Principal asked me if I wanted to leave my school, my friends, my teachers, my Motherland. I told him I didn't have any choice. I had to obey my parents. I thought that sounded plausible. They loved it when kids talked about obedience. I didn't want to be having this conversation and wished that it would end as soon as possible. I actually liked school and was sad to be leaving. Even he, with his priggish appeals to the Motherland, wasn't too bad; at least he had never been cruel to me. I did feel a little that I was letting him down. I understood my parents' reasons and agreed with them, but I would never be able to explain this to him. I kept telling myself that it wasn't really him talking but the Party. He didn't really care about me. This was Brezhnev speaking, that dangerous presence we always and never saw, the man who bored us every day in the newspaper and on television.

He asked me what I knew about Israel. Did I know about the conditions there? As well as the wars, there was starvation. He said it was not like me to do something like this, especially without researching it properly first. He could get me some literature on it if I liked. There had been many cases of Russians, in particular, going there and starving, of young women being forced into prostitution to support their families. Did I know about this? The idea of prostitution sounded fun to me but I didn't believe him. He told me that one of my teachers was thinking of recommending me for the Komsomol which would have made me, in effect, a trainee Party member. I was flattered. One did not become a Komsomol till fourteen or fifteen, and I was a bit younger than that. I remained polite but firm. I would go where my parents were going.

There was an almost automatic suspension of reality the day my mother launched our international careering. At least, that's the way it seemed to me. All of a sudden I didn't have to pass exams. If we were lucky, I would soon be in Rome en route to Israel, or wherever we were really going. If we were not successful I figured we would be in Siberia. Either way, the currency of my elite education would be devalued. Of course, in order to have any chance of getting out, we had to have a direct relative in Israel. This also contributed to the air of unreality because it had always been considered ill-advised for Jews in Russia to receive correspondence from Israel: it brought you under suspicion. Now we needed it. But since we didn't have any direct relatives there, we had to invent them. My mother made us memorize a false family tree. Aunt Hannah was born in Budapest and lived in Tel Aviv and so on. She tested us on it.

To apply for the exit visa my parents had to hand in their passports. But without a passport you were not a citizen, and you could not work for the government if you were not a citizen. I didn't have to renounce my citizenship because, being under sixteen, I didn't have a passport. As my Principal reminded me, I could still turn back. But my parents could not work. They were expelled from the Party. We lost our apartment. It was given to someone else. We were split up. Pavel and I stayed with different friends of my parents, and my mother and father stayed with different relatives on my father's side. These were the people to whom we had given our possessions. My parents had distributed them variously, my father trying to figure out who was most likely to help us, to put us up, to feed us. He moved about the most. Spread out around Moscow, we waited for our visas.

There was no point keeping anything, since you were permitted to take no more than the equivalent of one hundred dollars per person out of the country. We barely saw my father. He went out in the days without any papers, running around the city trying to find out what was happening with the visas and trying to make some money to live on by offering to do things for people. After seven months we got them.

My mother was quiet at the airport. My father tried to joke with the friends and family who had come to see us off. The customs officer, an older overweight man with a walrus moustache and bags under his eyes, slowly went through everything. Opening all our cases, he took out skirts and shirts and shoes and ripped them apart, ostensibly looking for valuables. The people who had come to see us off stood back. My mother remained silent. My father closed his eyes more tightly with each rip. Then he started on my father's little television. He said he had to search it and we watched him destroy it, this box my father had treasured. Pavel was fascinated by its disembowelment. He had never seen inside a television before. Stepping away from his handiwork, the customs officer caught a glimpse of me standing behind my mother and beckoned me to come closer. He smiled and then ripped the tiny gold hoop earring my mother had given me from my ear. I screamed. My ear was bleeding and my father could not contain himself any longer. He started shouting and threatening the customs officer, moving towards him menacingly. He jostled him and swore at him. Pavel started to cry. A couple of my parents' friends moved in to separate them but not before the customs officer was able to land a blow to my father's cheek.

The customs officer regained his composure rather quickly and disappeared out of view, saying he had to take our papers with him to be checked by his superior. I watched him leave us, taking our papers with him and, my hand to my ear, I remember thinking that the world was too narrow. There was not room enough for us. It was November, already cold, and my ear ached. The television sat in front of us, embarrassingly reassembled, a shadow of its former self. Our torn clothes and shoes, the first of our possessions to be humiliated, were already repacked in their cases and on their way to the plane. I started to trade chocolate with Pavel while my parents traded recriminations. "Why couldn't you keep your mouth shut? You provoked him," my mother said.

"He tore off her ear."

"Don't shout at me."

"Shut your mouth, just this once."

I looked at the time. The plane had just gone. It was snowing in Moscow and all our clothes were torn and on their way to Rome.

The customs officer came back and told us our visas had been confiscated. His superior had said that one of the required stamps was missing. We couldn't leave without it. He told us we could pick them up the next day from the offices of the Immigration Department. Then he called "Next" and as we passed muttered "Jew" under his breath at my father. Pavel's shoelace

was broken. He thought we might have to walk. It was snowing. There was nothing to say.

The next day my mother went to pick up the visas from the
Department. We went with her and waited. Eventually a woman
told us that they couldn't return the visas yet. She said her superior had been consulted and wanted to look at our case more
closely. I remember the woman saying, "It won't take long," as
though our dry cleaning wasn't quite ready.

"Why not?" my mother asked.

"Why not what?"

"Why won't it take long?"

"It just won't."

We had the equivalent of four hundred American dollars but
no rubles. We couldn't buy anything. Of course, hard currency
was very much in demand, but it was illegal to be carrying it. My
father was concerned not to do anything that might jeopardize
our case. But we needed to eat. It was an offense merely to go out
without identification. We were wearing out our welcome with
all the people who had put us up over the previous months, and
we had no possessions with which to sweeten the aftertaste of
their kindness. No answers were forthcoming from the Department. My father's family felt the whole thing had been ill-
advised. They had heard how it had come about and blamed it on
the woman who never could keep her mouth shut. Why did we
have to go anyway? My father had spent his whole life building
up contacts. They had served him well. Wasn't it good enough
for her?

We were getting desperate. It was hard enough to meet up
and when we did we fought, in front of someone else in their

apartment. I went to school just to visit. Prowling the corridors in search of friends, I was discovered by the Principal. He told me to go. I was not welcome in his school, my school, anymore.

We all, in our separate ways, visited the scenes and places of our lives from the time before our application to leave. Even without identification papers my mother felt compelled to risk visiting the streets, just to see people, the queues, familiar signs, the ubiquitous COMMUNISM IS INEVITABLE. We saw everything with the clarity of outsiders. We were like the disembowelled television. Small, never anyone's prize to begin with but with certain capabilities, almost attaining grace in that we functioned, we were being crudely taken apart, destroyed, to no other end than to be tossed about by the wind until dust, then forgotten.

In desperation, my father crawled into work. Without any information, how could he develop a plan? Perhaps someone had heard something? Even if they hadn't, until he had been told that nobody knew anything, he was doing something with a purpose. He spoke to a friend who happened to be non-Jewish. Yes, this man knew something. How good it was to see a friend. What did he know, just quietly? My father's boss, Zwier, had written a letter to someone he knew at the Department of Immigration. In the letter Zwier had warned that my father was extremely wealthy from his dealings in art and antiquities and that he was smuggling or going to smuggle paintings for diamonds or drugs. It was suggested that, given the overrepresentation of Jews in the Ministry of Culture, my father should be made an example of. He had always been too smooth.

My father told us this in an unemotional tone as if he were recounting the assembly instructions to some gadget. He had gathered us together in someone's apartment. It was during the day and no one else was there. The weather was fining up. It was the time of the Twenty-fifth Congress of the Party and the U.S. President, Jimmy Carter, was due to be arriving in Moscow. My father seemed relieved by what he had heard at work as though at last he had something on which to base a plan. My mother was furious. Deep into cursing Zwier, she saw my father pick up the telephone. She stopped. Why should he start calling people? There were things to discuss. This was the first real news since "It won't take long." Who was he calling?

We sat watching him dial. He was calling Immigration to ask for the person with whom we had been dealing all along. Identifying himself, he asked after her: Yes, she was well. That's good. We looked at each other in disbelief. Any news on our case? No, nothing yet. They're still looking at it. My father spoke very politely. If I hadn't seen it I wouldn't have believed it was him. He said that he understood that she had said that the visas were not yet ready but that he would be coming down to-morrow to collect them anyway. If they still were not ready he would be pouring petrol on himself in order to set himself on fire in front of the American presidential cavalcade so that they could see what a fantastic flame a Jew can make. He thanked her for her time and wished her a good day.

We were horrified. My mother asked if my father had gone mad. Whether he had or hadn't, I cried. Pavel just sat there stuffing his torn shoe with newspaper. After a while my mother stopped shouting. Everything she was seeing she had already seen before at night, night after night. Her voice became calm trying to comfort me. Whatever happened we would be all right, Pavel and I. My father walked around the room. How heavy he could make the air. Neither of them tried to tell us he didn't mean it.

There is a kind of laconic stoicism that may be said to be part of the Russian character. It's born of putting up with things, of living *anyway*. When a Jew lives in Russia for a minimum of one generation, this is one of the national traits that is absorbed easily, since we're used to doing everything in spite of everything else. The laconic stoicism is then mixed with an innate self-deprecating humor until there exists a highly refined tonic which insulates you from a world that seemed to hate you from before you were born. But as successful as the tonic might be in insulating you from the everyday insults, obstacles, irritations and affronts to your dignity, it has almost no effect when confronted with the probable death of someone you love. Nothing can take away this terror, nothing but death itself, your own death. That's what I was thinking. There we were, hapless figures, pathetic ambassadors of a more or less insignificant people, trapped like mice, powerless inside this rotting superpower. As with people, those countries whom the gods would destroy they first make mad. Everything was a sham fuelled by fear. It would really have been quite funny had my father not promised to self-immolate the next day so that Pavel and I might live beyond the lies, the shortages, the midnight knocks on the door and the sudden disappearances.

Who asked him to do this? What was he doing? Better here with him than the unknown without him. Was this how much he loved us or just how much he hated them? In his calm I saw his rage, the rage of a man who had seen himself all of his life the lone victim of a jostling crowd. Can a lifetime of humiliation and intimidation dumped comprehensively on hopes and dreams, a bloodied shirt from a random drunken explosion of hate, can all of this be assuaged only by his incineration? I could see him burning. He would burn well. He did everything well. My father has so much to teach me. Don't teach me this. I will not see it as love, I promise you. Don't risk it. There will be nothing to remember. I would have to end the uncertainty myself. I would be next. Don't try me. Stay, you who have always fought, and love me overwhelmingly in your inadequate way.

The following day my father, true to his word, went to the Department of Immigration alone. When he got there the visas were waiting for him. They were in the same state they had been in when they were confiscated. Nothing had been stamped or added to them. He was assured they would be sufficient to get us to Rome. We went to the airport the next day.

My mother had made my father promise to let her handle everything at the airport. She was afraid we might have to deal with the same customs officer. This time we had far less to get through customs. Most of what we had ever owned had either been sent to Rome seven months before, traded for something or given to someone to prolong our welcome. There was one thing my father had not packed the first time, something he had hung on to throughout everything that had ever happened to him: his stamp collection. The original customs officer was on duty. Perhaps he wouldn't remember us? We knew he would. My mother waited until he was occupied with other people so that we would be seen by somebody else. This other man was younger and not particularly interested. He went through our things absentmindedly, as if he had soccer or his girlfriend on his mind. Then he came across the stamps.

Some kind of form or certificate was needed to get the stamps out of the country if they were more than twenty-five years old.

My father had been collecting since he was a small child and had stamps from before he was born. I could never understand what he liked about them. Stamps in Russia were badly printed and looked faded as soon as they were issued. The younger customs officer told my mother matter-of-factly that we could not take them with us.

Excusing herself, my mother came over to explain the situation to my father, who was waiting with us. But he would not hear of leaving his stamps. He would get the necessary certificate. He could get it that day. The flight was scheduled to leave in an hour and a half. Let's not take any chances. It would be all right, he assured her. He knew someone who could arrange it for him on the spot. Who cares? Forget the stamps. But he couldn't. They had been with him all his life, and anyway, did she know how much these stamps will be worth in the West? No, she didn't, and neither did he. He would try to get the certificate. If he wasn't back in time to catch the plane, we were to leave without him. He would follow us as soon as he could bring the stamps. My mother pleaded. She was not leaving without him. I told him he was a fool and that I hated him. He slapped my face. The first customs officer was free now. Pavel saw him talking to his younger colleague. There was only one flight per day from Moscow to Rome. We stayed.

It took my father just under one week to get the certificate required to take the stamps out. A week later we were back at the airport. There was no one to see us off this time. But finally we were leaving Russia and going to Rome. No one said anything except Pavel, who wanted to explore the plane. My father told him to take his seat and not to say a word until the plane had taken off.

When the plane took off I wanted to cry. I looked at my mother and she squeezed my arm. Every day that we had been alive, every person we had ever met and all the words we had ever spoken, their purpose had been merely to fill in the time before this. None of us had ever been on a plane before. It felt as if we were being projected into heaven and that if we died on the way that would be all right too. My father had tears in his eyes. The stamp album was under his seat. It seemed remarkable that the plane could lift so heavy a cargo of yearnings and hopes off the ground.

In Rome we were met by a man from a Russian emigrant welfare agency. He was clearly the only person around who had any idea how momentous the day was for us. He arranged for us to be given a certain sum of money and be driven to Ostia Lido, part of greater Rome, where, with three other families, we rented a pension by the beach. There we resumed our waiting. Rome was only a temporary staging place for Russian emigrants. We applied to go to New York. My father wanted to start anew, without lies, figuring he no longer had anything to hide. When he disclosed that he and my mother had been members of the Party, he was told that New York was out of contention. We applied for Canada, which was extremely popular with people in our situation.

We were a small but shifting community. To supplement the allowance we were given by the welfare agency, my parents did what they could. My father took whatever laboring work was available. I don't think he ever really thought he was cut out for it, but he seemed to enjoy the pain. My mother got work as a nanny and from then on we saw much less of her.

My parents didn't force me to go to school and I pitched in with my earnings from various jobs. Initially, I did some babysitting. Later, I started teaching English to the other waiting Russian emigrants. At its peak, I had six groups going. Men and women, some older than my parents, grappled with grammar and handed me homework to correct, some with bravado, some with trepidation, just like schoolchildren. I tried to teach them sentences I thought might be useful to them in the early days of their new lives. *What is a mortgage? Why don't I work here anymore?*

I was learning a lot despite not going to school. My parents insisted that I keep up with my subjects. It was on that condition that they let me work. Maths, physics and chemistry were just a matter of going through the textbooks. The bigger problem was getting the textbooks. If ever I had any problems that I couldn't work out on my own, there was always a physicist or a mathematician on hand in our small transposed Russia on the Mediterranean able to help out.

The hardest thing to teach myself was history. Of course, it was possible to buy history texts as well, even in English, but to swallow all of it, particularly anything pertaining to the Soviet Union, required almost a paradigm shift. In Moscow, under the tutelage of my parents, I had always been reluctant to accept uncritically what was in the standard history texts, but nothing could have prepared me for the gulf between what I read in Italy and what I had been fed in Moscow.

Now I learnt just how different the world was from the one I had been taught about. There were new perspectives to be gained on such things as the treatment of the kulaks, the trials of the thirties, the efficacy of the Five-Year Plans, not to mention the Cold War we were then still in the middle of. It seemed that less than twenty years earlier, while Marilyn Monroe was singing happy birthday to the head of the free world from the middle of a cake, Khrushchev was taking off his shoe at the UN and banging it on the table. Heel trouble. I empathized. He obviously wore locally made shoes. A true patriot.

Our new life in Italy seemed to coincide with my sexual awakening. Boys came and went in Ostia Lido, and mostly that was fine. Everyone was aware they could be resettled in different countries at any moment, and that leant an air of abandon to our liaisons. Most of the people I hung around with were slightly older than me but they treated me as their equal. Having a little money helped. In addition to the natural sciences, I was learning all about the social power of money. It made you more mature. Your jokes were funnier, your opinions more considered. Then, of course, there was the power of a woman's sexuality, particularly over young men. This was fascinating. It was as though I were a well-connected member of the Party with every young man needing favors endlessly. There were no lies they wouldn't tell and nothing they wouldn't do to secure your patronage, a tremendous system.

There was one boy whose departure, when it finally came, I was not so cavalier about. Mitya was his name. He was much quieter than I was and that always made him appear soulful, at least to me. Unlike almost everybody else in the émigré community, he was a stranger to anything practical. All the mathematicians and physicists and engineers were capable of unjamming doors, mending bike punctures or fixing radios. Not Mitya. He was a dreamer. Of course everyone there was dreaming, but Mitya did not dream of a job in Canada, making money in New York or defending the Jews in Israel. He dreamed dreams about words, not just in words, *about* words. At that stage they were other people's words, but he hoped that one day they would be his words. I suspected he was writing already. I sometimes caught him scribbling in a little black book, but whenever I came near he put it away.

Mitya would have studied literature had he stayed in the Soviet Union. He had hoped to teach it. But now he would have to take any job he could get in whichever country it was that he and his family could get into. He had the deep round eyes of Kafka, about whom he was passionate. In his wallet he carried around a small picture of Kafka. It was not an affectation. He didn't ever show it to me. I found it one day while going through his wallet. Most boys had condoms squashed between their notes of different currencies and spare passport photos; it wasn't so much out of their need for them as out of the Russian habit of hoarding things of good quality. Italian condoms were so much better than the Russian ones, which broke so often it was cheaper to have children. But Mitya didn't carry condoms. He had Kafka.

Mitya barely pursued me. He was too shy. That helped me to love him. In his weakness was his strength. We would go out together with whatever constituted the group at the time and he would hardly say a word. I couldn't bear to watch him trying to fit in with the other boys at a disco or party. It was painful. He thought that I wanted him to fit in. In this he didn't know me at all. I have a lot of trouble with people who fit in, even if they're fitting in with people famous for not fitting in. I get this from my mother. Mitya was happiest showing me the books he was reading. He spent all of his meager funds on books and on me. We still wrote to each other. He went to Israel: just what they needed. His English was terrible. I don't want to imagine his Hebrew. Like his friend Kafka, he will never have a home.

I've seen a photo of him in uniform. He looked ridiculous. His gun seemed to regard him curiously. He loves better than anyone I've ever known.

I have every confidence that loneliness will one day be recognized for what it is, a pathology. Whether it will be psychiatrists, neuropsychologists or even philosophers who discover this I can't say, but in the same way that it is now thought that various types of depression have something to do with the presence or absence of serotonin in the brain, so loneliness will one day be correlated with the absence of something other than people. It is possible to be lonely in a crowd at a party, in a marriage and, of course, by yourself. Clearly, other people have almost nothing to do with it. Loneliness is an illness.

It was probably around that time that Pavel first manifested the symptoms. Or was it simply that that was the first time that anyone had noticed them? I noticed them but I didn't do anything to try to help him. Pavel's loneliness had been a recurring theme, a motif, dominant for him but just a subtle harmony below the surface of our own crashing melodies. Sitting there waiting for the private investigator to phone, it drowned out everything else and I was unable to hear myself think, unable to hide my anxiety. It was not easy to admit that perhaps it could have all been avoided.

After three years of rejection, suddenly Switzerland was said to be a possibility. My father was overjoyed. During the war he'd been evacuated from Moscow and taught watchmaking as his trade. Ever since he had been in love with Switzerland. What could be better than an entire country dedicated to hygiene, temporal precision and chocolate, not to mention their stamps? And if that weren't enough, there were the banks, those almost mythically discreet and mysterious financial institutions allegedly run by gnomes.

But while all this was still only talk, four visas arrived, uninvited, from Australia. It seemed impossible. We didn't want to go to Australia. Who knew anything about Australia? We had only applied because the Russian emigrant welfare agency said we had to and because we were assured we wouldn't be allowed in. (They had promised us that Australia accepted only direct relatives, that even first cousins were too distant.) Australia was our last choice. My parents were in shock. This was not alleviated by the seminars on Australia we attended. I remember the four of us sitting motionless in a darkened room watching documentary movies about Australia. So much wildlife, nothing but wildlife. My father was speechless. He had heard stories of Russians arriving in Perth and then trying to go back to Russia. No one knew anything about the country. The Soviet government didn't even vilify it. But our choice was simple. If we didn't go to Melbourne we would lose our subsidy and all forms of assistance in Rome. It was going to have to be our home.

It was autumn in Melbourne when we arrived. Autumn, I have since discovered, is Melbourne's season. Of all the seasons, it best suits that sprawling metropolis about which all of Europe has heard virtually nothing. It is when the antipodean former outpost of England takes time out between the un-European heat of a tropical summer and the impending log fire and cocoa season. Melbourne, I have learned, has always been more English than Sydney, and the climate has a lot to do with it. The streets are long and straight. They do not meander randomly the way the streets in most European cities do. Someone planned them.

From being a case for the Department of Immigration in
Moscow, we became first a case for the Russian emigrant welfare
agency in Rome and now a case in Melbourne for a Jewish welfare society. After a few weeks in a motel they found us a unit in
an inner suburb. It was a 1950s-style reddy-orange brick block
with terrazzo common stairs, corridors and balconies. Our unit
was on the third floor and our balcony overlooked the driveway.
The hallways and stairs smelled of cats, fried food and cigarettes.
But there were three bedrooms. For the first time Pavel and I
slept in separate rooms. When we first moved in he wasn't so
happy about this, but later, as he got older, it became his sanc-
tuary. This was around the time he got his cassette player. For a
long time he had only one cassette, a Deep Purple tape. Someone from the welfare society had donated it. He played it over
and over. It drove my parents and me crazy. My father argued
with him about it, and everything else, all the time.

My parents were not happy. After my mother had learnt in
Italy that we were coming to Australia, she had applied for a position with a Russian newspaper in Melbourne. The pay, she
knew, would not be much but it would be better than nothing
and could lead to other things. (Always they looked for the possibility of *other things*.) But by the time we were set up in Melbourne she learned that the paper had recently moved to Sydney.
She told us this matter-of-factly, as though she had just discovered that we had run out of milk.

My father was also having trouble getting work. There just
wasn't much call for Soviet-trained economists. But he refused to
apply for unemployment benefits, claiming that it would "look
bad." Things were different here. The State was not expected to

look after you, he insisted, and we haven't been here all that long that we should feel so comfortable putting our hands out. My mother called him a fool. Did he feel so comfortable with two children growing out of their clothes? My father told her that we would be all right, we always were. He said he had been thinking about investigating the antique market here. He would even investigate the value of his stamps. It was a mistake for him to mention the stamps. I knew he wouldn't do anything about it and it only made her angrier. Pavel said he didn't really need new clothes. But he thought his Deep Purple tape might be about to break. The unit was becoming so small, none of us could move. The Soviet Union had seeped into every spare inch. We had never been all right.

If I was to go to university, I had to finish school. I argued that I should be permitted to take an entrance exam and only if I didn't perform well enough should I have to go back to school. I was almost eighteen and, after Rome, felt about thirty. I really didn't care what I studied as long as I didn't have to go back to school. But no one was terribly interested in my European sophistication or what I wanted. Wherever you are in the world, authorities are still authorities. I was told I would have to sit an exam just to get into final year in secondary school. It was demeaning. They gave me a week to study for it.

I passed easily and got into a government high school for girls. Although it was a good school, I was very unhappy there. I don't think I've ever felt that alone. Not one person said hello to me for the whole of the first term. I cried every day when I came home. Pavel, who got home from his school earlier than me, was already crying by the time I got there. My mother didn't know what to do with us. My father looked at us incredulously. We had moved halfway around the world to escape the misery of Russia, and yet, we were more miserable than ever. I slowly shrank into myself. If it weren't for letters from Mitya, I think I might well have forgotten who I was. I thought of moving to Israel. Mitya had just gone into the army and I wanted to be with him and his photo of Kafka.

Pavel was often getting beaten up at school for being a *wog*. We had all been taught that a wog was a Greek or Italian Australian but not a Russian or a Jew. My father thought about this. As deplorable as it was for any child to be the victim of intimidation and violence from his peers, in his son's case surely it was all the result of a misunderstanding. Pavel had to have the courage to explain to his tormentors that he was neither Greek or Italian. When, in his tortured accent, he did explain his origins, they called him a spy and subjected him to a pogrom. Being a spy was a charge levelled at me, too, first at school and then at university in various inane undergraduate attempts at some kind of geopolitical humor. Nevertheless university signalled a marked improvement in my personal circumstances. There was the end of the daily humiliation suffered by an adult forced to wear a school uniform. But more than that, a university is intrinsically a more tolerant world. The very institution itself is a testament to pluralism, at least it is in theory.

I think it was Evelyn Waugh in *Brideshead Revisited* who wrote that we spend much of the second year at university trying to lose the friends we made in the first year. But I have always been advanced for my age, so already by the end of first semester I had begun to discard people with the callous disregard of a veteran socialite.

Of course, there were boys now and again, but most of them were lobotomized haircuts in gray windcheaters. I don't know what it was about the men at that university, but their cultural aspirations and social graces tended to gravitate to the lowest common denominator: namely, to those of the engineering students. Naturally, I made the mistake of attempting a relationship, however briefly, with an engineer.

He was the only boy at university I ever brought home. In an attempt to be hospitable and friendly to him, my mother went on at great length about how much she loved living in Australia. And, in a way, she had. Depending on what this private investigator told me, perhaps she would again. There and then she held it responsible.

Throughout my time at university, I had a series of jobs to help pay the rent and whatever else needed paying. Often that was everything. My father refused to apply for unemployment benefits and everyone else refused to employ him. Trained in Marxist economics two or three decades before and with broken English, he did not give the impression of a man going places. He was getting older and heavier, in bulk and in manner. But the truth was, there was almost nothing he couldn't do. No one would give him the opportunity, however, and gradually he was breaking. My mother, still trying to get some kind of language-based job with anything local and Russian, got a little dressmaking work from time to time to help out. Pavel worked after school as a janitor. He had started smoking and missing school, both with increasing frequency. My father sang Russian songs, initially when he was alone in the shower, but then in the lounge room when we were trying to watch television, or in the middle of the night, if he couldn't sleep. We were at each other's throats, shouting in anger at something or at nothing. The walls moved in closer to each other, and every shout set off in each of us an unscheduled train of thought to the edge of some or other precipice.

My mother fought with Pavel and he looked to me, crying so seductively, entreating me to take his part in disputes in which he was invariably wrong. Was I any less his friend, his soul mate, for wanting him to finish school, to turn the radio down, not to smoke, at least not in the flat, or for wanting him not to grab my father by the scruff of the neck and thrust his face into our impoverishment? His unintelligible English was also a real problem for him. He said he was so sick of trying to prove he wasn't stupid, he just wanted to smash everything. He was languishing in our tiny flat and he cursed my father for it. Take the government's money. It is for people like you. You are no antique dealer. Don't make us laugh. You are a disgrace to every real antique dealer. No stock? There is never any stock. There never will be because you have no money to buy it. And it went on nightly, my mother and Pavel joining in a mutual lullaby at each other or else in harmony against my father. And he sang, too, just any time, alone, in winter with the doors and windows closed so that he might be anywhere, and then in summer with the balcony door wide open to the street. I looked at him and at the railing on the balcony. In a genuine tragedy there is no hero to die finally, but the stage itself falls apart, beginning at the edges.

I was already working at the book and music shop part-time when Pavel left home. He desperately needed some self-esteem and he wasn't mustering any staying with us. I felt his English was the problem. He spoke well enough for shopping and for the street, but he was a long way from being able to study in English at a tertiary level, and—without ever having quite said it—my parents had brought us up to revere education above everything else.

Pavel saw the relative ease with which I coped academically, and because he loved me so much, he couldn't hate me for it or even be jealous. I was proof that, even in our circumstances, with our lack of money, one could still get on. So why couldn't he and when would he ever? It ate at him. He did not even have the consolation of a special talent that might just see him through anyway—no musicianship or artistry. I could see this fine young man hollowing before me: my brother, who in some other time or place need not have looked ridiculous to the world. He loved me. And I loved him, but because of the way he saw himself, he could never believe that my love was not pity or duty.

It was decided that he would move out, rent a one-bedroom unit in St. Kilda and, while working part-time, study a trade by night. Hadn't my parents worked by day and studied by night? Tradition! At least it was a plan. My father drew comfort from this, and in the days before Pavel left we began saying that it was *for the best.* My mother had thin tears along her face as we stood in the passage near the front door on the day he left. Pavel hugged each of us, including my father, with new strength, and when he came last to my mother, she heaved for breath. He was closing the door and only I heard him: "I am not worth your tears."

How Russian it was of us to turn his moving to a separate unit into a scene from *Doctor Zhivago.* Or perhaps it was very Jewish of us. In the first couple of days my mother moped around the unit between outbreaks of tears as though he had gone off to war, rather than moved three kilometers away. But before very long he was visiting with his laundry and eating everything in sight, waiting for his washing to dry. He was visiting once or twice a week, and my parents—usually my mother—spoke to him on the telephone almost every day. There's nothing like doing someone's laundry to eradicate sentiment. His new lifestyle seemed to bear fruit almost immediately. Pavel was a different person: he was lighter. The autonomy had given color to his demeanor. When he came to visit he would laugh and joke with us, even with my father. After a few months he started bringing us gifts, telling us that his hours at work had been increased and that he had more money. My father cross-examined him as to what this meant for his course. Was he still working hard? Where previously this type of questioning would have been interpreted as belittling, an invasion of his privacy and a lack of trust, now Pavel remained calm. "I have it all worked out," he told my father.

"How so?"

"Everything will be fine. I'm not going to go into the details. I know that you're happy about the extra money: don't pretend you're not. You're beginning to be proud of me. I can tell. Now you're going to have to learn to trust me."

My mother also started bringing in a little extra money. In addition to the occasional dressmaking, she started working in a little shoe repair store a few days a week.

"What do you know about shoes?" I asked her.

"It's like clothes. You just sew a little harder."

The shoe repair shop was a tiny leather-smelling place not far from where we lived. It was owned by another Russian Jew, a Mr. Kuznetsov, Sergei to my mother.

"This man knows shoes," my mother said, impressed. There was plenty of scope for people to have talked about Mr. Kuznetsov and his new assistant, spending all those hours alone together with nothing but the finer points of leather craft to keep them apart. But who would want to waste their time speculating about a relationship between two middle-aged Russian Jews?

"I don't trust him," my father said when Kuznetsov asked my mother to go full-time.

"But we need the money and he's got the work."

My mother sounded Kuznetsov out about taking my father on part-time. My mother explained in a roundabout way that my father was going crazy and that she would take a reduction in pay for the period it took to train my father. Kuznetsov agreed on the condition that she accept a pay increase before my father started.

My father was adamant. "I'm not working for him. That's it! Do you want to discuss something else?"

But he wasn't working for anyone else, either, and when my mother suggested that they examine the possibility of getting a car, my father looked at her in horror. Not only could they not afford one but it had always been his role to want things first.

"What has got into you? What do you need a car for?"

"Well, it *would* make things much easier but perhaps you're right, Sergei can give me a lift."

At about the time they were talking of cars, Mitya wrote to tell me he had taken a job in Israel driving buses. It wasn't what either of us ever had in mind for him, but there was no bitterness in his letter. I assumed he must have been so disappointed with his life that this was a positive thing. If anything, he seemed to quite like the idea of driving a bus up and down Israel. He had been a driver in the army, after all. I wondered if Kafka was going with him.

Pavel visited us in different clothes each week, clothes we

had never seen before. My mother scoffed at his taste or lack of it. My father questioned his priorities.

"Do you have so much money you can squander it with equanimity, or does your vanity lobby with more conviction than your future?"

But Pavel told him the future was always there. "The future can take care of itself."

"Maybe it can, but who will take care of you? All of a sudden you know everything," my father said.

"Just like you do, only you got to know it gradually. I am spending money I earn, like everybody else. Perhaps it has been so long that you have forgotten what people do. You earn, you spend."

"I should slap you down. You fool, what about saving something?"

I tried to intervene; I could see it escalating. "Let him spend all his pay for a little while. He's just excited to have some money for a change. You'll start to put a bit away soon, won't you?"

But he didn't, and to my father, who had always been besotted with contingencies, Pavel was a cowboy. He stopped coming as often as he had and he was more frequently out when my mother or I phoned him. She worried about him, and my attempts to attribute his increasing absence to some youthful phase of muscle-flexing machismo did little to pacify her. When he did visit he was usually sullen and disaffected. If he wasn't actually volleying barbs at my father, they barely spoke at all. But it was not due to my father that he was coming less, nor was it due to my mother's increasingly emotional expressions of concern for him. There was nothing at all at our place that made him feel better about himself. Everything there reminded him of the time before he had moved out, and I could see that whatever it was he had experienced after that had not made him look at us differently. His despair at the smallness of the place, at the wretchedness of our lives, the shabbiness of the furniture, the fetidness of the cooking odors that never went away and the irritating tap of our shoes on the linoleum floor, was still there, even if tempered by a kind of pity.

But worse for me than any of this was that Pavel was not coming to see me. He has never realized how much I need him. We are each other's personal historians. Without him my past is uncertain and my future is forlorn. We are each other's children, having spent our childhoods sitting together on so many different floors, laughing wildly at nothing when there was nothing to laugh at or crying about something when there was something to cry about, which was often. We have hidden together behind couches pretending to be other people or sometimes animals come alive from something we had read. Were my disapproving glances too strong or not strong enough? Did they come too early or too late? In the face of his rage, his burning desire to get on, to rid himself of his feeling of inadequacy, my love had been a too-faint breeze. No wonder he turned his back on me.

When my father refused to work in Sergei Kuznetsov's shoe repair store, my mother began working there full-time. By this time I had finished the Diploma of Education I had been advised to do after my first degree and was waiting for a teaching position to become available. I didn't want to teach but I was getting restless in the bookshop where I was now working full-time, and moreover teaching was better paid. The one benefit I would miss would be the discount on books.

My father had taken on the purchasing of a car as a personal project even though my mother had stopped talking about it. In the morning she walked to work and at night Sergei Kuznetsov drove her home. It seemed to my father that the shoe repair store was close enough for her to walk to and too far for her to be driven home from. Kuznetsov had a car and all day, six days a week now, he was with my mother while my father was at home or out trying to get work. Eventually Kuznetsov offered to drive my mother to the supermarket to help her with the shopping. At first she declined. Her husband could do the shopping. He has time. Yes, but he doesn't have a car.

One afternoon my mother called me at work from the shoe repair store. Her voice was interrupted by the syncopation of Kuznetsov hammering away at somebody's sole. It had been over a week since we had seen Pavel and days since any one of us had spoken to him. She was worried about him and asked if I would stop by his flat on the way home. Kuznetsov would have driven her there but she didn't feel right dropping in on Pavel with him unexpectedly. I was not to mention any of this to my father.

I knocked on the door and waited. There was no sound from inside. I went around looking through all of the windows. Fortunately his unit was on the ground floor. The place was emptier than it had ever been, emptier than it should have been. I stood on my toes and peered in, face flat against the glass, looking for something I hadn't yet articulated to myself, something I didn't want to see. There was nothing. A few boxes and some rags my mother had given him for cleaning lay on the floor. He had gone.

Where was he? What was I going to say? I needed time to think, so I just walked around the streets of St. Kilda near Pavel's unit. I called the real estate agent responsible for managing the block. It was late and I got his answering machine. In desperation I went to the agent's office hoping to find an after-hours number somewhere on the building. I did and called from a café, but another answering machine announced in a Groucho Marx imitation voice that no one was home. I told my mother that Pavel was out when I had got there and that the place was a mess as usual.

The next day I telephoned the agent again and spoke to a woman in their rental section. She said Pavel Gamarkin had been late with his rent for a few months and had not paid it at all that month. He had said he would make up the arrears but it seemed he had shot through, forfeiting his bond. Would I like to see the unit?

It was morning and I had a full day at work to think of some-thing before I had to go home. I couldn't tell my parents that he had just gone. My mother would have panicked and my father would have blamed himself, neither of which would have been much help. I was fairly frantic myself but I had customers, col-leagues and employers from whom to hide it. We were busy, I was out of ideas and kept imagining horrible squalid scenes with my brother at the center of them. It may sound comical but it was while restocking the Crime/Mystery section that I came up with an idea. I would hire a private investigator to find him.

How do you do that? How do you choose a private investigator? Do you interview them, find a competitive price? Who can advise you on something you don't want to tell anybody about? I looked in the Yellow Pages and chose one with a Jewish-sounding sur-name: Leibowitz, Bernard Leibowitz. It didn't sound much like Philip Marlowe or Sam Spade maybe but I wasn't Lauren Bacall, either, and it was an emergency. A woman's voice on the answering machine told me I had reached the Leibowitz Investigation Agency and to please leave a message after the tone. Then there was the tone. I waited for me to say something but nothing happened. How much time was there before the machine would cut me off? There was so much to tell him, I didn't know what to leave out. How much does Bernard Leibowitz need to know? I called back. This time I left my name and work number and asked him to use discretion, whatever that means, when he called me back.

He phoned me back the next day. I briefed him to find my brother. Bernard Leibowitz requested a photo of him and undertook to call me in a few days. Those few days were hell. I was no longer as good at waiting as I had been. The nights were worst. I lay there wondering how I had not seen it coming, my throat tense in remembrance of all that I had not said to keep him with me. What kind of mother would I be? What kind of friend was I? I had not been my brother's keeper and so he had not been kept. In the torpor of the sun's absence I scrambled the bedclothes till they lay heavily on me in complete disarray. I was so frightened for him.

My mother was in the process of rejecting sanity. She had no time for it, notwithstanding that I had managed to keep Pavel's disappearance from her. A few days after calling Leibowitz, I had the emotional equivalent of the experience of a newly toilet-trained child who is struggling to hold on but who trips and falls while running on his way to relief. In a sleep-deprived state I lost control of myself. But I hadn't tripped. I was pushed over, and the realization of my family's eternal vulnerability and of my inability to do anything about it spilled out of me all over the street.

I was walking home down Acland Street after work. It was a

fairly crowded early evening. The restaurants were already busy. The middle class, the offspring of an earlier wave of migrants, was hungry. I think I heard him first. Yes, that would be right. I would have heard him before I saw him and, had he not been singing, I might not have seen him at all. But the baritone was unmistakable. It was rich. Outside the travel agency my father was singing in the street. Some people had thrown money at his feet. I wanted to turn back, as if to un-see what I'd seen, to make it not him there. But it was him. The songs were Russian. The tears were his. I recognized them. They were like the fat rain-drops of summer. He was wearing a checked shirt of Pavel's, one he had criticized him for buying. Under one arm he held his stamp album tightly to his side. I came up to him but he kept singing. People stared at us as I took him in my arms, but he didn't stop singing. His tears mixed with mine and he let go of the stamp album. It fell open at his feet. I remember that one of our tears must have hit an exposed stamp and the print ran a lit-tle. Stalin lay smudged in Acland Street.

My father told me he would sing there each day until he had the money for a car. I picked the stamp album up from the ground and as we walked he told me about his day. He had taken a tram into the city to the General Post Office in Bourke Street. He had stood in a number of queues; all of them, it had turned out, were the wrong ones. The people serving at the end of each queue had difficulty un-derstanding him. Finally he was given the advice he was seeking, the name and address of the most expert philatelist in Melbourne. With his stamp album he took another tram and from the end of the line he walked to the address he had been given and showed a man the stamps he had been collecting all his life. The man offered him a cup of tea and said that he found them very interesting, nicely preserved. He did not want to buy them but knew of some people who might. The philatelist advised my father not to part with them for anything under one hundred and forty dollars.

I still hadn't told my parents about Bernard Leibowitz, the private investigator. This was partly to save them waiting for news in the event that he didn't come up with any and partly to save them from whatever news he did come up with. Perhaps a few days was a figure of speech to him meaning more than one week and less than two. What if something else came up? He couldn't be expected to drop a lead in another case to return my call punctually. How many cases did he work on at one time? Every time the phone rang I jumped. But when it wasn't him I was relieved. At times I didn't want him ever to call.

We were busy. Sometimes there was no one in the shop and we just stood around waiting. But not then. It was late afternoon and I was supposed to be emptying cartons and stacking shelves, but I kept getting interrupted when they needed help at the front counter. No one else sold an art diary quite like me. Would that be cash? I was sorry, there were no books specifically on the indigenous trees of South Australia. It didn't seem he would call.

Yes, I was coming. They needed me up at the front again. What was it this time, a brass band recording of "Amazing Grace" or this year's guide to movies on video? For fifteen ninety-five you could buy your own opinion or prop up that table in the lounge. What did we have here, a smart young man or an illiterate moron wanting music for a dance party? Couldn't he just amplify the fridge hum? His face was red. He'd shaved too closely. I could hear the phone. Good for you, boyo! He wanted Kafka. I didn't think we had any. He said it had to be Kafka. Well, all right, then. Did *he* want to drive buses too? I heard them calling: "Phone." It was for me. This guy must be loaded. He was carrying around half the shop. Why was he bothering me? Had he tried looking under *K*? Could I check out the back for Kafka? Out the back the phone had been hung up. I found a copy of *The Trial*.

The young man was happy, although it was not the translation he wanted. Life could be tough. The phone call, did he leave a name? How did I know it was a *he*? Did Rose have a secret? No name. Said he'll call back. When? Didn't say. I had to wait.

2. Melbourne

The private investigator did not call back till the following day. When one of the girls in the bookshop told me there was a phone call for me, I felt the faint stirrings of hope which, however deluded, however misguided, so often kicks in to keep us going and distinguishes us from other animals. Yes, this is Rose Gamarkin. Thank you for returning my call. It is a little difficult, I'm at work. Could I, perhaps, come to your office? Yes, I have a pen and paper.

Bernard Leibowitz's office had a door which had someone else's name on it. I knocked on it anyway. The man who opened it was a soft, late thirtyish bear with big hands and a loud tie. He introduced himself as Bernard Leibowitz and offered me a seat on the door side of the smaller of two desks that took up most of the room.

"I wasn't sure I had the right address."

"Oh really, why?"

"Well . . . the door—"

"Oh, the door, right, of course."

"This *is* your office though?"

"Oh yes, sure is . . . unless there's something I don't know."

"Mr. Leibowitz—"

"Please, call me Bernard."

"Bernard, why don't you have your name on the door?"

"Oh, I'm sorry. I should explain. I share the office with an-other PI, but you should feel completely free to say anything in front of him."

I looked around the room. There was no one else in it.

"When he's here. Feel free to speak confidentially when he's here."

Then Bernard Leibowitz looked around the room. "He's not here now. I'm not actually expecting him, not that I keep tabs on him. I mean, I keep a lookout for him generally, as I would imag-ine he does for me, but really we just share the office. But if he does come back, or if on some other occasion you're here and he's here, you should feel completely free to say anything you might have said were he not here. Here's my card, Miss Gamarkin."

"Rose," I said, taking the card.

"This really *is* my office, Rose. I really *am* a private investi-gator."

Of all the PI's in all the Yellow Pages, I had to find this guy. Was this the man in whom I was meant, by some divine design, to put my trust? I was looking for my brother. I needed to find him in a hurry to save a life or three. Even if there was nothing more sinister in Pavel's disappearance than a bout of juvenile delinquency, my parents were not in a position to take any such phase with equanimity. They never had been. In the absence of any real political or philosophical creed, in the absence of any religious or spiritual conviction, I had turned, in desperation, to the telephone directory and this was what I had been sent: a dancing bear. Why had I chosen him? Because he was Jewish.

What the hell did that mean? Did I think we would have something in common? I didn't really know what being Jewish meant, except in Russia. In Russia it meant exclusion, suspicion, ostracism, looking at the ground when you walked in the street. It meant quotas, denial of opportunities over and above that suffered by the other poor bastards. It meant blame for things beyond your control, fear for the safety of your children, unstoppable race hatred growing in people like cancer. It meant violence, seeing your own blood or that of your family unexpectedly against the snow on your way home from somewhere. What did it mean to this Menachem Marlowe in front of me here?

"Would you like a cup of coffee, Rose?"

He left the room to get it and that gave me a chance to look around. His desk, the desk at which I sat, was completely empty. There was nothing on it but dust, a telephone and an answering machine. His roommate's larger desk, however, had half-scrunched-up papers strewn over the tops of more neatly piled paper. On the roommate's side of the room was a bookshelf with motoring, sport and girlie magazines. That was more like it. Leibowitz came back empty-handed.

"Bit of a problem, I'm afraid. There's a place across the street. It's on me."

I was still thinking of leaving when we sat down in the café across the street and he ordered. Then he launched into a much-needed explanation.

"Look, Rose . . . Do you mind if I call you Rose?"

"No."

"That's right, you said that before. I've got to level with you."

"You're not a private investigator."

"No, no. I am."

"You are?"

"Well, sort of."

"What do you mean, 'sort of'?"

"I *am* a private investigator but—"

"'But'?"

"But you're . . . you're probably going to find this very funny one day, hopefully."

"What?"

"You're actually . . . my first client."

"Oh Jesus."

"Now listen . . . we can work something out here. Tell me why you need the services of a private investigator."

What Bernard offered was essentially a contingency-fee arrangement. He would not be paid unless he found Pavel. "It works for both of us: you need help and I need . . . experience."

Bernard Leibowitz was thirty-eight years old. He looked like he needed both help and experience. In his time he had been a construction worker, a ditchdigger, a cabdriver, a salesman in a menswear store, a shipping clerk, a carpet layer, a salesman in a department store, a waiter, a short-order cook, an insurance salesman, an aluminum-cladding salesman, the personal assistant to the spokesperson for a mining company, a real estate agent (of sorts), the personal assistant to a trucking magnate, a gardener and the guy who held the boom mike for the production company that made late-night television advertisements for one of those discount furniture kings who had gone crazy and was practically giving things away for unheard-of low, low prices. From all this he had managed to save a little money, which he put into the establishment of his very own antique shop. Twelve weeks before I met him he had sold the antique shop at a loss. Resolving to try his hand as a private investigator, he had just managed to get himself into the "Private Investigators" classification of the latest Yellow Pages minutes before they were printed. He really needed me.

"I've had a very rich life already. Believe me, I'm not complaining. It's not that I deliberately set out to eschew the conventional things—"

"You mean like a spouse, children, a house and a job?"

"Well, I am actually, in effect, part owner of the house. You see my mother was a joint owner, with my father, of course, of the family home. So when she passed away she left half of her half to me and half to my brother, Adam. Now that he's in Israel, there's only me and Dad, and since my father would want me to call him just about every day anyway . . . you know we may as well—"

"Live together."

"Yes. Why not?"

"Does your father still work?"

"Oh yes."

"What does he do?"

"He's a . . . teacher."

"Really?"

"Yes . . . for years now," he said, taking a sip of coffee and swallowing a capsule he had taken from a little plastic container in his pocket.

"What does he teach?"

"Bar mitzvah."

"Bernard, I hope you won't take this the wrong way, but I'm really worried about my brother. I don't know where he is or what's happened to him and I think I better get a real . . . I mean, a more experienced private investigator."

"Listen, Rose." Bernard Leibowitz cleared his throat. "I know you're worried about your brother. I really want to find him. I mean that. I'm not as stupid as I look. Give me two days. I have a car. We'll work out a plan. I'm more motivated than the next guy in the phone book. We'll find him."

He took my hand just below the wrist, not in a sleazy way but in the way that I had not realized I needed. I was tired. I thought that perhaps he had tears in his eyes when he spoke, but I couldn't be sure. Without warning I had tears in mine, for Pavel, for my parents, for myself and for this thirty-eight-year-old bear in a bright tie who was offering me two of his days to drive me around so that I could find my brother.

"Bernard, don't you need some kind of license to call yourself a private investigator?"

"You know . . . that's probably right. That makes sense. I think that's right."

The first thing he said he would do was call around all the hospitals and police stations to see if there was any word on Pavel. Bernard said that if the hospitals and the police had no record of him, it meant he was all right. I wasn't so sure about this but it

was comforting to hear it. He said I should go home and act normally in front of my parents. He would go back to his office and
start making the calls immediately. I wanted to go with him. I
needed to know that Pavel was alive and well as soon as possible.
But Bernard said it would take a while and that I would just sit
there, tense and nervous, which wouldn't help anybody. He said
he would call me at home if there was anything to report.

"No, no. You'll have to call me either way, otherwise I'll sit
there thinking you didn't call because what you'd heard was
so bad."

"Okay, but won't you have to explain to your parents who
this man is who's calling you all of a sudden?"

"Yes, you're right. I'll tell them you're someone I met in the
bookshop. You're a regular customer and I've given you my
home phone number. We're friends."

"I could be your new boyfriend."

"It's a bit sudden."

"How about a shy and gentle suitor?"

"They probably won't ask that many questions."

"It's settled, then. I'll call you tonight."

I went home and began waiting for him to call. I tried to read
but couldn't concentrate. I kept seeing my brother's sad little
face. Whenever the phone rang I raced to it. If my mother got
there first I was quick to inquire whether it was for me.

When she noticed my interest in the telephone she asked,
"What are you expecting? Is it Pavel? Is it about Pavel?"

"I'm not expecting anything."

She gave me a look that said she didn't believe me.

"Well," I added, "not exactly *expecting*, and it hasn't anything
to do with Pavel."

"Is it about work?" she asked. "Is it a boy?"

"It's nothing, really."

It was lucky we had gone through this because when Bernard finally called it was my mother who took the call. Fortunately she misunderstood my eagerness to talk to him and was later even a little distracted by it.

Bernard told me there was nothing to suggest Pavel was either in trouble with or known by the police, nor had he been admitted to hospital. He said that he had checked them all. Over the phone he did not seem so much like a bear. I was relieved that he had heard nothing.

We met the next morning before I was due at work. When I arrived at Bernard's office he was waiting for me in the hallway outside the door. His roommate was in conference with a client so again we went across the street for a coffee.

"Bernard, do you have to leave the office every time he has a client there?"

"No, no, of course not. It wouldn't really be my office, then, would it? No, I knew you were coming any minute so I thought, you know, save time and everything if I—"

"Waited for me in the hallway."

"I think it probably did save a little time but, anyway, I've had an idea."

"Yes?"

"I know you said that you'd already been to your brother's unit, but I think I should go there and have a look around myself."

"That's your idea, Bernard?"

"Yes. I'll call up the agent pretending to be interested and see if I can get them to take me through it this morning. I'll look for clues. He might have left something behind."

"He didn't. I've looked."

"You looked through the windows but you haven't been inside. I'll get inside to see what I can find."

He could see that I wasn't impressed with his idea. "Rose, you never know. You can go to work and I'll call you when I've been through the place. Have you had breakfast?"

I hadn't had breakfast and I didn't have a better idea. I didn't have *any* other idea except perhaps the nagging one of calling another private investigator, so I found myself going along with him.

My father was spared any anxiety over Pavel's disappearance. His relationship with Pavel had so deteriorated that he was unaware Pavel was missing. He was getting up later and later each day. It had become too much for him to watch my mother leave for work at Kuznetsov's shoe repair business. At the end of the day, when I came home from work, I would often find him in his old-world gray pleated trousers and his freshly ironed shirt, mopping the kitchen floor or scrubbing the bath.

"The place gets dirty," he told me once when he caught me looking at him.

Bernard called me at work and told me he would meet me during my morning tea break to show me what he had found.

"Do you get a morning tea break?" he asked over the phone.

"Yes."

"Good. I'll meet you in the alley out the back."

"Bernard, what did you find?"

"Can't talk now, Rose. I've only got two days. Meet you in the alley."

Why couldn't he talk? I was his only client.

When we met out the back it was in his car. He had brought along two cups of coffee, one of which he gave me when I got in next to him.

"Bernard, what happened? Did you find anything?"

"Rose, do you know if this is a loading zone?"

"I don't know. Bernard, did you find anything?"

"Yes, I'll show you in a second. How much time do you get?"

"Fifteen minutes. Why?"

"I thought so. That's enough time. I'll show you what I found and then we'll have the coffee. It needs to cool. I got the agent to let me have a look around and then, while she was occupied, I put all the stuff I could find in my travel bag."

"How was she occupied?"

"She had a very distracting call come in on her mobile phone."

"What if she hadn't had that call?"

"I made sure she did. I called my roommate and gave him the agent's mobile number. It was printed on her business card. Then I had him call her and threaten her with legal action."

"Legal action? Over what?"

"Everything. Under the general complaint that her firm had misrepresented the state of various properties, he complained about the plumbing, the presence of vermin, leaking toilets, cat urine on the carpet, that sort of thing. He just made it all up but it gave me all the time I needed. Now, come and see what I've got."

We got out of the car and he led me to the boot. He looked around, as if to see whether someone was watching, and then opened the boot to reveal his green travel bag. He unzipped the bag and pulled out the rags I had seen days earlier through the window of Pavel's flat.

"That's it? That's all you've got?" I asked him.

"And this," he said, pulling out a long piece of metal pipe.

"Jesus, Bernard. This stuff is useless."

"What about the pipe?"

"The pipe's not his. Pavel doesn't know anything about plumbing."

"I think he used it for something else. I've seen kids around, at the station, in car parks at the back of supermarkets; I've seen them with bits of pipe. They're using them to smoke crack."

"Pavel doesn't smoke crack."

"Rose, I think we're starting to make some progress here, but you're not necessarily going to like what we find."

"Bernard, what the hell are you talking about? I know my own brother."

"Rose, even if I'm right, it's not the end of the world. I really think your brother was doing crack. Look here," he said, directing me to the bend of the pipe with his finger. "That's not tobacco ash or dust, Rose. It's crack."

"Are you sure?"

"I'm pretty sure. Now, get in the car, drink your coffee and we'll talk about this in the time we have left."

He held on to the pipe and we went back to sit next to each other in the car.

"Look, the first time you find out someone in your family is using drugs, it's always a shock. Your first impulse is to deny it."

"Bernard, you don't know that this is crack residue."

"Yes, I do."

"How do you know? When have you ever seen crack before?"

"Rose, I've seen it. Believe me."

"I don't believe you."

"No, you mean you don't trust my judgment. You do believe me."

"Okay, then I don't trust your judgment."

"Trust me," he said, drowning in coffee a capsule he had placed on his tongue. "This is a pipe with crack residue which I found in the unit your brother was living in before he disappeared. Think about it. Somebody was using crack at his place. You said he was buying new clothes in the period before he disappeared."

"Yeah, so what?"

"It means he had money."

"Wait a minute. You find a length of dusty pipe among some rags in my brother's flat and now all of a sudden he's a drug dealer?"

"Well, I don't know. Maybe something like that. It would explain a lot."

"What would it explain?"

"Rose, I think his disappearance is something to do with crack."

"How addictive is crack?"

"Extremely addictive. You said he'd been pretty unhappy. He could have gotten hooked on it very quickly," Bernard said soberly.

"What's that capsule you just took?"

"It's an antibiotic. I've had a really nagging chest infection. Started as a throat thing . . . well, first a flu-type cold that really hung on, then a throat thing which has now gone to my chest. I'm okay, though."

"Well, even if it *is* crack, what do we do now? How does it help us find him?"

"If it *is* crack, and I'm almost certain it is, then, Rose, we have to find the local source of it because it's probably the reason he's gone missing. Where was he getting it? Since he didn't have a car or any money, at least at the start, chances are it was someone who operated in the vicinity of where he was staying who was supplying him with the stuff. If this guy was supplying him, he'd be supplying other users in the area. People will know. We have to find those people."

"Who, the other crack users in the area?"

"Yes."

"How are we going to do that?"

"You go back to work and I'll get out of this loading zone. I'll meet you back here after work. When do you knock off?"

"Five thirty."

"Will you want something to eat?"

"Bernard, what are you going to do between now and five thirty?"

"I can't tell you."

"Because you don't know."

"Look, I've got a day and a half to find your brother. I think we're making excellent progress. You haven't even had to take the day off work. You really should try to be a little more supportive . . . perhaps even encouraging."

"I'm sorry, Bernard."

"I understand. You're under stress. This is not about me, except in a peripheral way. I'll see you back here at five thirty."

I didn't know anything about crack or metal pipes. I knew very little about Bernard and I was starting to think that I knew

even less about Pavel. The more I thought about it, the more it
made sense. Why couldn't Pavel use crack? What was there to
keep him from using it: a sense of well-being, friends, a girlfriend, a job with a future? His father was falling apart. Why
not the son? Every day he went out and cracked his head open on
the English language. Every day he saw people looking at him,
and what they saw was young, foreign, poor and stupid. That's
the way he saw it. His father was a public embarrassment and a
private source of eternal conflict. His mother was a fountain of
anxiety about which he felt guilty and powerless. And I? In the
pursuit of my own survival, I had let him go.

Bernard had bought me a salad roll for dinner.

"I hope you like salad. Do you like salad?"

"Yes."

"Good. I didn't know whether to get them to leave out the
beetroot. I like beetroot myself but I can't eat it."

"Why? Are you allergic?"

"No, I always get it all over me. Especially in a car situation.
Beetroot is very dangerous around me, also chocolate-coated ice
cream. I really should only eat certain foods with a plate. Even
then—"

"Bernard, have you found out anything?"

"Yes, I have. There is a group of kids, teenage boys who hang
around the station not far from Pavel's flat. They probably know
something."

"About Pavel?"

"About crack. They probably know how to get it locally."

"How do you know they know?"

"There are empty vials around the station. I've seen them on the ground. If those kids aren't actually taking it themselves, they know who is."

"So what are you suggesting we do, go and wait at the station?"

"Rose, you don't have to go. I can call you if I find out anything."

"No, no. I'll come with you. What else should I be doing?"

Within twenty-four hours of meeting him, I found myself trusting Bernard Leibowitz with the safe return of my brother. Should I have gone to the police? Should I have told my parents? Was Pavel using crack? Was that why he had disappeared? Why did I think that waiting in a car outside a suburban railway station for a group of disaffected adolescent boys would help me find my brother?

The sun had gone down. We had already waited forty minutes and seen nothing but people getting off trains: men and women in suits, mothers trying to carry their babies and hang on to small children, the adult children of immigrants and the young unemployed in stonewashed jeans. Schoolchildren had come and gone. Tradesmen were rare, office workers more common, each with a briefcase or a bag of some kind. They took themselves each day to and from that part of their lives that was evaluated by reference to their age. Not yet a junior manager, but then, not yet twenty-seven. Still a junior manager and almost thirty-seven. They took the train every day and never spoke to anyone. They never had the chance to while away the hours sitting in a car with Bernard Leibowitz.

"Bernard, how do you know about vials and pipes? How do you know about crack?"

"I've been around . . . more than you think."

The flashing light of the pizza place across the street lit and unlit one side of his face. It seemed unusual, in my recent but concentrated experience of him, for him not to want to talk of his past, not to want to shed light on his experience.

"Was it through one of your jobs? You've told me all the different jobs you've had, but none of them . . . well, none that I can remember, sounded like it offered an opportunity for close contact with any drugs."

"Well, actually that's not right but . . . that's not where I learned—"

"Bernard, have *you* used it?"

"No, no . . . been offered, though."

"Where?"

"Oh, you know . . . here and there . . . nightclubs."

"Do you go to nightclubs?"

"Why is that so surprising?" he asked, a little hurt.

"Do you?" I repeated.

"Not anymore . . . used to . . . when I was younger."

"Bernard, you've never really seen any crack, have you? It's all right, you know. You can admit it."

He turned to face me. The light from the pizza place lit and unlit the back of his head. On and then off, on and then off. I saw in his face for the first time the look of a man who has lived more than once that hour when worlds collapse.

"Adam was mixed up in it."

"Adam, your brother, the one who lives in Israel?"

"Yes."

He took a deep breath of the kind one takes before telling a story one almost doesn't tell.

"I don't think I have told you much about my mother, have I? Where do I start? Both my parents went through the Holocaust. They didn't know each other before the war. They met in a displaced-persons' camp, married and came out here in the late forties. They didn't know any English before they got here, didn't know anything about this place, didn't really know anything about each other. This seemed the farthest place away from Europe. They were teenagers. That's all they were. They couldn't have known even themselves.

"They had come from . . . I can only try to imagine it. You know, they say there are two common responses of survivors to the Holocaust: one is never to talk about it, the other is to talk about it incessantly. That's obviously an oversimplification, but my father reacted by almost never talking about it while my mother always wanted to talk about it. My father, who had come from a secular home, became increasingly religious after the war. Apparently he was barely observant at all before the war. My mother had no time for religion at all. She said that she had seen huge chimneys belching out smoke from the burning bodies of the people from her town, from the town next to hers, the town next to that and from every town she had ever heard of. She saw it, Rose. Day after day, hour after hour, it never stopped. We cannot imagine it. She saw people come in and smoke go out way up into the air where God was supposed to be.

"As children we heard her in the middle of the night. She would wake up screaming. She used to sleep in a separate room to my father because she needed to sleep with the television on."

"Why?"

"In case she had a nightmare. She often had nightmares. The television would immediately remind her that her screams belonged to the past and that this was the present, the death camps were behind her. She had a husband now, two sons, a job."

"Where did she work?"

"In a bakery. Posner's bakery."

"Near the shoe repair shop?"

"Yes, that belongs to a fellow called Kuznetsov now. He's Russian. Do you know him?"

"My mother works there."

"For Kuznetsov?"

"Yes."

"Really! He's a good man. Kuznetsov! What a . . . world."

"You were telling me about your mother. . . ."

"She was one of those who was always talking about it. She would tell us, Adam and me, stories, hundreds and hundreds of stories. She told the story of the two-year-old boy who was smuggled out of his parents' house after his mother was shot there. The mother had been ill when the Germans came and when they saw that she was unable to get out of bed, they shot her as she lay in bed. The father took the child to the house of a nearby Polish woman. The Polish woman didn't know what to do with the two-year-old boy so she put him under the bed. He stayed under the bed or else in a cupboard for four years. He had to be taught to walk. The children of the Polish woman were afraid their mother would be found out and shot in the street, as they had seen happen to other Poles who were hiding Jews. They hated the little Jewish boy. They would beat him.

"A story like this we might hear at breakfast before going to school. Then at night some more with dinner and then she would put us to bed. Sometime in the middle of the night we would hear her screaming. My father would come in and try to comfort her, but if he mentioned God or if she heard him pray for her, she would throw something at him. I think it wasn't that she didn't believe in God, it was rather that she blamed him."

"What about her?"

"What do you mean?"

"What's her story?"

"Well, it's funny to say this but, as many stories as she would tell, she was always sketchy about the details of her experience. We knew how her family was rounded up, we knew about the ghetto. She lost a lot of her family in the ghetto from disease and starvation. A brother was shot trying to escape. A sister was in the resistance. We knew she was in Auschwitz, like my father, but we don't know how she survived. Adam and I speculated privately but we couldn't bring ourselves to ask her. She was in the part which had factories, not in the extermination part in Auschwitz II, or Birkenau, as it was called. Nobody survived from there. Despite all the neuroses she was left with, she was a great mother. Does that sound strange?"

"No."

"I mean . . . she was obsessed with her children. Every little thing we did was important, special. Our friends, our school results. It wasn't enough just to bring home drawings from school. She wanted us to explain them. There was nothing to explain but she wanted meaning. Usually there wasn't any. It was a very intense household. Nothing was ever light. She stuffed us with food, with stories of the war . . ."

"And with love."

"And with love. Yes, so much love you could touch it. That's why, when she died, Adam just fell apart."

"Was she ill?"

"She committed suicide almost nine years ago."

What must that day have been like, the day he learned of his mother's suicide? Or did he find her? I was unable to ask him this, just as I was unable to ask him how she committed suicide. It really didn't matter *how*. I thought of him reliving it in his mind in the years since she did it. And I thought of this as he talked. It was not long after this, he told me, that he came to learn the difference between rock salt and crack and about the use of L-shaped domestic plumbing pipes of the kind he had found loose in my brother's unit. His brother had taught him all about it. This was how he knew what my brother was doing. I had chosen well out of the phone book.

Bernard told me how Adam had started coming to him for money. Adam would have known that Bernard was unlikely to have any, working one or two of his precarious jobs and having just started studying a trade at night school. But he came anyway because he needed it, and when he came he looked gaunt and distracted. He was moody, sullen or else obnoxious in a way he had never been before. At first Bernard had taken all of this to be Adam's reaction to his mother's death. But the mood swings were so wild. Then he found the vials.

Bernard hadn't known what to do. He knew that it would finish his father off to find Adam like this. His father was in a deep depression as it was. He had blamed himself for his wife's suicide, at least for missing the signs. But there had been signs since 1945. Bernard was afraid of forcing his brother to seek proper medical attention in case there was some mandatory legal requirement for doctors to report crack addicts to the police. What did he know about any of this? Whose brother uses crack? His. Mine.

In desperation he bundled Adam into his car one day while Adam was high and took him to Bernard's then girlfriend's place. They locked him in a room there while Bernard made discreet inquiries about the length of time it takes a crack user to detox. His girlfriend took it upon herself to look after Adam whenever Bernard went to check on his father. After five days Adam had cleaned out his system, but Bernard knew that it would take more than five days to turn his brother around completely. Having made some calls to an old school friend then living in Israel, Bernard borrowed money against his portion of his mother's share of the house and sent Adam to his friend in Israel. It seemed that Adam has not looked back. Nor has he been back in nine years.

Since then Bernard has looked after his father by himself. His father had become more difficult and taciturn in recent years. If he talked at all it was generally to himself.

"What does he say?"

"Often I can't tell, because it's not in English. But for years I've heard him rumble to himself, 'I am eighteen and I have a trade. I am eighteen and I have a trade.' Just like that. You understand what he's saying, don't you?"

I didn't understand but I let it go. "It can't be easy living with him," I said.

"It's not so hard. And in the absence of anyone else in my life, how can I leave him alone? He's getting older faster than most people. He's seen his family shot. He's been through Auschwitz. His wife is dead and he blames himself. I'm all he's got now."

There was so much more to Bernard Leibowitz than I had suspected. I thought that if I had been half as strong as he was, my brother would have been safe and we would not be parked outside a railway station, waiting for scraps of information to help us find him. This man next to me, with his ridiculous ties, had learned to take his distress, bundle it up and store it somewhere away from himself so that he was able to tackle each day anew. Now he was trying to help me find my brother.

"And the girlfriend?" I asked.

"We're still in touch. She's a really good person but . . . I can't really blame her." He looked at his hands. "I'm pushing forty and not looking . . . Well, she's with a guy who can take care of her now, not in some distant future. He's a nice guy, too, from what I can tell."

"'Take care of her'?"

"Don't you want someone to take care of you, Rose?"

"I've never really thought about it."

"She'd thought about it. She's a lot older than you. She wanted children before she got too much older, and I've never really looked like the kind of guy who could be counted on to feed them."

Bernard sat forward and leaned on the steering wheel. It was dark by then. He was looking toward the station. Seven or so boys were smoking, skateboarding and shaking up cans of spray paint. There was no one else around. Bernard told me to stay in the car and I did, until I saw him go to the boot and take out the metal pipe. We were in the shadows of a railway station, where all the Met warning signs and designated safe areas did nothing to dispel even the menace of a well-aimed spit from a kid with a baseball cap turned back to front.

I got out of the car sufficiently behind Bernard for him not to hear me close the door. If he had heard me he would have sent me back to the car. It shouldn't have been dangerous. Wasn't he just going to ask these kids some questions? But it looked dangerous. I wasn't going to watch from the car.

Bernard walked toward them at an even pace. He carried the pipe nonchalantly by his side in one hand. Up closer, these boys were more like men. Two of them were leaning against a wall, one lighting the other's cigarette. Another one skateboarded around them, doing tricks, perhaps trying to get the attention of the one who'd had his cigarette lit. A little further along two others were spraying something on the wall, talking to each other and laughing in bizarre staccato bursts. Bernard approached the smoker but was addressed suddenly before he had a chance to speak. The others stopped to watch.

"What the fuck do you want, mister?"

"I just want to ask you a couple of questions," Bernard said, far too politely.

"Why don't you read the timetable, like everybody else?"

At this they all laughed. Bernard continued walking up to him.

"I don't want to talk about the timetable," Bernard said.

"Yeah, well, I don't want to talk to you at all, so why don't you piss off before you regret coming here."

"Just a couple of quick questions, okay?"

"You're not a cop, are you?"

"No, I'm not a cop."

"Shit, I didn't think they'd got that desperate."

They all laughed again. Bernard was out of his depth. He moved even closer.

"I want to talk to you about crack."

"Yeah, well, I don't want to talk to you about anything at all, so why don't you get the fuck out of here before I knock your teeth down your throat."

"Where can you buy crack around here?" Bernard asked, still in a quiet voice.

"Don't you understand English, you fuckwit?" he said, pushing Bernard in the chest.

"Look, I don't want any trouble."

"Well, you're gonna get a whole lot of trouble any second now," he said, pushing him again.

"Look, I'm trying to be polite to you boys. I just want to know where a person could buy some crack around here."

At this, the kid grabbed Bernard by the scruff of his neck and, between clenched teeth, snarled, "I don't want to talk to a piece of shit like you about crack or anything, ever, understand?"

"See, I'll go if you'll just tell me."

At this the boy released him, pulled out a knife and put it to his throat. I called out Bernard's name but he was the only one of all of them not to look at me. He stared straight at his tormentors. If I had not seen what happened next I would never have believed it.

In a fluid instant Bernard raised the metal pipe in his hand and, moving back one step, knocked the knife out of the kid's hand. Then he leaned forward and pressed the pipe against the kid's neck, pushing him against the wall, and said in the same quiet voice, "Listen, you little neo-Nazi piece of shit, if you tell me where I can buy crack around here I'll remove this from your neck and let you breathe again. If you don't tell me immediately, I'm going to kill you. Now, it might occur to you that I'm bluffing, but then it should also occur to you that not all crazy sons of bitches look like you, so I might not be bluffing and it is absolutely not in your interest to find out. Your friends won't help you because if I'm crazy enough to kill you just for some lousy information, then I'm crazy enough to go after them. Of course, I won't get them all. I won't even get most of them. But I'll probably get at least one of them and that's what they're thinking right now and that's why they're not doing anything except waiting to see what I'm going to do to you if you don't tell me where they sell crack around here. So now that you're fully apprised of the situation insofar as it concerns your continuing to breathe, I'll ask you again: Where can I buy crack around here?"

"Take it easy, will you! Y' can get it at Ziggy's."

"Ziggy's on the junction, the karaoke place?"

"Yeah."

"Well, that wasn't too hard, really, was it? If you had only been cooperative to start with, you wouldn't feel so bad right now." With that, Bernard stepped back and forced the air out of the kid's chest with one end of the metal pipe. The kid immediately doubled over while the others looked on in horror. Bernard turned around, kicked the knife off the platform onto the tracks and started walking back towards the car, swinging the pipe wildly in front of him. The others parted for him like the Red Sea. He grabbed my hand and opened the car door for me. He had already started the engine before I had a chance to say anything.

"Bernard!"

"Thank God the car started."

"Bernard!"

"What? I think that was useful."

"What made you think they're neo-Nazis?"

"They're not neo-Nazis. They're dangerous but they're not neo-Nazis," he said dismissively. "Why d'you ask that?"

"You called him a neo-Nazi piece of shit."

"Oh yeah. I always find it helps me in sticky situations to depict an antagonist as a Nazi. I lose my inhibitions that way. I don't have anything against Arabs."

"You just became someone else."

"No I didn't. I'm still the guy you called to find your brother. Have you ever tried karaoke?"

———

I had seen Ziggy's from the outside many times but never really registered what it was. By day it was a broken-down watering hole for dribbling old men in need of a shower, a shave, new clothes, some food and a past that did not send them back to Ziggy's every day. By night it was much sadder than this. Not all of its flashing lights flashed every time. Some of them stayed off. Even its mirror ball was sad. Suspended from the ceiling, it looked atrophied and told the story of the club's owner at the time of refurbishment opting for the cheapest and smallest of everything. This included the television screens suspended in front of the stage for the karaoke singers. Good eyesight was more of a prerequisite for aspiring singers here than a good voice.

The carpet was thin and sticky, so that when we walked in my feet stuck to the floor and every step was a distinct effort as though small weights had been attached to my shoes. The air was thick with cigarette smoke and beer. We sat down at a table in the middle of a rendition of "Let It Be" by a fifty-something Japanese man in a suit. He had loosened his tie and in my hour of darkness he was standing right in front of me. Our table was next to the one he had come from. I inferred this from the fact that there were four other fifty-something Japanese men in suits sitting there. Three of them had young blond women in tight short skirts sitting on their laps.

"How does this work?" I whispered to Bernard, gesticulating towards the young women on the laps of the Japanese men.

"For a little extra you can pay them to sit on your lap."

"Are they prostitutes?" I asked.

"Sort of. Not really . . . little bit."

"You don't know, do you?"

He didn't respond and instead was looking around him. The place was crowded. We were lucky to get a table. There were people there of all ages. Our table had a drinks menu on it with the usual array of overpriced sticky drinks named after parts of the human genitalia or else after variations of the sexual act. But the titles didn't seem to promote their purchase, since most of the men appeared to be drinking beer and the women white wine or else champagne. Only the Japanese men and the young women on their laps appeared to be drinking anything sticky with milk in it. This was presumably due to the strength of the yen.

Bernard looked at the drinks menu and offered to buy me one.

"Just a mineral water, thanks."

"Really, that's all?"

"Yes, but you have whatever you like."

"No, I'm working, remember . . . and driving."

I thought that Bernard probably couldn't hold his drink, but then, he was full of surprises. I watched him get up and make his way through the crowd to the bar, such a strange mix of almost childlike politeness, a certain naïveté, zen acceptance of his lot and unexpected flashes of streetwise cunning and determination. Was this going to get me to my brother? The Japanese man had almost finished. *There will be an answer. Let it be.* He missed the top note but his compatriots didn't seem to mind. They, along with the blond women in their laps, cheered enthusiastically on his return to their table. How was any of this going to lead us to Pavel?

Bernard returned with two mineral waters and some sort of

cocktail. He placed them on the table with the cocktail between the two glasses of mineral water. The DJ was shouting for more volunteers.

"What's this?" I asked Bernard.

"I thought we could share it. I'm past the contagious stage."

"What is it?"

He had forgotten and had to consult the menu.

"It's called a . . . Purple Vulva."

"Bernard, what are we going to do?"

"We are going to drink our drinks and then show Pavel's photo to the bar staff, see if any of them recognize him."

We finished our drinks to the accompaniment of two under-age girls singing "Fernando."

"The one on the left was quite good, I thought," Bernard said as they got off the stage to drunken applause and catcalls and we made our way to the bar. We had to wait to get the attention of the bar staff. Bernard had the photo of Pavel I had sent him in his hand. It was dark, crowded and noisy at the bar, and it took more than five minutes to have the two men and one woman serving shake their heads and volunteer that they had never seen my brother in all of their sun-filled lives.

There was one member of staff we had not approached. She had served at the bar earlier but was now going from table to table collecting empty glasses. There was something about her that made me think she was the least experienced of the bar staff. Bernard pointed her out and told me she had been the one who had served him. Three men got up to sing "American Pie," much as the DJ begged them to reconsider and choose something else.

"I love this song," Bernard said as we made our way to the last member of the bar staff.

"Excuse me, have you ever seen this man?" said Bernard, showing her the photograph.

She looked up without stopping, as the men sang, *A long, long time ago* . . . Bernard followed her to the next table with the photograph still displayed before she said no and moved on to the table after that.

"She's lying," I said to Bernard.

"What?" he asked as the men sang, *Oh I knew if I'd had my chance* . . .

"She's lying. I can see it. Give me the photo."

He gave me the photograph and I followed the woman to the side of the bar where she stacked the empty glasses she'd collected on a wire grille tray and put them in a dishwasher to be washed. As soon as she had programmed the dishwasher I tapped her on the shoulder.

"Excuse me, have you seen this young man?"

"No," she said without looking at the photograph.

"Please have a look. It's important."

"Are you from the police? I don't know that guy. I've got work to do."

"Please, miss. I'm not from the police. I think you know him."

"What if I do?"

"I'm trying to find him. He's my brother."

She looked at me for the first time and told me to wait there. She went to the dishwasher and removed the clean glasses. I gestured to Bernard across the room. The woman came back to me and told me to follow her. She led me behind the bar, out through the kitchen into an alley and asked to see the photograph again.

"Are you really Paul's sister?"

"Pavel. My name is Rose."

"Everyone here knows him as Paul. I'm Yvonne."

She stuck her hand out for me to shake before lighting a cigarette, which she kept behind her back.

"So you know him? Is he all right? Do you know where he is?"

"When did you last see him?" Yvonne asked.

"About ten or so days ago. Is he all right?"

Yvonne let out a long stream of smoke through her nostrils. "He's a really sweet guy, your brother."

"I know. Is he all right?"

"No," she said, "he's not. He's in trouble."

"What kind of trouble?"

"It's not uncommon around here . . . at least . . . part of it."

"What is it?"

"He's been using."

"What? Crack?"

"Yeah, they get it here. Paul was using pretty heavily."

"Is he addicted?"

"I'd say he was. . . . I know he is. But it's worse than that now."

"Why?"

"He didn't have much money to begin with, but his habit got so bad the dealer offered to let him start selling for him. Paul was going to sell this guy's stuff to pay for his own use. Problem was, when he took his first supply, three thousand dollars' worth, he got jumped just taking it home. Now he's three thousand in debt to a dealer who'd promised to get him if Paul cheated him."

"But he didn't cheat him," I argued.

"No. Of course not. Paul wouldn't cheat anyone. I don't think he'd know how. He's one of the nicest people I've ever met. But as far as the dealer is concerned, Paul owes him three thousand and now he's gone missing on him."

"Missing?"

"Yeah. Paul is scared. He's gone into hiding 'cause this guy promised him trouble if Paul went out on his own or used it all himself."

"Do you know where he is?"

She did not want to tell me. She thought she was protecting him. He had been ignored by the world until all of a sudden he had woken up in the eye of a hurricane. What Yvonne knew was no rumor. She knew where he was. She cared where he was. She cared too much to tell me.

"It's not you," she said apologetically.

"No, it *is* me. I'm his sister. I'm not going to hurt him. I want to help him."

"It's just that he's scared to death that they're going to find him and he hasn't got the money. He's scared of what they'll do to him and he's right to be."

"Yvonne, I'm his sister. Do you think I'm going to tell people where he is? Who's going to help him if not me?"

She looked up at me. "I'm trying to help him."

"Is he with you? Is he staying with you?"

She thought for a moment and then nodded. She did care for him. I looked at her anew. No one had ever cared for him in the way that she did. I could see it in her eyes. Slightly older than he, she had been around the block a few times, stopping off to pick up empty glasses at a karaoke bar here and there, but she had a soft spot for my brother. She was putting herself at risk for him and she knew it. She scribbled her address for me on the back of his photograph.

Bernard seemed a little reluctant to leave the bar, and under the circumstances I didn't feel comfortable telling him what had happened until we were alone.

"You know they don't use the actual video clips."

"Really?" I said, trying to get him to hurry.

"No, and I think the words on the screen shouldn't be relied on, either. Take 'American Pie.' You know 'American Pie'?"

"Not really," I said, dragging him towards the door.

"Everyone knows 'American Pie.'"

"I'm Russian."

"Well, I think they got the refrain wrong. It read on the screen: *Well I know that you're in love with him 'cause I saw you dancing in the gym.* I don't think that's how it goes."

"Bernard," I said as he closed the car door, "I've found him."

If someone phones to tell you that your child is in a certain hospital, you will drop everything and get to the hospital as quickly as you can. And to survive in the meantime you pull a blankness over your mind's eye to try to block out the blitzkrieg of images that lie in ambush. You want to put off knowing, to hang on to hope, and yet, you want to know as soon as possible. I was in a hurry, not merely to know all the grim details but to know whether there was still time for me to help him. It was a miracle that we had tracked him to Yvonne's home, and it was all Bernard's doing. It should not have annoyed me when he wanted to stop off at the 7-Eleven before going there. I tried not to show it.

"This won't take a second. Really it won't. It's just around the corner from the address she gave us. I just want to buy something to drink. I'll be quick. Do you want something?" Bernard asked.

"You just *had* a drink."

"I know, but I forgot to take the antibiotic and I try to take it at exactly the prescribed intervals so that if the infection doesn't clear up, at least I'll know I've done everything I can."

"Okay, okay. We'll go." It wouldn't take long.

He swung the car into the empty car park of the 7-Eleven and parked. He asked me again if I wanted anything as we approached the automatic sliding doors. There was no one else around. Bernard went to the refrigerated section at the back and the world stopped. The world that I knew stopped. Frozen-yogurt cups, glossy magazines, potato chips, tinned spaghetti and doughnuts under glass, all bathed in a yellow light. I had seen them all before under that light but never had I seen him that way, my brother and not my brother, about to change everything irrevocably.

Skinny, in a loud orange-and-black-checked flannel shirt with his back to me, he moved in slow motion. Though his voice was thin and reedy and his behavior bereft of all reason, I could see it was him. I could see it in the way he stood, slightly bowlegged, another thing we were always going to look into as soon as we could, as soon as we got to the end of the tightrope, as soon as the fire was put out, as soon as we were each somebody else. By the time I got close enough to touch this skinny, distorted man that was my brother, but before I could say anything, I saw him pull a kitchen knife on the 7-Eleven clerk and insist in a nervous Russian English that the clerk empty the till. I put my hand on his shoulder and called out.

"Pavel, no!"

He turned to me. The clerk moved back towards the wall behind the counter and picked up a golf club. Pavel's eyes were glassy. There was stubble on his face and he seemed to have

THE REASONS I WON'T BE COMING

regressed physically. He was smaller. He was stoned. The clerk took a swing from behind the counter. He missed Pavel only by chance when Pavel moved away from my outstretched hand.

"No, no, no," Bernard called out, running from the back of the shop. "This is all wrong. This is the wrong place. This guy thinks you're serious. It's not the right store."

I had Pavel's hand in mine and the kitchen knife lay on the ground by his side as Bernard took center stage and we watched him.

"You thought this was a real holdup, didn't you?" he said, addressing the clerk.

"It looked pretty real to me."

"Well, in a way I'm glad you say that, but I'm afraid we owe you a very big apology. My name is Bernard Leibowitz. I'm a playwright and theatre director and these two are actors in the cast of my new play *Hold Up*. Well, that's the working title. It's a little, I don't know, stereotypically urban but . . . We have permission to rehearse in a 7-Eleven store in East St. Kilda and these two have turned up in the wrong store. You see, the whole thing takes place in a 7-Eleven store. I really am so sorry. Did you really think it was the real thing?"

"Of course. A guy pulls a knife on you—"

"Yes, but he was too slow, too timid." Bernard picked up the knife and began to demonstrate. "Empty the till!" he shouted. "Empty the till!"

"No, that's *too* much," said the clerk. "People don't really do it that way."

"Really?"

"No, no, the kid is right. Armed robbers always give away something, some sign that shows they're scared."

"You've been robbed here?"

"Oh yeah. A few times."

"That's terrible. Do you like the theatre?"

"I do, but I usually see movies 'cause they're cheaper and you can fast-forward the bits you don't like."

"That's so true. Well, look, I'm terribly sorry for the mixup. But you were scared, a bit? You're not just saying it because . . . we have to know . . . we've got to get it right."

"A little bit scared."

"That's great. You were good playing along with the whole golf club thing. Have you ever acted? Let me get these Cokes, 'cause we're actually running a bit late. What was your name?" Bernard asked, giving the clerk his money.

"Paul."

"Paul what?"

"Paul Chandler."

"Pleased to meet you, Paul. I'll write that down. Bernard Leibowitz," he said as they shook hands. "I'll send you two tickets when we open. Should be in about three weeks."

"Great."

"Come on you two, let's go. We're late. See you, Paul. Again, we're really sorry."

"Hey," the clerk called out as the three of us walked out, "what happens in the end?"

"We're workshopping it. You take care of yourself," Bernard called.

Bernard started the car. I sat in the back with Pavel and started yelling at him until Bernard told me to stop.

"He's stoned, Rose."

"Who's he?" Pavel asked.

"His name is Bernard. He's your guardian angel."

"Is he your boyfriend?"

"I'm a private investigator," Bernard called from the front seat.

We drove to the edge of a park where I could interrogate Pavel without disturbing anybody. Everything Yvonne had told us was true. Bernard let me ask the questions, mostly in Russian, although it seemed that Pavel's English had improved. He had developed a crack habit he couldn't sustain. He had first bought a few vials from the tough guys at the station. They were the ones who taught him about pipes and then sent him on to Ziggy's when he needed more. The pipe Bernard had found in his unit was the first he had ever tried. It was too big, an inefficient use of the rock, so he left it behind. If Pavel had got it right the first time, we would never have found him. Unable to pay for the quantity he was soon using, he agreed to sell crack for the dealer from Ziggy's in order to support his own habit. He had taken delivery of three thousand dollars' worth to sell on the streets but he was robbed by someone whom Pavel suspected knew the dealer at Ziggy's. It had to be a setup. He was jumped on his way home from Ziggy's. All of it was taken. Now he was a crack addict, three thousand dollars in debt to his supplier, strung out and in hiding. The dealer at Ziggy's had warned him that he would be "just so much raw meat" if the stuff was used or sold without being paid for. Pavel had been a probationary dealer, a learner dealer, and had failed.

"If it wasn't for Yvonne, I might be dead already," Pavel stuttered between sobs.

"I don't think they'd kill you for three thousand dollars," Bernard sought to assure him.

"Why not?" he asked.

"'Cause when someone is as desperate as you are, they'll do nearly anything, and a person who'll do nearly anything is worth more than three thousand dollars to the people you're afraid of."

I felt numb. I vacillated between anger, sadness and fear for him. I was angry because it was all so unnecessary. He had brought it on himself in some pathetic adolescent assertion of his independence. How could he have done it? How could he have brought this on us? I was not as open-minded as I thought. It had seemed to me throughout my life that every uncertainty, every obstacle, every disaster that we had ever faced had been due to an authoritarian regime that the whole world knew about. Everybody knew about Stalin. Everybody knew about Brezhnev. But crack—who would understand this? Why should someone feel sorry for him? He had brought it upon himself. His problem was beneath us. I was angry.

Yet, looking at him in the backseat of Bernard's car, his body swimming in his shirt, his face pale and wet with tears, I managed at the same time to feel sorry for him. He was a sad little boy, my brother, an average boy of stifled adequacy, unblessed, whose normalcy was stolen from him by circumstances not only beyond his control, not only beyond his parents' control, but beyond his understanding. He did not even know how far back in time he would have to go to explain this almighty European river of hatred for a group he found himself born into, a group whose existence was for so long marginal, as marginal as his existence within it. Pavel was a prisoner of his foreignness, a little boy impersonating a man permanently in exile. The exile who succeeds through hard work and talent gains everybody's acceptance and even acclaim. But no one gets any acclaim for just getting out of bed day after day, for having a talent only for attracting derision, with his clothes, his looks, with the spittled noise that he tries to pass off as English. This was a boy who was never good at anything. At school he sat at the back and learned only to be himself. No one chose him to be in the team, in the play, in the club, in the band, to kiss behind the bike sheds. His clothes never fitted him. They smelled of Russia, of close living in small apartments. He was either invisible or else ridiculous. This was a scared and lonely young man who had never felt confident about anything and, on the basis of everything he had experienced, had no reason to expect that he ever would. With just a little bit of crack he could forget the way he always felt, forget his parents' shouting, their house-proud impoverishment. With just a little bit of crack he could feel the way he had heard a man is supposed to feel. He could speak better. He could be not afraid. He could be capable. He could go on to achieve something. Why would he ever want to be without it?

I was scared for him. I knew nothing about addiction, nothing about what it took to tear yourself away from the only thing that ever made you feel worthwhile, nothing about how long that took or what you had to go through to come out on the other side. Bernard knew. He knew from Adam.

"So what do we do now?" I asked him.

"He has to detox. We have to take him somewhere where he can detox."

"I can't go back to my unit. They'll kill me," Pavel whimpered.

"He can't be left alone," Bernard said.

"How long will it take him to detox?"

"Anywhere from two to five days. And they won't be fun days."

"I can't take him home to our parents like this. I don't know what it will do to them. I don't know what my father will do to him."

"Do you know anyone who could watch him for two to five days?"

"*I'll* watch him. That's not the problem. The problem is *where* to watch him. Where would I tell my parents I was staying. What do we do afterwards?"

"First things first: he has to detox," Bernard said.

"I can't go back to my place, they'll kill me. I owe them three thousand dollars."

"We'll take him back to my place," Bernard said.

"Really?"

"Why not. It's safe for him."

"What about your father?"

"It will test his religious convictions. It's a mitzvah," Bernard said.

"What's that?"

"A good deed."

"Bernard, it's not fair on your father."

"Rose, it's an emergency. Do you have any better ideas?"

Bernard's father lived in the middle of a narrow street of weatherboard houses guarded by trees planted by the early European settlers to drain the swamp they were building on. The street was crowded with old cars. Bernard parked in their driveway. The house was dark. The refrigerator hummed. The clock in the hall ticked. Bernard let us in while I tried to keep Pavel quiet.

We went to the front room, where Bernard switched on a lamp on a side table. There were black-and-white photographs in frames. It was too dark to make them out.

"You can stay in my brother's old room," Bernard said to Pavel. Then to me: "You're going to have to tell your parents something, Rose."

"I know," I said, looking beyond the light of the lamp and into the darkness. "I'll tell my mother something. Whatever I tell, I'll tell her first. What about your father?"

"I'm going to wake him now."

"Now?" I whispered in alarm.

"Rose, I have to. Pavel's not going to go to sleep and—"

"No, I will, I will," Pavel interrupted.

"Can't you wait till morning?" I begged him.

"Pavel may not let me. Detox is . . . well, it's not pleasant. I don't want my father waking to some strange sound in the middle of the night. He'll think he's back in the camps unless he realizes it's fifty years on and the noise is coming from the other room. Either way, I have to wake him."

I remained with Pavel in Adam's old room while Bernard went to wake his father. I heard him knock on his father's door and my heart sank. I could hear their muffled voices. A little while later Bernard called me into the kitchen and there was his father, sitting at the table in his summer pajamas, with the light off. I don't know why I was so unnerved by him. His arms, resting on the table, were illuminated by the light from the window. Beneath the hair on his left forearm I saw the number. I had never seen one before. I had heard about them, of course, read about them, but had never seen one. Bernard grew up seeing it at breakfast. His parents had been branded like cattle and he saw their numbers every day before school. One day, without warning, he saw his mother's number for the last time.

"You are Rose?" his father said in a quiet, accented voice.

"Yes."

"Bernard tells me you need help."

"Yes, Mr. Leibowitz, my brother is unwell."

"Drugs?"

"Yes."

"Do your parents know?"

"No."

"Do they know where you are?"

"No. When my mother hadn't heard from my brother for a number of days, she sent me to my brother's place to check up on him. I came back and told her he was fine, but the truth was he was missing. He'd moved out of his unit and I was worried something might have happened to him. I didn't know what to do. Bernard— Bernard helped me find him. When we found him he was . . . he'd started taking . . . it's called crack. . . . Nothing with needles."

"You are Bernard's friend?"

"Yes."

"Where do your parents think you are now?"

"Out with friends. I'm not sure where they think I am."

"Your family, you are Russian Jews?"

"Yes."

My eyes had filled. A tear spilled out onto my cheek. I did not want him to see it. I didn't know why I was crying. It annoyed me. I hadn't known I was even close to tears. He stood up, a shrunken man, too small to be the father of a bear. He got up from the table and put his hand to my face. It was warm. The skin on his palm was wrinkled and I cried even more.

"Rose," he whispered, "I want to help you. I will turn the light on and make us a cup of tea. You will tell me how I can help you." He turned the light on and went to the sink to fill the kettle.

"Your parents have two, yes? You and your brother?"

"Yes."

"No more?"

"No."

"Well, a boy and a girl. That's it, isn't it? There are no other kinds. I have two boys."

"Yes, I know. Adam is your other son."

"You know Adam?" His eyes lit up.

"No, Bernard has told me about him. He's in Israel now?"

"Yes . . . he's there and I am here."

"With Bernard."

"Yes. It's a hard life for him in Israel."

"It's a hard life everywhere," I offered, regretting it immediately. This man knew about hard lives. He didn't need any wisdom from me. He put the kettle on for a cup of tea.

"Well, Rose, if you are Russian you will know something about hard lives, even one as young as you."

I smiled weakly, not knowing what to say. My brother was high on crack in the other room and this man's son was watching over him. My parents were at home, my father probably in his chair watching late-night television, not understanding it all, my mother probably in bed staring at the ceiling, wondering where her children were. I was being made a cup of tea by a man who had seen, who had experienced, the worst the species had to offer. My eyes kept resting on the number. I tried not to let him see.

"You are a good sister to take care of your brother like this."

I didn't know how to answer this, either. I couldn't say anything that didn't sound trivial to this man with the number on his arm and the sad sunken eyes. Those eyes had seen it all. They had seen the dead piled high on top of each other. They had watered when ashes blew into them, the ashes of the Jews of Europe.

"You are looking at my arm, at the number." He had noticed.

"No, I was—"

"It's all right, Rose. I have had it a long time now. I was fifteen when it was given to me," he said bringing over the tea. "I was fifteen. I had already seen my father, my mother and two younger sisters lined up against the wall and shot. I saw it through a gap in a neighbor's fence. By the time I was on the train to Auschwitz I was long an orphan. There was time to think on the trains. I thought of my family, just gone. I hallucinated. All those people crammed together, no air, no water. I kept mistaking shapes in the dark at the other end of the cattle car for my father, my sisters, my mother. By the time we got there I had seen men and women die standing up. I had seen children smothered under the weight of people struggling to be near a crack in the wooden doors for air, for moisture. The train slowed. We could hear the dogs in the distance. When they opened the doors the light was blinding. We shielded our eyes. The dogs were straining on their leashes to get at us; they were deafening. The SS were shouting at us to hurry off the trains. They beat us into a formation for the first *Selektion* to see who would go straight to the gas. Most were to be gassed within twenty-four hours. You cannot imagine the scene. No one could invent this nightmare.

"People had brought suitcases with them on the train. They carried them into line until they were ordered to drop them. We saw skeletons in striped uniforms, their eyes bulging out of their faces. They came to pick up the belongings people had dropped. I had nothing but a coat. An SS guard ordered me to drop it. One of the skeletons came to take my coat. He came very near to me. All the while the dogs were barking and the people from the train were being beaten, crying, screaming, into a line. He came to me, this skeleton. I don't know why he chose me, but without looking at me he muttered underneath his breath, 'I am eighteen and I have a trade. I am eighteen and I have a trade. You must say it or you will not see the morning.'

"I have said it every day since, like a prayer. *I am eighteen and I have a trade. I am eighteen and I have a trade.*" He sipped his tea. He lifted his eyes from his teacup and spoke as if confessing, "I have said it every day. It's worked so far."

It was agreed that I should go home. I wanted to walk. It was only a couple of kilometers and I didn't want to leave Mr. Leibowitz alone with Pavel. But it was unthinkable to both Bernard and his father that I should walk home alone in the dark. Bernard's father had suddenly become a member of the cast. Mr. Leibowitz told me that Pavel could stay with them for the period of his detoxification on one condition: that I told my parents where he was and why. I tried to bargain with him. I told him I would tell them *where* he was, but not *why.* This was unacceptable to him. We settled on *one* of my parents and *why*, and it had to be tomorrow. I did better than that. I was forced to.

Bernard drove me home and when I got there my father was asleep but my mother was up, sitting in the dark. She didn't know whether to hug me or shout at me. Where had I been? Who had I been with? How had I got home? Had I seen Pavel? I sat beside her in the dark and told her everything: about

Pavel's empty flat, Bernard's listing in the telephone directory, the crack pipe Bernard found in Pavel's flat and how he used it on the tough kids at the station, about Ziggy's, the dealer and about Yvonne. I told her about Pavel's attempt to rob the 7-Eleven and Bernard's impromptu theatre workshop and, of course, about Mr. Leibowitz.

At first she wanted to go to the Leibowitzes' immediately but I managed to talk her out of it. She asked why Pavel was there with them and not recovering at home. I told her that I didn't think Pavel and my father should see each other until Pavel had gone through the detoxification period.

"But I'll have to tell him. He's his son, too, and if I tell him he'll want to see him."

"It won't do either of them any good, Mum," I explained. She thought about this and I took her silence as tacit agreement. It was two o'clock in the morning. The only way I could get her to go to bed was to promise to take her to Pavel in the morning.

She called Kuznetsov at home first thing the next morning to tell him she would not be coming in that day. Why? Was she sick? What was wrong? Kuznetsov would not rest. He wanted to know everything. My mother was whispering. She didn't want my father to hear.

"It's my son, Pavel. He's in trouble."

She hung up in a hurry when she heard my father getting up from the kitchen. He would have seen her putting the phone down. She tried to preempt any questioning from him about the phone call.

"Oh, you're showered and dressed already," she said to him.

"Who were you whispering to so early in the morning?"

"It's not so early."

"Was it him?"

"Who?"

"You know who I mean. It was, wasn't it? It was Kuznetsov."

"Yes."

"What are you whispering to Kuznetsov for? Isn't it enough that you'll spend all day with him?"

"You're being ridiculous. You know that."

I heard all of this and came in to try to help my mother but I couldn't think of anything to divert him, so I just asked whether she wanted the shower before me. The radio news was on. I couldn't hear it properly. There had been a bombing somewhere. My mother was floundering in the face of my father's interrogation. She tried to turn the conversation towards the question of who should use the shower next.

"Well, your father is already up and dressed," she said.

"What were you whispering about?" he continued.

"Are you running late, Rose?" my mother asked.

"Not especially," I answered uncertainly, not knowing what I was meant to say.

"What were you talking about?" my father persisted.

"What's wrong?" I asked, stalling for time.

"I was calling to tell him I wouldn't be coming in today."

"Why not?" my father demanded.

"Was there a bombing?" I asked.

"Yes," my father answered dismissively before continuing to my mother, "Why aren't you going to work today?"

"Where was the bombing?"

"Where do you think?" my father answered. "In Israel, on a bus. Why aren't you going to work today?" he said, turning his attention back to my mother.

There was a thud in my chest. Mitya. Nobody was more vulnerable than my bus-driving Kafka.

Somebody knocked at the door. My mother looked at me.

"Because I feel sick," she said.

"I'll get it," I said, walking to the door, the two of them waiting behind me to see who it was. I opened the door and then turned to see my parents' reaction. It was Kuznetsov.

"What are you doing here?" my mother asked in horror.

"You can't go one day without her?" my father shouted.

"Would you like to come in?" I asked him after a moment, and he did, brave man.

Kuznetsov was a small man. He wore round wire-framed eyeglasses in the style of Trotsky and, later, Lennon. He introduced himself with an apology, always a bad way to start with my father.

"I am sorry to visit you . . . unannounced . . ." he began.

"I think the correct English word is *uninvited*," my father interrupted.

"Yes . . . perhaps you are right . . . and I am sorry to have to meet you under these circumstances," he continued.

"What are 'these circumstances'?" my father inquired.

I looked at my mother, still in her nightgown, and thought she looked faint.

"I have only come like this because . . . I was worried . . . and thought that . . . perhaps I might be of some assistance."

"I cannot thank you enough for worrying about my wife the way you do. Every husband should be so fortunate as me in this regard."

"I was worried about her . . . and also—"

"Thank you, Sergei. We are fine," my mother interrupted.

"Also what?" my father demanded.

"Also . . . your son."

My father looked at my mother, who hid from his face by looking at me. I knew we had to tell him. I told my mother to have a shower and get dressed. I would tell my father and Mr. Kuznetsov the story. She agreed. It was, after all, my story. There was no alternative. The two of them sat next to each other in the living room listening to me without saying a word.

"But is he all right?" my father asked about Pavel when I had finished. He was stunned.

"Well, he's at the Leibowitzes' house with Bernard and his father."

"Why is he there?"

"He has a number of days to detoxify."

"Why can't he do that here?"

"Because you two don't get on at the best of times. If he were going through withdrawal around here, there would be a murder. Either he would kill you or you would kill him."

"No, it's not true." My father turned to Kuznetsov. "I love my son."

"I am sure you do," Kuznetsov volunteered, putting his hand on my father's shoulder as my mother reappeared.

She told me to go and have a shower. I heard Kuznetsov volunteer to drive us all to the Leibowitzes' house.

"What about the shop?" my mother asked.

"This is more important," he said.

My mother and I sat next to each other in the back. Mr. Kuznetsov drove and my father sat next to him. No one knew what to say until Kuznetsov spoke.

"Have you heard the news . . . about the bomb in Israel?"

"Yes," my father said, "yes, I heard."

"What happened?" my mother asked.

"There was an explosion on a bus in Israel."

"There were people killed?"

"Eleven, many more injured."

"It never stops," my mother said to herself.

It occurred to me when we got there that I should have called Bernard first to tell him we were coming. But the way it had happened, I just hadn't thought about it.

Bernard came to the door. I had asked the others to wait in the car. He told me his father had not slept.

"Because of Pavel?"

"No, because of the bomb in Israel."

Whenever there was a terrorist attack, Adam would call home. It was a promise their father had extracted from him. Adam had not called. I had forgotten that the Middle East conflict touched them personally. It was more true to say I had never thought about it. I had brought our hell to their place and the radio had home delivered their own. What made it even more frightening than usual, Bernard told me, was that the bus was on the Jerusalem–Tel Aviv route. Adam took that bus frequently. He lived in Jerusalem and had a girlfriend in Tel Aviv. Perhaps the buses Mitya drove went between Jerusalem and Tel Aviv. The thought filled me with terror. Bernard's father had not slept all night. He had listened to the news not long after I left. Pavel had slept through. He was taking a shower.

Bernard went to explain my situation to his father while I waited at the front door for instructions. He came back. His father said I should bring my parents inside. He would warn Pavel. I went to the car to explain things to them.

"The poor man," my mother said.

The first thing she said to him when she saw him in the kitchen was, "So you haven't heard anything?" They had never met.

"No," he said, sitting in the kitchen, unshaven and still in his pajamas. "I am waiting."

I looked at the number on his arm.

"He will call," Bernard said. My father and Kuznetsov introduced themselves. There was an immediate unspoken bond between these people. My mother put the kettle on.

"Your son is taking a shower. Bernard, will you check on him?"

We sat in silence in the kitchen, from Russia, from Poland, survivors of Stalin and Hitler, strangers. My brother was in exile, in the shower. He was trying to get off crack. He owed three thousand dollars to a drug dealer. Eleven people had been killed on the Jerusalem–to–Tel Aviv bus, many more were injured. Outside the sun was shining. How could any of this be explained to the neighbors, to the people in their cars, in the shops, factories or offices, people who did not come from where we came from? How do you take a normal person and put them at this kitchen table? Perhaps, for us, this is normal.

Of course, there is so much more to say. It was not quite like this. There was more. But this is the way I will tell it.

The kettle boiled. Kuznetsov looked at his leathery hands. My father looked at Mr. Leibowitz's arm. My mother got up to make tea. Mr. Leibowitz looked at my father.

"Your daughter tells me you collect stamps," he asked my father.

"Yes," my father answered.

"Postage stamps . . . from around the world?"

"Yes."

"Isn't that . . . for children?"

"Yes, I think so."

Bernard came back into the kitchen. A few steps behind him was Pavel, with wet hair and a towel around him. The telephone rang. It was louder than usual.

ACKNOWLEDGMENTS

For their help, in various ways, the author wishes to express his gratitude to Nikki Christer, Wendy Koleits, Virginia Lloyd, Julian Loose, Fred Ramey, Natasha Pahoff and Trevor Hildebrand.

ABOUT THE AUTHOR

Elliot Perlman is the author of the novels *Seven Types of Ambiguity* and *Three Dollars,* for which he cowrote the screenplay. He lives in New York and in Melbourne, where he works as a barrister.